Judith
יְתִידוּהְ

Leslie Moïse

PEARLSONG PRESS
NASHVILLE, TN

Pearlsong Press
P.O. Box 58065
Nashville, TN 37205
www.pearlsong.com
www.pearlsongpress.com

Painting of *Judith and her Maidservant* by Artemisia Gentileschi used with permission of the Uffizi Gallery in Florence, Italy.

Trade paperback ISBN 9781597190756
Ebook ISBN 9781597190763

Library of Congress Cataloging-in-Publication Data

Moise, Leslie, 1960–
   Judith / Leslie Moise.
      pages cm
   Summary: "In the ancient Middle East a pious, wealthy young widow saves her town from a besieging army in this novel based on the apocryphal Book of Judith"—Provided by publisher.
   ISBN 978-1-59719-075-6 (trade pbk. : alk. paper)—ISBN 978-1-59719-076-3 (ebook)
   1. Judith (Jewish heroine)—Fiction. 2. Bible. Old Testament—History of Biblical events—Fiction. 3. Women in the Bible—Fiction. I. Title.
   PS3613.O40J83 2013
   813'.6—dc23
                                        2013016589

To courageous women everywhere;
you know who you are.

Glossary

Pronunciations based on Hebrew and ancient Aramaic.

Abra. *AH-bra.* Judith's maidservant and close friend.

Achior. *ACK-ee-or.* Former commander of the Ammonites and Judith's friend.

Ammonite. *Ah-MON-ite.* Member of the country that ruled the ancient world until Assyria defeated it.

Assyria. *A-SEER-ee-uh.* King Nebuchadnezzar and Holofernes's land, which rules the ancient world.

Bagoas. *Ba-GO-ahs.* Holofernes's body slave. A eunuch.

Bethulia. *Be-TOOL-ee-uh.* A Jewish town in the mountains. Judith's homeland.

Chabris. *CHA-bris.* One of Bethulia's elders, or judges.

Chana. *CHAN-uh.* Young wife of Joakim.

Dorcas. *DOOR-kas.* Judith's kitchen maid.

Ezra. *EZ-rah.* Naomi's grandson, and son of Uzziah.

Hilkiah. *HILL-key-uh.* Naomi's servant.

Huldah. *HOOL-dah.* Judith's elderly maidservant and cook.

Holofernes. *Ho-LOW-fern-ees.* The leader of the Assyrian army. Judith's enemy.

Gothoniel. *Go-TOHN-eee-el.* A goatherd. Judith's neighbor. Husband to Rebekah.

Joakim. *Ye-HOH-keem.* One of Bethulia's elders.

Judith. *Ye-HOO-duf.* The heroine.

Mannaseh. *Meh-NAH-sheh.* Judith's deceased husband.

Melchior. *Mel-KEY-or.* Commander of the troops from Esau.

Naomi. *Neh-OHM-ee.* Uzziah's elderly mother. Judith's friend.

Nathaniael. *Na-THAN-ee-el.* Son of Rebekah and Gothoniel.

Sendal. *SEHN-dahl.* A commander in the Assyrian army.

Sirach. *SEE-rach.* Bethulia's priest.

Sol. *SAUL.* A handsome young potter.

Shoshana. *Sho-SHAH-nah.* Wife of Chabris.

Rebekah. *RIV-kah.* Judith's neighbor. Wife of Gothoniel.

Ruth. *ROOT.* A rare female potter.

Uzziah. *Ooh-YAH-uh.* Bethulia's magistrate, son of Naomi.

Part One
The Preparation

Chapter One

JUDITH PAUSED WHERE TREE SHADOWS met the sunlit path. She loosened her woven belt, and with her sackcloth robe no longer clinging to her damp skin, stayed in the shade a moment before the long walk up to her village. The long walk from her husband's tomb. *Blessed art thou, oh Lord of my people. Thank you for the peace of this place. Thank you for my friends, my household, and for—*

Lips pressed together, Judith stalked into the glaring heat and up the rough track. Stirred by her wide sandals, dust rose and drifted. On the hilltop, Bethulia's mud-brick walls gleamed gold in the sun. The summer sun that had killed Manasseh two years ago today.

Today she missed her husband too much to thank the one true Lord for their brief marriage. Not when she had been a widow almost as long as she had been a wife.

Judith lifted her long, dark hair to wipe her neck with a square of linen. Her maidservant and friend, Abra, would have water waiting in the courtyard. Water for the ritual cleansing after a visit to the tomb, and a cool drink to follow. Tonight Judith would send these limp robes to the fuller to be washed. If she spread her garments on the flat, heat-soaked roof afterward they would surely dry by morning.

At the turn near the top of the trail, Judith paused. A clamor of voices came from the place of judgment just outside the village gate. Every day but Sabbath the elders met there to advise people with family or business disputes. Broad-shouldered Chabris passed judgment quietly, while stringy Joakim always fussed.

Now an adolescent's tenor piped above the babble of male voices. When an older male moaned, a raspy sound full of pain, Judith lunged over the brow of the hill. Several men, their backs to her, stooped over someone stretched out on the ground in the shadow of Bethulia's wall.

"Which of you is strongest?" Chabris clapped his hands when neither of the goatskin-clad men beside him responded. "Come, we must get this man into the village at once."

Manasseh's friends had carried his limp body into their house two years ago.

Judith trembled, breathing harder than the climb or the heat warranted. She rushed across the sun-crisped grass of the gathering place and tripped on her ungirdled robe. "Who's hurt? How can I help?"

Four men swung to face her—Chabris and Ezra, the slender adolescent son of the town magistrate, as well as a pair of shepherds who must have come to the elder with a complaint. No matter how urgent their disputes, those congregated around the elders usually greeted her when she passed on her way to or from Manasseh's grave.

This time no one spoke. Chabris shifted to block her view, as did the two shepherds. Neither man worked on the lands she had inherited two years ago today.

"Who is it?" She pressed closer, but Chabris held up one square hand to hold her off. Stomach clutching, Judith rose on her toes to see past him. The prone figure lay groaning on the dirt, his bare legs splayed. Silly of her, with Manasseh and her family all dead, but—"Please, Chabris, tell me what's wrong."

Ezra gripped her arm, his touch reassuring though his long fingers barely circled her wrist. "It's all right, Judith, he's a stranger."

"Yes, a stranger. Do not fear." Chabris tugged off his outer garment and tossed it to Ezra, who caught the length of brown wool handily.

The youth ducked out of sight behind the two shepherds. "Let me help you dress, sir."

The stranger was naked? Judith blushed. "Who is he? Where is he from?"

A voice she had never heard before answered in muffled accents. "I am an Assyrian messenger, lady."

"Assyrians?" Chabris's graying head lifted sharply. The two shepherds edged away until the short one stood to Judith's right, the other in rank-smelling goatskins on her left.

The messenger unfolded himself with Ezra's support. Though the man clutched Chabris's discarded garment against his front, the edged furrows of his ribs and one bony hip showed on either side of the cloth.

Judith ducked her head, though not before she saw the dried blood down his chin and swollen lips. She covered her own mouth with one hand.

While Ezra struggled, one shoulder thrust under the messenger's armpit, the smelly shepherd braced the man's other side.

"Thank you." The stranger formed the words with care. He swayed toward Chabris. "As I crawled up your hill, I heard you passing judgment. You are a man of some authority here?"

Chabris nodded, calm even in his linen under-robe. "I am one of the elders."

"Then I will give you the message I was sent to deliver." The messenger bowed, wincing. "I am Achior, former commander of the Ammonite forces under the command of General Holofernes.

He orders me to offer your people two choices. You will surrender or you will die."

Surrender. Die? For an instant Judith didn't understand.

"Our magistrate must hear of this, and Sirach the priest." Under-robe brilliant white in the sun, Chabris brushed the boy aside and tucked one arm around the messenger's waist. "Ezra, run tell your father we're on the way."

The magistrate's son dashed through the low arched gate. The shepherd and Chabris led the gaunt messenger after him, one slow step at a time. The second shepherd scurried close behind as if to hide the stranger's nakedness. Within a few heartbeats, the men had disappeared inside.

Only Judith remained, alone with the chirr of insects and the echo of the messenger's words. *Assyrian army. Holofernes. Surrender or die.* She raised one wide, shaky hand to shade her eyes and study the horizon, where a broad plain stretched to distant mountains. When had Holofernes sent his messenger, and from where? Babylon was a long journey from Bethulia. But what if the Assyrians had started soon after their messenger?

A billow of dust drifted above the pass. Fresh sweat broke out inside Judith's scratchy robe. Was the world's mightiest army already on their final approach to Bethulia? They would catch her out here, alone. Everyone knew what Assyrians did to captured women. Young or old, maiden, married or widowed would make no difference.

Sweat or tears stung her eyes. Judith made herself focus on the drift of vapor above the pass. It was only a wisp of cloud. She shook her head at her folly and forced her numb legs to move. At the shrine set inside the wall she stopped and sat down. Her fingers itched to close the gate, but only Uzziah, the magistrate, had the great wooden key that would lock it.

Holofernes would not attack before her people answered his demands, would he?

Footsteps pattered along the narrow street. Ezra bounced through the archway and tripped over her extended legs. "Sorry we left you like that. I came to see if you'd gone home."

Judith gripped the boy's skinny arm. "What did your father and the elders decide? Have they consulted the priest yet? Will we submit or stand?" To stand, it must be. To hold Bethulia against invasion.

Uzziah's son laughed, high and thin. "Achior and my father had just greeted each other when my grandmother sent me back for you."

Beloved Naomi, always so kind. But— "Achior?" Oh, the messenger.

"Everyone's assembling in the market square." Ezra skipped backward. "Come on, don't you want to hear what the priest has to say?"

Judith slumped on the narrow bench. *Manasseh. Manasseh, why did you die? Why did you leave me alone?* "Run ahead, Ezra. I'll follow you, soon."

"Thank you!" Ezra was thirteen, perhaps fourteen. Five years younger than Judith, but as his sandals slapped around the corner, she felt decades older.

She stood, then plucked the sackcloth away from the back of each thigh before she plodded toward the village center. *I'm not alone. I'm not.* To think so was to doubt the strength of her people, to doubt the One who had chosen them. *Blessed art thou, oh Lord. I know you will guide us.*

The magistrate and elders would heed that guidance. Uzziah, Ezra's father, was learned and astute. He would keep faith with the Lord, just as Sirach the priest would interpret the Lord's word.

Judith entered the main courtyard of her house, built against the village wall near the gate. No voices called from the kitchen, and Abra did not appear to remove her sandals or offer water. Her household must be in the square with everyone else. Judith dipped water to wash her hands, dried them and drank from a fresh container. Then she set out for the village square.

A thick-bodied man in goatskins strode along just ahead of her, beside a woman whose delicately woven scarlet robes billowed beneath a cinched girdle. Judith stopped. Her neighbor Gothoniel wore his shepherd's goatskins every day including Sabbath, though his wife Rebekah was one of Bethulia's finest weavers. Their son, in his second summer, rode easily on Rebekah's hip.

Judith held back until the family reached the square. She followed slowly, only to halt again and stare around her. Except on the busiest market day she had never seen the place so full. Village men and shepherds from outside the walls crowded the dusty grass at the center. Young women and mothers huddled together in the shadow of the buildings, children held close. With a rattle of bead bracelets Rebekah pushed her way into the shade cast by a house, then cradled her son against her breast.

Had Manasseh lived, might she have borne him sons? Judith turned her head away from the sight of the young mother. Around the square, older women clustered in doorways or stood above the crowd along the front edge of the flat roofs.

Judith nodded to Shoshana, Chabris's willowy wife. She returned Judith's silent greeting, but no one spoke until Ezra's grandmother Naomi, a few dark hairs sprouting from her chin, called down from her rooftop.

"Come stand with me, Judith." Her elderly friend crooked a finger.

The villagers turned toward the sound of a lifted voice. Judith met Naomi's faded gaze, then tipped her head toward the fig tree in the corner of the square nearest the High Place. Naomi's eyes vanished in a web of wrinkles as she grinned and waved Judith on.

In the shade of the fig, Judith stood apart from the young wives and mothers, yet separate from the men. Hands clasped behind backs, her townsmen faced the High Place or the courtyard of

Uzziah's house opposite. Halfway between the children and the men, Ezra hopped on one foot, bobbing toward the adults, then away.

Sirach, the priest, appeared on the top step of the High Place. Sunshine lit through the edges of his priestly garments, a blend of white linen and wool. A moment later, the door of Uzziah's house opened with a grind of wood against the stone socket. Long-jawed and somber, the magistrate crossed his courtyard, flanked by the elders. Dressed in his brown robe again, Chabris appeared composed once more. Joakim strutted along, hollow chest poked out as far as possible. A fourth man limped along behind them. Achior, the messenger.

He wore one of Uzziah's garments, and though the magistrate stood taller than any man in town, the hem barely reached past Achior's knees. His injuries appeared more serious than Judith had realized. Beneath eyes bruised purple, his pale cheeks bore scrapes and uneven patches of stubble. His mouth puffed out like hideous fruit.

She frowned. Why had the general sent a messenger in such condition? Why not an Assyrian soldier, helmeted and heavy with armor? Achior had said he was a former Ammonite commander, but he looked worse than any slave, beaten, barefoot and naked.

The priest met Bethulia's leaders on the lowest step of the High Place. Sirach and Uzziah conferred together, and then the priest stepped aside. Uzziah climbed the two lowest stairs, turned and faced the villagers.

A ripple swept through the crowd as people leaned forward to listen. Judith shook her head and stretched to pluck one of the fig's soft fruits. It would take Uzziah a moment to speak. It always did. "A good quality for a magistrate," Manasseh once told her. "Justice listens. Justice can wait."

I would rather not wait now, Judith thought. Like the good judge he was, Uzziah did more than mete out verdicts. He offered opportunities to learn. In this case, patience.

She bit into the fig, its juice cool in her dry throat, and glanced toward a swift movement across the square. Abra, in motion as always.

Wiry curls poking out like sprays of anise, her friend joined Judith under the fig tree and fanned herself with a flap of her linen robe. "The Assyrians have sent—"

"A messenger. Yes, I know, I was at the gate soon after he arrived." Judith picked another fig and passed it to her friend. Their fingers clung together as Uzziah spoke at last, and even Abra grew still to listen.

Chapter Two

UZZIAH LIFTED HIS HANDS and his dark robe slid down his stringy arms. "For many years, the Assyrians have attacked and destroyed tribes from the Euphrates to the frontier. And now—"

Now they turn on us. Judith wished another bite of fig could sweeten her thoughts.

"—now the Assyrian king, Nebuchadnezzar, has sent us a message." The magistrate paused. "We surrender, or we die."

A babble of voices burst out around the square. A number of women clung together, crying.

"Why can't we fight, father? We will fight and die gladly!" Ezra's young voice cracked on the last word. He blushed and flattened both hands over his mouth.

Uzziah shook his head. "We have no need to fight or die, dear one. My brothers, my sisters, do you not know we are safe here in our mountains, safe in the hands of our Lord?"

Yes. Judith dropped her half-eaten fig in the dust. Her people could stand against any danger as long as they kept faith with the One.

"Well said!" Naomi's clear call bounced off the house fronts. Her fine black garments drooped to reveal a figure as wiry as her son's.

Uzziah acknowledged his mother's shout with a swift glance, then lifted his arms higher. "The priest and I agree you must hear Achior, former advisor to the Assyrian general, Holofernes."

Beside her, Abra's muscular fingers closed over the fig Judith had given her. "Advisor? I've seen firmer looking milk."

"Please." Judith touched a fingertip to her lips. "I want to listen even if you don't."

Abra snorted, but bit into her fruit.

Near the center of the square, the goat herder Gothoniel peered uneasily at his red-robed wife, then fingered his bristled chin. "Why should we listen to him? He's our enemy."

"Yes, our enemy!" At the center of the grass another man shook his fist. "The Ammonites attacked and killed peaceful peoples for years, until the Assyrians finally defeated *them*."

"And forced them to fight Nebuchadnezzar's battles." Gothoniel's grating voice grew louder with every word.

"Let's send him back to Babylon now!"

Yells of protest spread across the square, not just among the men. A few women added their shrill cries to the growing tumult. "Send him to Babylon!"

"My people, please." Uzziah spread his hands in a soothing gesture. "Better to listen and learn before we do anything rash." He stood, eyebrows raised, until most of the outcry quieted, and then paced down the steps and away from the High Place. Chabris followed at once, Joakim more reluctantly.

Sirach kept still an instant, then pivoted so the tails of his linsey-woolsey tunic flared. He ascended to the altar that topped the High Place. Hands tucked into his white sleeves, Sirach studied each person in the crowd one by one. When his narrowed eyes passed over her, Judith clasped her hands.

With the same measured elegance he used on Sabbath, Sirach

said, "Our Lord's laws are clear. We are to welcome strangers in need."

As her fellow citizens hushed, Judith smiled. *Blessed art thou, oh Lord of my people. Thank you for giving Bethulia's magistrate such wisdom. And our priest such good judgment.*

"He is an Ammonite and unclean." This time the muttered complaint came from a woman. Rebekah? Judith squinted, but could not see her neighbor's face.

"This stranger needs our care," continued Sirach. "But our Lord also emphasizes the need for knowledge. Not only would it be against the One's law to turn Achior away uncomforted, it would be ignorant."

Sirach lingered a moment, nodded, and climbed down to join Uzziah and the elders.

Judith noticed Gothoniel squirming through the grouped townsmen, away from his wife. Why did Rebekah refuse to see that he was not a leader of men? Without her urging, he would happily rule nothing but his goats and sheep.

Achior limped toward the steps of the High Place. Unlike Uzziah or Sirach, he did not climb a single one. Instead he kept level with the villagers while the closest townsmen formed a loose semi-circle around him.

Judith expected the messenger to look only at the men, or stare into the air above the heads of the crowd. Instead Achior gazed at one of the men closest to him, then at a woman up on a rooftop. He met Judith's eyes next. The messenger inclined his head, straightened and drew a breath.

"I no longer command the Ammonites in the Assyrian army. Now I am only Achior, a man with no people, no land and no home." The tall messenger spoke quietly, as if seated before his hearth fire with his wife or a close companion. His eyes, pale inside their puffs of bruised flesh, focused on Gothoniel. "My friends—"

"Friends?" Gothoniel grunted.

Thin, dark eyebrows flattening, Sirach took a step away from the magistrate and elders. "Peace, my son."

"Yes. Listen for now." Behind the priest, Uzziah spread his hands once more. "We will each speak our minds soon enough."

Judith kicked dirt over the fallen fig with the toe of one sandal as Achior bowed to the crowd as a whole.

"When the king commanded Holofernes to attack you, the general asked his commanders to share what we knew about your people. He's a strong leader, cunning and fierce—"

A hiss rose from the crowd.

"I do not mean to brag, only to warn you." Achior's split lip broke open when he raised his voice to be heard.

Judith winced. The man was an impure foreigner, a killer. Yet Sirach spoke truly when he said Achior needed their help.

The Ammonite ignored the blood seeping down his chin. "The other commanders described you as weak, sheep ready for slaughter. But I reminded Holofernes what all well-traveled men know. 'The Israelites follow only one god. Their god parted the Red Sea to help them escape enslavement in Egypt.'"

Across the square Naomi swayed in place, twisted hands against her breast. Judith clutched a gray-barked fig branch as the messenger's voice grew stronger.

"I warned Holofernes. You Israelites prosper because of your faith. I told the general, 'The Assyrian army will be disgraced if we—' if they—'attack you.'"

Abra swallowed a bite of her fig as if savoring more than its juice. "I expect that pleased the general," she murmured. "About as well as a flea bite."

Judith chuckled, only to sober at sight of the wounds on Achior's face. How many more bruises did his borrowed clothing hide?

"Holofernes clubbed me to the floor with one fist. 'You dare tell me not to go to war?' His fringed robe slithered across my face while I lay there, gasping for breath. 'The god of the Israelites cannot save them. Their blood will soak the mountains and their dead fill the valleys before I am done!' Then he laughed. 'I will cut my message to them into your flesh.'"

The fig dropped from Abra's limp fingers. All across the village center, mothers reached out for their children. Even Ezra sped out of the square to the rooftop, where he huddled against Naomi's breast. She clutched him tight, but Judith could not say who supported the other more, grandmother or grandson.

Her fingers worked together. *Manasseh. Manasseh.* If only she could clasp her husband's hands, even bigger than her own.

Achior staggered. Chabris moved closer, but the messenger shook his head with a slight smile, and took a breath rough as a plough cutting through hard ground.

"Holofernes cursed me. 'You act like a woman—no, a eunuch.' My brothers in arms stripped me naked, like a captive, and pinned me while the general's body slave shaved off my beard. Then Holofernes whipped me while Sendal, my second-in-command, sat on my legs and held my arms."

Judith wished she had not eaten today.

"My own men dragged me from the palace on a forced march." Achior flipped back the neck of his borrowed robe to reveal the rope burn scarring his neck. "The march ended when they dumped me on the plain in sight of your village."

And from there, he crawled. Judith remembered the messenger's torn feet, and could not look away from the cut knees his too-short robe did not hide. Beside her Abra wept, as did some of the adolescent girls and young mothers.

"I come to you in the hope that we can help each other. Together, maybe we can be ready when the army comes."

The hush sizzled like a new fire. Then Ezra bounded away from Naomi's embrace. Balanced on the low wall that fronted their rooftop, he thrust both fists high. "We stand! We're safe here, with our Lord!"

One by one, the people joined in. With tears running into the corners of her smile, Abra slipped both arms around Judith's waist. She danced them around in a circle, then leapt away to join a ring of other maids, all singing.

Few people seemed to notice when the magistrate and elders joined Sirach again. The priest motioned at Achior, then toward the altar on the High Place before he nodded.

Uzziah raised his voice. "We're in agreement, then? We stand."

"We stand!" The men's voices boomed off the walls of the square, echoed by the high-pitched cries of the women. "The Lord is our defense!"

Only as long as we keep perfect faith! Judith glanced at Rebekah and her hands chilled. If she bore so little respect for her neighbor, how could her people's respect for the Lord be true? Abra skipped up to whirl Judith in another brief dance, and her fear faded. *I love my friends and honor the One.* That mattered most, at least for a woman.

All around the square families hurried together, laughing, shouting, crying. Uzziah crossed his courtyard to join his son and mother on the roof. Joakim, the second of the elders, motioned for his wispy young wife to join him near the High Place, and Chana darted to obey. Abra danced away again, this time to urge Dorcas, the little kitchen maid, to spin in dizzy circles while Judith's old cook looked on and almost smiled.

Only Judith stood alone. A fever had taken her parents the year before she married. Less than a week after Manasseh's death, his mother died too. "Old age," some said. Of a broken heart, Judith knew. A month later, Manasseh's father followed his wife and only child into the tomb.

Judith's throat pinched shut. *I'm the only person here with no one.*

Then she realized Achior also stood by himself, injured face sallow now his tale was finished. As if he felt her attention, the messenger's pale eyes stared into hers.

With her jubilant neighbors swirling around her, it seemed that only this commander who no longer commanded anyone understood. Judith dipped her head and bowed to him. Achior's swollen mouth curled upward as he bowed to her in return.

Chapter Three

JUDITH SPREAD HER FRESHLY WASHED GARMENTS across the sun-warmed roof. Heat burned through the wet material even as the night wind cooled her neck. Yes, her widow's robes would dry by dawn.

A clash of noise burst out and she pushed up onto her knees, only to sag again. Just some distant neighbor playing the sistrum. Footsteps scuffed up the steps to the roof and Judith gasped, then steadied at the familiar sound of Abra's voice.

"Why do you keep servants?" Her friend's hair fuzzed around her head and shoulders. "Send me to the fuller's if you want your clothes washed. A lady should never visit such an unclean place. And I should be spreading them to dry, not you."

"I've spent more of my life doing for myself than letting others wait on me." But Judith shifted so Abra could help arrange the heavy fabric. "I started grinding flour for my mother the day I was strong enough to pound a rock in the mortar."

"I know—" The sistrum rattled and chimed again. Abra dropped low to the roof, only to straighten again. "I know. Still, it's been five years since..." She lifted her chin and tried again. "Since you wed."

Judith jerked the edge of the sackcloth but couldn't make the seam lie flat. She sat back on her heels, arms around her bent knees.

Abra tidied the garment so it would dry into the right shape. "Remember when you helped me carry water from the spring?"

They had both been about six. "I remember." Her mother had sent her to play in the shade, but Judith heard crying and went deeper into the trees to investigate. By the spring she found Abra, the curly-haired serving maid of a rich merchant, struggling with an urn as tall as she was.

Now Abra rocked onto her heels as well. "Huldah had sent me to collect water by myself for the first time. You helped me wrestle that urn up the hill, all the way to Manasseh's father's house and Huldah's kitchen." She chuckled. "I've never seen the old woman so surprised, before or since. You helped me do that. You, a merchant's daughter."

"A poor merchant's daughter." But Judith smiled, as always at thought of her father, Merari, unpacking goods off the donkeys the instant he returned from a buying trip. "Esther! Judith! Come, see what beauties I found."

It didn't matter if the pots, the lengths of cloth or leather turned out to be chipped, unraveling, or wormy. Her father saw only the intricate carving, the bright colors, or the smoothness of the hides—

Out on the street, shouts and laughter burst out. Judith crouched down, Abra plunged upright. They glanced at each other, then settled again.

"You asked me to play when other merchants' daughters ignored me. In the eyes of the world you're my mistress. I'm nothing but your maidservant. But you know I'll do whatever you need without complaint."

They listened as some men passed by outside, joyous as a Sabbath celebration. This time, neither woman flinched.

"My parents kept no servants. When Manasseh—" Judith

rolled onto her knees to jerk and tug at the wet robe. "When I first wed, I tried to copy his way with the household."

She had found it impossible. Manasseh never gave an order in his life. He just grinned and requested help from the nearest servant. Eventually Judith managed to pretend authority, at least with the workers on Manasseh's lands outside town.

"I never saw any problem." Abra's soft cheeks rounded in a smile. "Mistress."

"Then you're the only one." Judith squinted at the mountain pass. Was that a spark of light? Torches? She rubbed her eyes. The spark was still there, against her shut lids. "Huldah still says I'm too lax with my household."

"That old complainer. She's even stricter than Joakim. She grouses about my hair until I wish I could clip it short like a man."

Her friend's voice carried, as usual. Were Holofernes and his army close enough to hear the echoes?

"Please, Judith. Stop looking at the mountains." Abra rubbed another invisible wrinkle out of the wet sackcloth. "The Assyrians won't be here for a long time yet."

Judith leaned over to tap her friend's plump shoulder. "I'll stop worrying if you will. Why don't you go celebrate?" While she still could.

"I danced as much as I wanted earlier, in the square." Abra sniffed. "Most of the people still celebrating are abed, and not sleeping."

"You're probably right." The clash of sistrums and drums, the laughter that remained sounded far away. Judith rested against the wall that formed the roof's balustrade, and part of the town's fortifications.

The year before their marriage, Manasseh had purchased two small houses on either side of the home Judith had shared with her parents. With the help of servants and friends, Manasseh built this larger, pleasant home on the site with a central courtyard that opened into the street. Servants' quarters and the kitchen lined one side of the courtyard, storage rooms the other, and a spacious reception room faced the entrance. A passage led to a second, private courtyard outside the master's bedchamber. Stairways from both courts gave access to the roof.

"I love my neighbors, but I don't want to look at them all the time." A few mornings after their wedding, Manasseh had stood on this rooftop, and slipped his arm around her waist. "I want to sleep beside you with air from the mountains blowing through our windows."

She smiled into the brown eyes so close to hers, and touched the dimple beside Manasseh's mouth. "I'd be happy anywhere with you." But it was good to live on the spot where her parents had lived. Good to live in the beauty Manasseh had created in this place saturated with her parents' love for each other and her. Saturated with their faith in the Lord.

Manasseh raised her hands, nearly as large as his own, to kiss one palm, then the other. "I feel the same about you." He drew her down the steps into their private courtyard. By the time they reached the bedchamber, they were racing each other.

"I won!" Judith bounded inside with a triumphant laugh.

"My long-legged wife, so swift." His fingers closed on her hips as he circled them toward the bed. "We're both winners. Let me show you—" He pressed her back onto the cushions.

Judith linked her arms and legs around him, only to tense and draw away a little. "Sirach says marriage must be rooted in friendship and love, not lust."

"Sacred law also requires we share our joy in each other." Beneath her hitched up robes, Manasseh's hand circled from her hip to her belly and down. "Our time together, pleasuring each other like this, is the best of love." He chuckled, and nipped her chin, her throat. "Shall I stop, or do you agree?

"Yes, husband, oh yes—" In the delight of his body bearing

down against her, into her, Judith's sense of duty faded. "I love you, I love you, I love—you—"

Now she pressed her forehead against her knees. She didn't want to remember the first intensity of her marriage, or how she and Manasseh had steadied into their roles as man and wife. But not as parents, though they never outgrew the privacy offered by the courtyard between their bedchamber and the world.

Lashes wet, she ignored the aching pulse deep in her body. An evening breeze flowed over her, along with the raised voice of her neighbor, Rebekah. "You are a man of the village, better-traveled than most. If only you asserted yourself—"

"If Gothoniel asserted himself with her, maybe everyone else on the street could sleep." Abra poked an errant curl behind one ear.

Judith nodded. "I hoped when the baby came Rebekah's fire might cool." And give Gothoniel, and everyone else, some peace.

"It would take a brood of dozens to smother Rebekah's fire. Now they argue so often, I doubt there will be more babes. She exhausts Gothoniel until he probably has no energy left for—"

"Abra, please." From the silence next door, Judith guessed her neighbors had unrolled their sleeping fleeces and settled to bed. Whether to argue in whispers or make up their quarrel she did not want to know.

She knelt up, one arm on the coping where Manasseh had rested his hands on that day so few years ago. Judith stared across the feathery cedar tops toward the mountain pass. Abra sat on the wall, her back to the plain. "When do you think they'll come?"

"I don't know, but we need to be ready." The mountain that provided Bethulia with seclusion and safety had stones too deep and thick for villagers to dig a well. "We need to collect and store water."

"Food, too." Abra bounced up and dashed halfway down the stairwell before Judith called her back.

"In the morning. We'll collect every jug and pitcher Huldah

can spare from the kitchen, and I'll send Dorcas along the street to suggest our neighbors do the same."

Abra prowled the rooftop, plain linen robe aflutter with her quick strides. "If we form a chain from the spring up to the gate, passing full containers hand to hand, we can store enough to last— how long?"

"Long enough." But the wind blew dry against Judith's face, with the worst of summer still to come. *The One is our protector. As long as we keep faith, harm cannot reach us.* "In the morning, bring my tent up here."

Abra halted. "Your tent."

"Yes." The tent of her widowhood. The shelter from her first long year of grief.

"I'll see to it first thing. Good night." But her friend crossed to Judith and held her close a moment before she withdrew.

"Good night." Judith shut her eyes. Tomorrow she must go to the High Place and offer a lamb for Sirach to sacrifice. Two lambs. One for her un-neighborly thoughts about Rebekah, and a second in gratitude. *Blessed art thou, oh Lord, for giving us time to prepare for the siege to come.* Bethulia had this breathing space, no matter how brief it turned out to be, because of Achior.

Judith climbed down to the courtyard. Perhaps she would brew herself a soothing drink. She crossed to the kitchen door, only to pause.

The Assyrian's messenger needed clothing. His wounds required care. As a woman of Bethulia, it was her duty to help a stranger in need.

Judith smiled as she entered the kitchen, with its comforting smell of old fires, olive oil and bread. When she offered clothing and ointment for the Ammonite's injuries, what could be more natural than to ask a question or two? Achior and her village shared the same future now. The same enemy.

Holofernes.

Chapter Four

SUNLIGHT BURNED BETWEEN THE PALM FROND ceiling of Judith's courtyard. The floor felt cool underfoot as she studied the jugs, bottles and urns her household had collected so far. As she bent to check an old container for cracks, the sharp odor of mint rose from her clean robe.

Judith sniffed the rough fabric. A few crumbs of pungent leaf drifted down. She frowned. Perfumes had no place outside the High Place, or the Temple in Jerusalem.

Huldah's cracked voice snapped out from the kitchen. "Watch how you handle that, you silly chit. We can't lose another jug to your careless fingers."

Giggles and a crash made Judith wince. Before the broken vessel stopped tinkling across the floor inside, Abra staggered out through the kitchen doorway, a stack of bowls nested in her arms. She shook her head at Huldah's outraged shouts and squatted next to Judith.

"Do you think Dorcas will ever learn not to giggle when Huldah yells at her?"

"Maybe someday. She's only eleven." Judith held out a fold of her garment. "Why did you rub dried herbs into my robes?" When her friend only tidied the already perfectly aligned bowls, Judith caught a snarl of Abra's hair and tugged gently. "Well?"

Abra smoothed the unruly lock into place the moment Judith let it fall. "Mint soothes the spirit and increases joy. I patted some into my robes as well, and offered more to Huldah and Dorcas. I'd give some to everyone in town if I could."

Judith traced the incised lines carved into a storage urn tall as her waist. "Perhaps you should save your remedies for later." After Holofernes and his army arrived. "Do you know what Dorcas broke this time?"

"Only a jar. Not very big either, though you'd never guess from the way Huldah scolds, would you?"

Inside the kitchen, the elderly cook ranted on. "Our region is famous for its pottery. Famous, do you hear? You should be proud of your village's artisans and their wares—don't titter like that, girl. Show respect for your elders. And stop giving me that silly smile. You're not a donkey."

"Dorcas." Judith did not raise her voice, but Huldah silenced at once.

"Yes, mistress?" The little maid appeared in the doorway, her delicate features pushed into a smile.

But Judith saw the tears in her eyes. "Go tell every woman who lives on our street that we plan to start gathering water soon." When the girl bobbed her head, Judith reached out to grip her fragile wrist. "We're doing important work today. Thank you for your help."

The child's smile bloomed. "Yes, mistress. Thank you, mistress." Dorcas skipped across the courtyard.

Judith watched her waver, then dart off down the narrow street. The girl's neck still looked too slender above her tunic, but at least her knees appeared less knobby. She was picking up some healthy weight at last.

Huldah poked her head into the courtyard. Light from the

pottery lamp still lit in the kitchen filtered through her thinning hair. "You don't train a child by coddling her."

"Or by terrifying her, either. Move and I'll bring out more pots. I promise not to break them!" Abra edged past the older woman with a friendly bump, rounded hip to thin one.

"Mind your manners, girl, or I'll raise my stick to you." Huldah glared down at Judith. "And as for you, madam—"

Manasseh would have known how to soothe the old woman. Judith just held up a hand, palm out. "Peace, Huldah. Now isn't the time to argue within our own household. Perhaps you and I give Dorcas what she needs to grow into a reliable servant—a balance between criticism and praise. Now." She ignored her cook's tightening lips and gestured at the pots that covered the courtyard floor. "Do you think we have enough vessels to last out the siege?"

Huldah hitched out of the kitchen, forked end of her staff propped under one armpit. "Measured against the thirst of everyone in Bethulia?"

"Hush your ecstasies, crone," Abra snapped. "Or I'll stop work to sing." She clattered across the courtyard, more containers in her rounded arms.

"Humph." Like an ungainly bird settling on its nest, Huldah wobbled down to her knees to help. The hands of both women wove back and forth as they arranged the pots, Abra's flesh smooth and plump as an olive, Huldah's withered knuckles strung through with knotted veins.

Judith knelt to help them. She picked jars from the heap four at a time, two in each hand. "While you start down to the spring, Abra, I'll tell Naomi what we're doing. She'll want to organize the women in her part of town." And Naomi would surely know where Achior lodged.

"Let's get on with it, then." Huldah's crutch flailed the packed earth. She muttered thanks to Abra for the supportive hand the younger woman pressed against her haunch. "The sooner we begin the better, before the heat grows bad."

"We'll spread the work over several days?" Abra squinted at Judith between wisps of her hair.

Judith nodded. "Until Bethulia runs out of containers." Or time. She turned to leave just as her neighbor Rebekah entered the courtyard from the street. Her son toddled after her, the hem of his mother's red garment crumpled in his tiny fists.

Rebekah must wash the robe herself every night, or it would show stains from caring for her child—Judith squeezed her eyes shut. *Blessed Lord, forgive me.* Rebekah wove fabrics lighter than any other woman in town. The scarlet robe showcased her skill, and the wool from her husband's flock.

"Good morning, Rebekah. You, too, little one." Judith bent to touch the boy's curls. As always, their softness startled her. "How strong you've grown. Will you help your mama today?"

"He helps me every day, don't you, Nathanael? Why should today be any different?" Rebekah scooped him out of Judith's reach and nestled him on her hip.

Judith stiffened. Even when they were girls living side by side, Rebekah had disliked her. Judith's family accepted her as a gift from the Lord. In arguments that carried up and down the street, Rebekah's parents let her and everyone else know they wanted a son.

No wonder Rebekah flaunted Nathanael. *Blessed art thou, oh Lord. Lend me strength. Help me live beside her in peace.* And with the emptiness inside herself, inside her house, as well. Judith forced a smile. "I'm sure—"

"I hear you expect us to collect extra water today." Rebekah sniffed. "Some of us have families to care for, you know."

Before Judith could think of a calm reply, Huldah nudged the nearest pots with her walking stick. "Gathering water is a woman's chore, one you may not be able to do once the Assyrians arrive. Best get it done now while you can."

"While we can." Abra hefted a pitcher onto her hip. "Don't you want water for your son, no matter what comes?"

Rebekah's mouth squared, ugly as a wound. "If you were my slaves I'd whip you for such insolence!"

"They're not slaves, they're servants. And the One bids us treat even slaves as human beings." Indeed, most of the people Judith knew treated slaves with the same respect due a family member. Distant family, who would inherit no wealth, but—

Rebekah thrust out her long chin. "I'd certainly control my household better than you do."

"Would you?" Judith's chest felt full of molten metal. She stalked away, barely pausing to stab each foot into her sandals.

"Mistress, wait." Behind her, Abra scurried to catch up, her own sandals flopping. They passed into the street side by side. Her friend wheezed with suppressed laughter. "I'd like to see that one try to control anyone, especially herself." With a wicked imitation of Dorcas's giggle, Abra sped toward the village gate and the spring beyond.

With a reluctant smile, Judith turned the opposite way. Other women flowed around her, headed for the spring to judge by the urns and pitchers most carried. Men trooped out of town as well, scythes over their shoulders, bunched halters dangling from their arms. Not everyone agreed with Rebekah.

Judith breathed deeply, only to cough when the smell of goat dung rolled from Gothoniel's stable. The shaky structure, of posts with a brush roof, stood just beyond her neighbors' one-room house.

She would give Holofernes every last gold piece she owned, every sheep to the tiniest lamb, every plump calf and bustling donkey, to have her husband alive and his child in her arms. To have the riches Rebekah took for granted.

Judith wheeled back the way she had come, ready to beg her neighbor for peace, only to collide with a man. For an instant, calloused hands gripped her arms. "Excuse me, lady. Did I hurt you?"

"Not at all, sir. I turned without warning—" She stared up into the gaunt, bruised face of Achior. Holofernes's messenger.

Chapter Five

"GREETINGS, SIR. I'M JUDITH, widow of Manasseh." To her surprise, she needed to tilt back her head to meet the stranger's pale eyes. "I hoped to meet you today and offer my help."

Achior still wore his borrowed, too-short robe, but ointment shone on his bruised face and the scrapes where his beard had been forcibly removed. "Thank you, lady, my hostess Naomi has tended my wounds." The messenger smiled more easily than on the previous day. "I owe everything to your people, from the food in my mouth to the roof over my head."

Again, the quietness of his voice startled her. "Our Lord bids us welcome strangers. And you lost everything when you defended our good name."

The stream of people hurrying by widened to a flood. Judith frowned after them, then at Achior. "Did you just come back into the village? What were you doing outside the walls, keeping watch?" It seemed likely for a former military commander.

Achior shook his head. "I'm grateful for the comfort your people offer me—"

"Yesterday Sirach, our priest, reminded us of our duty to you." But how much of the priest's talk had Achior truly understood? She thought Ammonites worshipped pagan gods and goddesses like their Assyrian rulers, though probably with different names. "You're staying with Naomi and Uzziah? I'm going that way myself."

Judith kept level with Achior's limping pace. For once, she only glanced at the pottery displayed outside the homes of her artisan neighbors. She must remember to replace the vessel Dorcas broke at the next weekly market.

Achior's steps dragged, and Judith stopped. "Am I walking too fast? You traveled a long way with those injuries."

"You're very tactful." He laid one hand over the roughened skin around his throat. "A forced march with a rope around my neck, a spear at my back. I hope never to 'travel' that way again!" In the angle of sun between two buildings Achior wiggled his scabbed toes in the dust. "My Assyrian rulers live by an unforgiving code. Everything in Babylon reflects that inflexibility, even their architecture."

The messenger had not answered her question. Why? "What do the houses in Babylon look like?"

Every time Achior smiled, his lips curved more comfortably. "The terraced gardens above the Euphrates are as large as this village, if not larger. White and yellow lions decorate the city walls." He studied the simple homes around them, and his smile faded.

Was he picturing the ramparts of Babylon, as she was, the flayed skins of conquered people dripping blood, red on the blue glazed bricks? "Please tell me why you went outside today."

Achior aimed those pale eyes at her. "Today your people come and go through the gate at will. I wanted time alone under the trees while I can have it."

Judith stared at him. After Holofernes arrived, would she ever visit her husband's grave again, or hear a dove's wings rise through the fragrant cedars?

"Are you unwell?" Achior reached out to steady her, then drew back before his fingers touched her.

She did not need to see her husband's tomb to remember their love. "Yes, thank you, sir. Achior." This time, when Judith moved on Achior kept pace with her. "You seem very—thoughtful—for a military leader."

Achior laughed, and a serving woman clad in a linen undergarment poked her head out of a doorway a few steps ahead. As Judith and Achior passed, she called to someone inside the house. "Come see, it's the Ammonite!"

Achior did not even glance toward the sound. "There's plenty of time for observation on a campaign. The different sounds made by armor or harness, the change in the plumage of birds with the seasons. In the night watches, I considered what I'd seen and heard that day. In the days and weeks before."

"I think I understand." Judith glanced back at the serving woman. On top of baking bread, cooking and weaving, the women of Bethulia prepared for siege—and still found time to observe Achior! Perhaps women and warriors, Israelites and Ammonites weren't so different from each other.

They rounded a corner and sunshine highlighted the fine lines at the corners of Achior's eyes. He must be nearer forty than thirty, perhaps even her father Merari's age when he died.

Ezra and his friend Ham trotted past. Ham bobbed his close-cropped head, and Ezra waved. "Good morning, Judith. See you at supper, Achior."

The messenger smiled so broadly the cut on his mouth opened a little. "Yes, at supper. Enjoy yourselves, boys."

Judith watched the two adolescents race toward the village gate. Were they going to help the men prepare for siege? Probably. And to run, to shout. To be outside while they still could, just like Achior. "I'm glad you're staying with Uzziah."

"Why?"

Before she could answer, footsteps pattered along a flat rooftop. The shadows of several heads appeared on the street just in front of Judith's sandals. When she looked up the three women—girls, really—ducked out of sight.

Achior halted. "Forgive me. Will it cause talk, our walking together? You're a widow, but young—"

"I've been a widow a long time." Judith strode toward the square. "Everyone knows I still—that I loved—" She would not weep here in the street. "Everyone knows."

At the edge of the square Judith realized she was leaving Achior behind again, so she paused to wait for him. A widow named Lila stood beneath the tree in the corner, picking figs. She stopped to watch Judith and Achior cross the rest of the way to the magistrate's house.

Achior bowed. "You don't have to escort me inside, lady. Thank you, but I can find my own way from here."

"I'm not escorting you. " She shook her head at the thought of a woman doing such a thing. "I told you, I want to see Naomi, to discuss plans for the women to collect water from the spring."

The messenger's brows gathered over his nose. "Uzziah and the elders met last night to make plans for provisioning the town. As you saw, your men are already gathering what they can."

Water was a woman's responsibility. Like so many other things about her people, Achior might not know that. Briefly, she wondered who collected water on a military campaign. Slaves, probably.

Judith faced him on grass trampled from yesterday's gathering. "You've witnessed sieges before?"

"Never from inside the walls until now." Again, his painful smile. "In any case, defense is the business of your leaders."

She wove her fingers together. "In times like this, surely food and water are everyone's job? We have wheat and barley to grind into flour, but if we're to eat bread after they come we'll need water, too."

"Very well." Achior jerked his head. "Uzziah tells me Bethulia has olives and olive oil put by from last year, and the men might find green olives to pick today. Your beasts need to be herded inside for safekeeping."

Judith remembered the stink from Gothoniel's goat shed and wrinkled her nose. "So many cattle locked inside would be unclean."

"Even so, you'll need lambs and calves for temple sacrifices."

Had Uzziah seen fit to explain such things to the messenger as well? "We usually eat meat only on holy days and festivals— oh!" Judith took a swift step toward Achior. "What if we kill the livestock? Now, before the army arrives? Without food they will have to move on and leave us alone!"

Achior shook his head. "I'm afraid they are well provided for. The Assyrians established storage posts throughout their territory long ago. They will stock up on the way here."

Enough for all of them? "How many men does he have?" He. Holofernes. King Nebuchadnezzar had ordered the attack, but the general was the one who had blackened the eyes and battered the body of the man before her now.

Achior dipped his fingers into the pocket made by a clever twist in the woven girdle at his waist. He drew out a fistful of pebbles and shook them in his closed hand. "I don't want to frighten you."

"It's better to know." Everything Sirach taught on Sabbath, all the Lord's sacred laws, emphasized the importance of knowledge. "Besides, I'm already frightened."

"If you insist." For the first time, his words came clipped, almost harsh. "On the march they're like the dust of the earth. One hundred and twenty thousand foot soldiers, twelve thousand mounted archers. Twice as many chariots—the Assyrians favor chariot attacks above cavalry. And cattle, sheep and goats enough to feed all the men for months to come."

"So many?" Judith took the last few steps into Uzziah's courtyard. There she pressed one hand against the rough bricks.

"I'm sorry, I should not have told you."

The Lord will guide us. This stranger, this messenger, would help. Still, she would lean against the wall a moment longer.

His voice gentled once more. "Your village is preparing. But your god watches over you and that's just as important. Your faith gives you strength."

Judith pushed away from the wall, and blessed Abra for rubbing the soothing mint into her clothes. "What's he like? Holofernes."

"Holofernes?" Achior squinted at the sky. What odd crossing of blood, what distant ancestor, had given him such unusual eyes? "Why do you ask about the general?"

"One hundred and fifty thousand soldiers." Judith shuddered. "That's more than I can imagine. But only one man leads them. If I can picture him, he becomes the only thing to fear." That was how she'd faced Manasseh's death. One minute, one hour, one prayer at a time.

"I see. Well, he's broad-shouldered, thick-necked and bold as a bull. Impetuous, too, especially when he's bored. And he can't imagine that anyone would dare defy him. That any people would fail to submit to him."

She considered the messenger's bruised face. "A proud man."

"Proud. Yes." Achior fingered the scrape marks on his jaw. "And empty inside. Constantly trying to fill that emptiness." The crinkles around his eyes deepened. "Holofernes would never pause to observe trees in the wind, or the tilt of an eagle's wings against the clouds."

"Thank you." As Achior had done the day before, Judith bowed from the waist. "Thank you for telling me."

He stared at her. "Why do you bow to me like that?"

"You bowed like that yesterday." For an instant she had forgotten he was a stranger. A foreigner. How could she forget?

His shaven cheeks flushed. "Yesterday you looked alone in the crowd, as if only you understood that your world has changed forever."

"My life changed forever two years ago." Past Achior's shoulder, Judith saw Lila under the fig tree, eating fruit. Did the older widow have nothing else to eat today? Would she have time to go out to glean the fields after the men finished, before the siege began? Not for the first time, Judith thanked the One that Manasseh had left her able to look after his household and herself. And, sometimes, others as well.

Now would be the right time to care for others, too—

"It's easy to offer ointment for wounds, clothing for the body." Achior spoke even more quietly. "Not everyone has the strength to ease the pains of the spirit. By allowing me to share, that's what you've done. Perhaps Holofernes did me a favor, sending me here."

"I'm sure he didn't mean to." Judith smoothed her sackcloth garment. "You seem to be handling the—the changes in your own life very well."

His feet didn't shift, yet Achior seemed to draw back from her. "What do you mean?"

"Yesterday, when you addressed us." How could she describe his ease at the foot of the temple, dressed in a stranger's clothes? "You sounded so calm."

"I felt like I was tumbling down a mountainside! I've been tumbling for weeks, bruised and sore. Yet it's exhilarating, too. Where will I land? How will it end? Until now, my life followed a pattern. No matter how different the place, how different the tactics of the people I fought, the pattern remained. Now the pattern is broken."

Was that the answer? Judith decided to focus on the new pattern, woven of tens of thousands of soldiers, chariots, archers and spears. And Holofernes. A new pattern, but still strung, as all things were, on the loom of her Lord.

"I'll go in now. Thank you for walking with me." Achior started across the courtyard, stopped to remove his sandals, and continued into the house.

Before she followed him, Judith frowned toward the mountain pass. If only she could see beyond them, into the Assyrian general's empty heart. It was too bad no one had ever found a way to use that void against him.

Chapter Six

THE CHATTER OF VOICES and the clash of pottery drifted from Naomi's rooftop. Judith removed her sandals and hurried up the steps, one hand on the sturdy banister hammered into the side of the building.

Every servant in the household, from the lowliest stable boy to the head servant, Hilkiah, scurried back and forth under Naomi's command. Brownish-gray urns, bowls, pots and jars spread in ever-expanding rings around the old woman's feet. The plain, burnished surfaces of some, the decorative lines carved into others, made it clear Naomi was considering every vessel in the household, no matter how precious.

"I don't think this one, Hilkiah." Naomi tapped a jug with one bent finger, then handed it to her chief servant. "Look inside, smell. It's held olive oil, and recently. Return it to the storeroom. If all goes well we'll use it for oil come winter—Judith!" Her wrinkled face creased deeper with her smile. Naomi scooted sideways to make room for Judith on the bench.

Judith sank down in the shade cast by a rectangular canopy. Several young quince trees, planted in pots as high as her hip, spread more coolness. Pungent herbs in lower, wide containers turned this corner of the rooftop into a garden.

A tiny maidservant scampered toward them, a tower of pots jingling in her arms.

"Careful, young one." Spine straight as a date palm, Hilkiah paced over to stoop and take half the pots from the girl.

Such a contrast with Judith's household, with Dorcas's giggles, Huldah's scolding and Abra's jokes. Hilkiah's stiff-backed ways always made Judith think he had been born of a date palm instead of a mother's womb. But as he placed the pots at Naomi's feet, Judith realized that things only sounded different here.

She squeezed her friend's bony knee. "We think alike, you and I."

"The women of your household are on their way to the spring?" When Judith nodded, Naomi laughed.

"I came to suggest you and your neighbors do the same." Judith gestured at the bustle around them. "I'm too late."

Naomi tipped her grizzled head toward the house next door. "My young neighbor, Chana, acted like I wanted her to confront Holofernes by herself! Poor little pigeon. It will do her good to take some responsibility, as long as that silly goat Joakim doesn't bleat and make her lose her nerve."

Like all Naomi's comments, 'pigeon' and 'silly goat' described the hollow-chested elder and his child bride perfectly. Joakim's judgments might be sound, but they always struck Judith as unimaginative. Or so it seemed to her, a mere woman.

"Chana's no younger than you when you wed, but she has half your spine and none of your spirit. The days ahead will test us all. Maybe they'll help our little bird discover her strength as well." Naomi wiggled her knobby toes in the sun. "Ah, that feels good. Even on the hottest day, there's a thread of cold in my bones."

Cold, on a day like this. Yet Judith shivered too, in spite of the heat spilling around the little patch of shade. Her friend was indeed growing old. "I pray our Lord has a gift for someone in the days to come."

"We've already received one." Naomi pressed her palms against the skinny ridges of her thighs and rocked in place, ready to stand. "Achior shared the Assyrian's battle tactics with my son and the elders."

One hundred and twenty thousand foot soldiers, twelve thousand mounted archers. Twice as many chariots. "We need every advantage."

"Indeed. Siege first, my son told me." Naomi peered at the servants busy nearby, and lowered her voice. "The Assyrians keep a village under siege as long as possible, to weaken the people inside with hunger and thirst, and destroy their faith. Sometimes—" She sucked in her lower lip, as if considering. "Sometimes they bring captives from recent battles, caged in wagons. The wagons drive round the town, while torturers torment the victims inside."

Judith nearly gagged. "They won't be able to do that here. Our hill is too steep."

While Hilkiah organized pots by size and type, Naomi drummed her fingertips on the bench. "You stood under the fig tree yesterday and listened to Achior. What do you think of our visitor?"

She could be honest here as nowhere else. "He has years of experience as a commander. Years spent committing—" Some things were hard to say after all. "Committing atrocities."

Naomi inclined her head. "Atrocities ordered by his ruler, a brutal king."

"True. Yet Achior is impure, because of where he comes from, what he has done, what he believes." Judith shifted on the bench. "But today I learned more about him. We walked to your house together."

"Oh?" Naomi frowned, then her lips softened. "We must remember our Lord is concerned for all the world's people, not just the chosen."

"I'm glad you're giving Achior hospitality. Clothes, medicine, a place to stay." Judith gestured toward the guest room off the courtyard.

"I ask again, what do you think of my guest?"

Judith slid one foot into the sunshine. "He reminds me of my father, I'm not sure why." Two men could not differ from each other more in experience.

"Merari had a flexible mind." Naomi tapped one fist on Judith's knee. "When a business venture failed or the Lord gave him a daughter, instead of a son to care for him in old age, your father chuckled and went on. Achior has the same gift. When life changes, he may take a moment to catch his breath, then moves to change as well."

"I wouldn't expect such a trait in someone who spent his life in the Assyrian army." Perhaps this was why she felt at ease in the Ammonite's company. Judith stood and offered a hand to her friend. "Abra and the others are probably at the spring. I need to join them."

Naomi's spindle-thin fingers clasped her forearm and tightened. "You always do what's necessary, don't you, my strong daughter? For daughter you are, daughter of my heart."

"Naomi." The name came out in a whisper that almost choked her. The clatter of pots, the voices of Hilkiah and the other servants washed away.

"Peace, Judith, I didn't mean to upset you." The older woman's faded eyes shone with tears. "But when should we speak the truth if not at times like these? Even before your mother died, I loved you like my own."

Judith sank to her knees, forehead against the hem of the old woman's robes. "As I love you now, and always will." Her tears splashed the sunlit roof and evaporated.

I was wrong to think I had no family yesterday. Wrong. Here is my beloved mother, and my sisters wait for me at the spring.

Answering tears flowed down Naomi's cheeks. "Go, do your

work. Share your strength with us all."

"I will." Judith kissed the bristled chin. Out on the street, she dodged men laden with the first of the harvest—what there was to harvest. *Thank you, Lord, that we brought in the wheat a full moon ago.*

A few women passed her on their way into the village, each with a sloshing jug on her hip. Water for their families. For their neighbors. For their town

Villagers clustered around Sol the potter's gate, and at his chief rival's across the way. Like the ordinary men and women of Bethulia, the artisans were doing their part to supply the town.

Judith hurried on, her sandals light. Holofernes had given Achior his freedom, though he didn't intend to. Maybe the general's threats against her home were another unintentional gift. Maybe Chana wouldn't be the only person to discover her strength in the siege to come.

Chapter Seven

FROM THE SPRING NEAR THE ROOTS of the hill floated the voices of Bethulia's women. Judith climbed toward the village, panting in the heat with an urn half her height gripped in both arms. She paused to catch her breath and smile at the sound of laughter far below.

At first she and the other women had worked in swift, anxious silence, as if Assyrian chariots might plunge into sight any moment. Now the chain of matrons, mothers and servant girls moved at a steady pace, meeting at each turn to hand up a jug, bottle, or bowl to the next woman in line.

Judith blinked sweat out of her eyes and shifted the urn to her other side. Bent at the waist, she trudged up the last stretch to the hilltop, where Dorcas was waiting for her. Her little maid would carry the vessel on the last leg of its journey. In the courtyard at home, Huldah would seal the container with a rough lid and wax, ready to be tucked inside a storeroom.

On the crest of the hill Dorcas stood, arms already outstretched. Judith hesitated. "Careful. It's heavy."

"Don't worry, mistress." Dorcas clutched the urn to her chest with both arms. "I can do it." She wobbled in a circle and tottered toward the gate.

"Ask for help if you need it!" Judith watched the girl safely through the gate, then stretched, fists braced at the small of her back. From her vantage point here at the place of judgment, she watched other women climbing the path. She lifted her chin. *When you come, Holofernes, we'll be ready.*

Beyond a line of algum trees, their sandalwood scent rich on the air, a man bellowed. "Stop that ram! Stop him, boy!"

Through the branches, Judith heard the clatter of fleeing hooves. A whisk of brown fleece darted out of sight. Ham, Ezra's friend, called out, "I see him, Gothoniel."

"Don't just look at him—catch him," shouted her neighbor. When Ham doubled back and stooped, Gothoniel shouted louder. "What are you doing? After him!" Here in his natural element, the goatherd's voice thundered off the hillside.

Ham tucked several stones into his shepherd's scrip, pausing to admire one fist-sized rock.

"Yes, you'll need those for your sling when the Assyrians come. But now—" Gothoniel's tone climbed again. "Get after that beast!"

Smiling, Judith turned and then rushed toward Chana just as Joakim's bride stumbled the last few steps uphill, an enormous bowl clutched to her budding bosom. The bowl slipped lower with every step, water sloshing over the edge to spatter the girl's dove-colored garments.

"Chana, stop." She should have met the young woman down the slope, at the last bend in the track. "This part of the hill is my responsibility."

"I have it—" Perspiration streamed down Chana's face. Judith lunged as the bowl fell with a splash and a thud. Water darkened the dry ground at their feet. Chana's pale lips rounded. "What will my husband say? He'll be so ashamed of me."

Most women married slightly older men, since a bit of age better prepared a man to guide and protect his wife. But Joakim was three times older than Chana. After her few months of marriage, the girl looked fragile enough for the wind to knock down—if there had been any wind.

"We won't tell him." Judith righted the bowl. "This is women's business."

Lashes wet, Chana stared up at her. "Won't—tell—"

"There's some water left. Drink it." She supported the heavy bowl while the trembling girl obeyed, a few tears sliding into the bowl as she did.

Shoshana appeared around the bend with a pitcher tucked under each arm. As always, Chabris's wife walked as if she trod on thick rugs instead of dirt. "What happened? Oh—" She grinned down at the fresh mud puddle. "You should have seen the mess I made by the spring this morning, before my fingers woke up. I dropped a lovely carved bottle that belonged to my mother, and her mother before her. Every drop spilled right back into the pool."

Chana's shoulders relaxed. "You dropped something too?"

"Dropped and broke it." Shoshana laughed, and handed Judith both pitchers. "It's so hot. I think I'm finished for the day." She raised her eyebrows.

Judith nodded. "Why don't you both go home? I'll send word downhill that we need to stop for now." If only someone had suggesting stopping to rest on the day Manasseh died—

As the elders' wives vanished through the arch into Bethulia, Rebekah sauntered up from the spring, bead bracelet clicking at every step. She carried nothing, not even the smallest bottle.

Rebekah owns one bracelet and it is never off her wrist—Judith changed her grip on the pitchers. *Blessed Lord, forgive me.*

"Those things look heavy." Her neighbor's footsteps grated closer. "That's just the kind of thing you'd do, carrying two things instead of just one like the rest of us."

"Shoshana brought them uphill. I'm only taking them inside."

Judith glanced at her neighbor's empty hands.

Rebekah shrugged. "I left mine at the end of my stretch of path. I'm sure someone will fetch it the rest of the way." She yawned. "Nathanael had a restless night. You cannot imagine how tiring it is, caring for a child. No wonder you're strong enough to sling heavy urns of water around, with no babies of your own."

Judith looked at her. "Yes." She swung away toward the gate.

"And you've already done so much today." Rebekah kept up with Judith's longer strides. "All this—" Another click from the bracelet as she gestured down hill. "After your stroll with the Ammonite this morning."

One of the pitchers bobbled. "I asked him about sieges."

"Lila told me the two of you talked a long time on Uzziah's doorstep. A very long time."

Lila, the widow under the fig tree. Judith said nothing.

Rebekah twitched her skirts. "My son will be waking from his nap soon. He always wants me the instant he opens his eyes."

Judith gripped the pitchers tighter. Would it be so wrong to dump the contents over Rebekah's head?

Then a tiny figure hopped through the gate. "I come meet you, Mama."

Rebekah swooped the boy into her arms. "Thank you, Nathanael." She sashayed toward home just as Dorcas came through the open gate.

"I'll take those, mistress." Her kitchen maid held out both arms again.

Judith shook her head. "I'll do it." She heard the sharpness in her voice and dropped onto the seat by the shrine in the wall. "I need you to go down to the spring and tell the women to stop for now. It's dangerously hot." *Manasseh.*

"Yes, mistress." Her little kitchen maid studied her a moment. "Rest. I'll help you with the pitchers when I come back." She hurried away.

Judith stayed in the musty chill of the wall until the women started to come through the gate by twos and threes. Each bore at least one water vessel. Eyes shut as if in prayer, Judith twisted on the bench so no one would trip over her feet and listened to their voices. Some were soft and young, others cracked with age. The slosh of water punctuated them all.

Warmth rose from her heart and pressed out of her eyes as tears. *Thank you for these women, Lord. Thank you for every soul in the village.* Then she remembered Rebekah. *Well. Almost every soul.*

Chapter Eight

JUDITH TURNED HER HEAD TO GAZE at the shrine. Outside the walls, grass shushed in a brief wind, and a bird fluted a few bright notes. Inside the village, men and women called to each other. Footsteps hurried past on the street, some slow and heavy as if laden down, others urgent and quick. Here in the narrow dimness inside the wall, she rested between the natural world and the rising urgency of preparation.

She breathed in the musty smell of mud brick and the tang of burnt oil from the shrine. "Thank you," Judith breathed, and stood to get back to work just as Dorcas trotted up.

"Here, dear one." Judith handed over one of the pitchers, then stooped to hug the girl's thin shoulders. "Bless you."

Dorcas colored to her hairline. "Of course, mistress. Of course I will help you." She set off for the house.

Judith let her go ahead. The more Dorcas accomplished on her own, the steadier she would become. Shallow baskets of green olives lined the foot of the wall, ready to be taken to storage rooms or buried in the cool ground, sealed inside big pots. Judith paused to gloat over the fruits. They would give no oil, but neither would these olives fall into the hands or bellies of the Assyrians.

"I hate pickled olives." Abra spoke just behind her.

"I know." Judith shifted her pitcher to grip it by the handle, then tucked her free arm around Abra. "Soon we may be grateful for olives, even the ones pickled because they're too young to eat any other way. The men have been hard at work."

"Nearly as busy as the women." Abra broke off as Sol, the handsome young potter, jogged around the corner toward them. She smoothed her hair and settled the urn she carried jauntily on one hip. "Hello, Sol."

Judith stooped over the olives again to hide her grin. So her friend liked Sol's looks, did she?

"Did you sell all your work?" Abra's voice rang out, a little too merry. "Are you going out to dig clay for more?"

He nodded and kept going, but as Judith stretched to test the firmness of an olive she heard his steps falter. By the time she glanced back to see if he meant to speak with Abra after all, the potter was moving away.

Abra grunted. "I should've known better than to try to catch his eye with you beside me." Urn dangling from one hand, she plodded toward home.

"What do I have to do with it?" Judith caught up with her friend at the entrance to the courtyard.

All Abra's merriment was gone. "With you to distract him, Sol doesn't see me. Can't see me, maybe. Only you."

Water splatted from the pitcher to soak Judith's toes. "What?"

Her friend lowered her urn to the ground, then crouched to remove Judith's sandals and her own. "I grieved for you, every moment you spent grieving in the tent after Manasseh died. I feared we would never laugh together again. That you'd never laugh at all."

"Abra, stop." The words scratched her throat like claws.

But Abra just squatted on her heels and looked up at Judith.

"Punish me if you want, you need to hear this. Sol is not the only man who hopes your grief will end soon."

Judith swerved to stare at the street, where Sol hefted several baskets in his arms, muscled from shaping clay every day. "He's not even looking at me."

"Not now." Abra spoke in a tone of weary patience. "But he paused to watch you walk by. Or away. And he stopped altogether when you bent over the olives."

"Nonsense." Judith kicked her sandals out of the way. Why would Sol—would any man—stare at her? "Nonsense!"

In a corner of the courtyard, Huldah picked up her cane and straightened away from a jar she had just sealed shut. "What's nonsense?"

"She doesn't believe Sol just admired her on the street." Abra carried the urn across to the old cook. "Doesn't want to believe it."

Huldah thumped her stick on the pavement. "Watch your tongue, girl. That's no way to speak to our mistress."

"And a widow!" Judith burst out. Had they forgotten that as well?

Huldah let out a huff of breath. "Yes, a widow. A widow with no men of her husband's family to marry her. It's time you wed again, or so others say." She lowered her eyes as Judith stalked over and set her pitcher down with a thud.

Abra stepped between them. "I'm sorry, I know this upsets you. Still, better to hear it from us and be prepared. Unless you would rather goggle like a fish when some fool asks you to marry him."

"Sol would never ask me to—" Judith sank onto the bench built against the wall.

"He might." For once the wrinkles around the cook's mouth curled up instead of down. "Whether he wants to marry you or not, he's going to look and wonder. And he won't be the first or the last."

"Or the youngest or the eldest." Abra nodded agreement.

Judith studied the faces of these two women, so dear to her. So maddening. Huldah, born into Manasseh's household as a servant, had known her long before she became a rich wife, then a wealthy widow. Huldah knew how things should be done, or at least remembered how they were done by Manasseh's parents, and his grandparents before them.

"Why would any man want to marry me? Why even look at me, when Shoshana's lovelier, Chana's sweet and tender. Even Rebekah's more dashing." Her voice rose, she couldn't stop it. "Abra, you're younger than I am—"

"By six months."

Judith ignored her. "You can marry. You will. I will not." Never again.

"Hush, the neighbors will hear you." Huldah waved her crutch in the air for Abra to take, then limped over to clutch Judith's shoulders. "Know this, mistress. You have qualities no other woman of Bethulia has."

"Or even those in Jerusalem!"

The old woman's wispy brows tightened at Abra's interruption. "Or in Jerusalem. You have something few women possess."

Now she understood. "Riches." Cattle and gold, lands and crops. What man wouldn't look at her and see what she owned? Not her self at all. Manasseh had seen her. He had seen her for who she was, and loved her for that alone.

Huldah shook her head. "Wealth has nothing to do with it. A man wants a woman who—" She hesitated, scowling.

"A man wants a woman with a body he can sink into when he lies with her, a woman with passion and strength to match his own." Abra stuttered when they stared at her, and turned aside to tidy her hair. "Or so I've heard."

"You think men desire me for my size? My strength?" Judith drooped against the wall at her back. For hadn't Manasseh loved those very things? *I can hold you so tightly and you don't wince or pull away.'*

The cook brushed one crooked finger down Judith's black robes. "Men see the passion in you, no matter how you bank it with the ash of mourning."

"Huldah—you—I never—" In her whole life, Judith had never thought to hear the older woman talk this way.

"It's no secret I didn't approve when my young master married you. Daughter of a poor merchant? He could have done better. And after you wed, the shameless way you both behaved. Not just the first week, even the first month, but almost every day. In the daytime, too!" Her wrinkled cheeks warmed.

Judith felt hot-faced herself. *Manasseh and I, sneaking off through our private courtyard. Embracing with love and joy.* All the time Huldah had known. Probably everyone in the house had known.

Feet spread to steady herself, Huldah leaned closer. "And you're too easy on your servants. Always have been."

Blessed Lord, not again. Judith fought the temptation just to roll face down on the bench.

"Is she too soft on you as well?"

"Yes, even with me." Huldah flicked one foot at Abra, who dodged and grinned. "That comes of being born into a household without servants."

Next the old woman would blame her for being born at all. Judith wrapped her arms around herself.

Abra rapped the cook's shoulder with her knuckles. "Our mistress is right here. Talk to Judith, not me, unless you just like listening to yourself complain."

"Mind your manners, girl. I'm not too old to beat some politeness into you."

Abra sputtered. "Me! What about you?"

"Oh, let her finish." Judith straightened to meet the fierce eyes under their hooded lids. "You've wanted to say this a long time, Huldah. Get it over."

The old woman glowered at her. "It isn't fitting for me to tell you what's in my mind. I would have kept it to myself until the day I died, if the Assyrians weren't on the way to our gate."

So this was thanks to Holofernes as well. Judith jerked her chin. "Go on."

"Even before the young master died, I knew why he had chosen you." The harsh voice softened. "Such love you had for him! His mother grieved loud and long, as any mother of such a fine son would. But you grieved quietly, unshaken in your love for him and your respect for our Lord."

Judith bounded to her feet. Huldah snatched up her cane and swung it so the end of the stick blocked Judith's escape. "Now you offer that love to everyone. Abra, who you've always treated more like a friend than a servant, to my shame—"

"It's none of your business, you crone!"

Once more, Abra might not have spoken for the attention the older woman gave. "And Dorcas, too. I've even seen you touch a tree branch with tenderness, or gaze at a piece of fruit before you take a bite, like the pomegranate is a beloved child."

Abra nodded. "Yes, that's true."

"Stop." Not since the day Manasseh died had Judith felt stripped so bare. Did she have no secrets from anyone?

"Now those filthy dogs, those Assyrian swine, plan to destroy us, and you gather water and distribute food to those too poor to put stores by for themselves."

A breath of herbs and baking wafted through the kitchen window beside Judith. "How did you know?"

"Oh, mistress. I am old, I sleep light and wake early. I saw you go."

"I want no one else to know." Then Judith sagged against the wall. "But since you already do, you may as well help. Tomorrow I planned to visit Lila, and see if she needs provisions." Abra snorted.

"Hush, girl." Huldah scowled at Abra. "Our mistress ordered

men from her farms to deliver food to the house before dawn. But she delivered the packages of flour and oil, olives and salt, herself at first light."

"I wasn't—I didn't mean to remark on what Judith—" Abra shrugged. "It doesn't matter."

In the silence the palm fronds that shaded the courtyard hissed. "Huldah, are you done?"

"One thing more." Huldah rubbed the flesh below her arm, where Judith suspected the crutch sometimes pinched her. "It's a pity all that sneaking off to bed in daylight never made any sons. What a mother you would have been! If you can marry again, do it. Make children with another man."

The cook stumped back to the water vessels as if nothing had been said. Judith stared as Huldah lifted a jar and held it out to Abra. "Come on, girl, help me carry these to the store room." Huldah raised her head, eyebrows knotted. "Where's that useless young thing? I need Dorcas's help, too, for what it's worth."

"Why are you so contrary?" The words burst out of Judith.

"Mistress." Huldah didn't even glance back from the storeroom door. "Is there anyone alive who is not?"

Judith shut her mouth. Abra lifted a sealed water container but did not follow Huldah into the storage room. "Men like beautiful hair, too. And yours is so thick and glossy. So tidy, even now you no longer wear it in combs."

"We're supposed to keep our hair and bodies clean." Especially women.

"Yours isn't just clean. It's gorgeous." Abra poked a lock of her twisty hair behind one ear. It sprang free at once.

Judith's lips twitched. When Huldah stepped into the courtyard again, she tugged the cook onto the bench beside her. The crutch crashed to the ground, and Huldah grumbled to herself. But one threadlike arm slipped around Judith's waist.

"It isn't funny." Abra's lips curled even as she muttered it. The next instant the three of them were laughing.

"If I could give you my hair I'd do it gladly." Judith squeezed Abra's hand.

"Thank you." Abra propped Huldah's fallen crutch against the wall, within the older woman's reach.

Footsteps thudded down from the rooftop. Ezra leapt the last few stairs in a single jump. "It's ready, Judith. Abra said I could set it up for you and I have."

Abra finger-combed her hair. "You raised the tent already? That was quick."

"First you help bring in the herds, then you work on my tent? You've had a busy day." Judith got to her feet and shook the dust from her robes. "Thank you, Ezra."

Behind the magistrate's son, her little kitchen maid skimmed down the steps as silent as smoke. Like smoke, she drifted into the kitchen.

"What's it for?" Ezra hopped in place, eager as little Nathanael. Today, in the excitement of preparation, Ezra chose to be a boy again.

"Come back this evening and I'll show you. Right now—" Judith peered at the sky. "I need to go." No one asked her where. She scooped up her sandals and left.

Chapter Nine

DUST LINGERED ON THE STILL AIR as Judith descended
the path. Heat shimmered above the distant mountains. She
moaned when she entered the cool twilight beneath the cedars.
Usually she hurried to reach Manasseh's resting place. Today she
intended to savor every moment. The trees rose high above her, the
air pungent with their scent.

Manasseh had loved cedars for their strength.

Judith sank into her accustomed place, back supported by a
wide trunk, legs folded modestly beneath her black robe. Not that
anyone could see her. Everyone was still busy inside the village or
resting between their labors. She faced the boulder that sealed her
husband's family tomb, cut into the rock face. Manasseh's bones
rested in the floor now, his parents inside the niche in one wall.

Hands curled in her lap, Judith closed her eyes and breathed in
the cedars' aroma. *Blessed art thou, oh Lord—* What was that? She
half-stood to peer down the slope, Achior's warning sharp inside
her. *'An army countless as the dust of the earth.'* No one from the
village would intrude on her, true. But how long before soldiers
walked the hillside instead of her fellow villagers?

She took her place again. *Blessed art thou, Lord of my people.* Strange that Achior, so different from her, also craved solitude. Judith shook her head. "Blessed art thou, oh Lord, for the messenger you have sent us—

A crack exploded overhead, followed by a hiss of foliage and a thud. Judith lunged to her feet, then stared at the raw, splintered end of a heavy branch, broken loose in last autumn's storms. It had fallen at last, its foliage already drooping. Shards of wood as long as her forearm scattered the ground, a spray of daggers around the fallen bough.

Judith sat once again and leaned against the familiar trunk. Her heartbeat thudded against the bark, as if someone or something in the tree hammered to be let out.

Silly of her to bolt like a quail at the hunter's footstep. With tens of thousands of men and cattle, Holofernes's army would make far more noise than a broken branch. *I will hear them if they come. I will hear them coming.*

Judith glanced around one more time, then shut her eyes to pray. A more serious petition than the one gabbled hastily after her disagreement with Rebekah.

"Blessed art thou, oh Lord. Thank You for the love I shared with Manasseh—" She touched the roots that cradled her, remembering her husband's laughter, low and tender when they were alone, or his great shout of enjoyment when something amused him during the day.

A bee hummed by close to Judith's cheek. The tiny wind of its wings brushed her skin, and she opened her eyes to watch the insect vanish in the direction of her family's burial chamber. Her mother Esther rested there with her father Merari, a decade older and four inches shorter than his wife. Judith remembered his glossy hair and wondered if Abra had ever envied him. His laughter had been soft and long. Judith had never been able to resist laughing with him, even when she was too young to understand the joke.

And Esther, with her great beak of nose. Tall like Judith, and so quiet compared to Merari. Her mother had taken pleasure in keeping house, in making it a place of comfort and love. She always used the best of her weaving for Merari's garments, waited to stitch her own clothes after Judith made her choice from the new cloth.

How Esther would have enjoyed the house Manasseh built from the roots of the one she created. Or would her mother weep because the place now sheltered only her childless daughter? A wealthy widow and her servants.

Judith thumbed sweat off the back of her neck. Huldah and Abra must be wrong. Surely Manasseh's wealth explained why men desired her. Sol wanted her house in town, the lands outside it, and the summer home built on those lands. All of it Manasseh's. *I am only the steward he left behind, Lord.*

So she shared his riches, not just by giving to the priests, as expected of people born to wealth. Not just quietly delivering food to those in need. She bought goods from all the potters in town. Handsome Sol, who embellished his pots with fancy carving—though perhaps, Judith thought with a frown, she should avoid Sol for a while. She liked the work of silent, sad-faced Ruth just as well.

Ruth spent long hours bent over every vessel she made, burnishing them until the clay shone bright as metal. Judith never passed the other widow's stall in the market without pausing to admire and praise. "People want more than money for their work," Merari had often said. "They want what they create to be appreciated."

Ruth learned the craft from her husband in the months he spent, slowly dying.

Judith wondered if that would have hurt even more, to watch her beloved waste away, day by day?

No. Nothing could have hurt worse. Judith curled her fingers around an exposed root and squeezed until she could focus her thoughts.

If Merari still lived, how would her father react to the Assyrian threat? What advice would her mother give? Judith rocked in place. She had been a wife three years, a widow two more. Right now she wanted her parents, missed them as much as her husband.

Blessed art thou, Lord— "Lord, help me! I miss them so much!" Judith crawled away from the tree, stretched out face down on the ground, and wept until no more tears fell. Exhausted, she curled on her side. No prayers. No plans. Nothing but the wind and the distant murmur of water down the hill.

When she opened her eyes, sunlight poured between the cedars in an amber flood, and tree shadows stretched across the clearing. Judith stumbled to her feet and brushed her robes with both hands. Ezra would be waiting for her to explain what she meant to do with the tent on her rooftop. She couldn't return home with dirt and dry cedar needles clinging to her garments, like some lazy shepherd—

A flare of white lanced toward her from above. When Judith lifted a hand to shield herself from its radiance, the shaft of light coalesced into an enormous sword. It flashed down in a killing arc. And vanished.

Judith swung in a circle, heart leaping in her chest. She was alone. Alone, with the splash of the spring below and the homely call of a wild donkey down the hill. Alone with the vision of a sword.

More than a vision. Judith gaped at her right hand. Her empty hand. She still felt something she had never experienced, a thing women were forbidden to know. The weight of a sword hilt in her palm.

In spite of the heat, Judith wrapped her arms around herself. *I dozed off. It was nothing but a dream.* Shaking, she stared through the feathery cedar branches into the sky. "Lord of my people—was that a vision?"

Impossible. The One chose men to be his messengers. Only men. Never women.

Chapter Ten

EZRA SAT ON THE TOP STEP TO HER ROOF, leaning back on his elbows, legs stretched down what seemed like half the staircase. His knobby ankles already stuck out below the garment Naomi had stitched for him less than a month ago.

Judith's black tent rippled behind him, entrance pulled wide. She smelled the goat hair, and the overpowering, familiar odor of loss and grief wiped away her dream vision like nothing else could.

"Why did you want your tent set up again?" Ezra lurched to his feet. "Judith? What's wrong? Do you need water or—" He froze, one foot on the roof, the other on the step below. "Blessed Lord, they're here. They're already here?"

"No! No, it's nothing to do with the Assyrians. Don't worry, I'm fine." But Judith stumbled across to the parapet where the air might move, and cool her face. Where she could no longer see the tent, though she could not escape its smell. "You know I visit—" Her throat clicked. "—Manasseh's tomb every day?"

Ezra fiddled with the sling tucked in his belt. "Everybody knows."

Everybody. Enough time had passed that no one commented any more, but everyone still knew. Judith took a shallow breath, one hand over her nose and mouth. "I didn't expect—the smell of goat hair—takes me back."

Back to the first days after her beloved died, with his mother Deborah's constant wails from downstairs. *"Manasseh, my son. My son—"*

Judith remembered her husband's naked body, waiting to be prepared for the grave by the women of the household. By her. She smelled the fragrant oils they rubbed into his cold flesh. She heard Deborah keening when the boulder boomed into place and sealed Manasseh inside the tomb.

That night when Judith had crawled into the bed where Manasseh had loved her so often, so well, the scent of his flesh still infused the room. His tangy, male odor made a mockery of the hours Abra and Dorcas had spent scrubbing the house and everything inside it. So Judith had dragged this tent up to the roof. Inside its shelter, she stretched her aching body on a simple mat instead of the cushions she and her husband once shared.

Now her breath hitched, the stink of goat hair making her gag. Ezra's breath quickened in response, and Judith turned like a poorly hinged door and forced a smile. "I'm just—remembering."

If our life together had lasted fifty years it would have been too short.

"Manasseh died to feed our village." The young man touched the tent with one fingertip. "Grandmother still talks about it sometimes. About him."

"I'm glad." Judith crossed to the tent one reluctant step at a time. She had asked for it to be raised again, after all. Then she stared out over the plains, rich with the scent of summer and twilight. "Before Manasseh died, I honored the Lord like a child. Unquestioning. After he died, I—" *I, what?* "That changed."

Was that why the sword of light appeared to her this afternoon? As a warning that she was not to question the ways of the Lord?

Ezra stooped to peer inside the tent. "Is that why you wanted your tent raised up here again?" His voice came muffled, as if muted by the fabric.

"What?" Judith stepped away from her view of the hillside. "No. After Achior spoke to us the other day, I thought the tent could provide shelter while we keep watch for our enemies."

Ezra backed out of the tent in a rush. "My father is meeting all the townsmen this evening, in the market square. The first volunteers will stand watch tonight at moonrise."

Of course the men of Bethulia would post lookouts. It was a man's responsibility to guide and counsel his family, and protect them as well.

But the thought of huddling inside the house night after night, waiting for the lookout's bellow when the Assyrians finally appeared, made Judith fist both hands. *I don't want to lie there and shiver, or bolt awake at the first shout in the darkness.*

She wanted to see them coming for herself.

"Can I help?" Ezra's whole body tilted toward her at a quivering angle.

"Help me how?" What was he talking about?

"My father won't let me keep watch with the men, he says I'm too young. But I can see a long way, even in the dark. Grandmother says I can spot a ripe fig on a tree all the way across the valley."

Judith laughed. "I'm sure she's right. Only—Ezra, I'm not keeping watch." Not exactly. But her household had no man to join the rest—

"Then why do we need the tent? Oh, I know! It'll keep us hidden from archers. Achior told me Assyrian bowmen are the best in the world."

Best—or worst? "And they could arrive any time." Judith contemplated the young man's face, so narrow. So young. "Uzziah already said you couldn't keep watch. I don't want to get you in trouble. I don't want to put you in danger." The tent had been a witless idea, as silly as imagining the One had sent her a vision.

Ezra patted the woven belt at his waist, twisted so it formed a small sack on one hip. The makeshift pouch rattled.

His friend Ham had his shepherd's scrip. Judith made the obvious guess. "Stones for your sling?"

Ezra nodded, sober as his father. "I carry it with me always now. Every man in Bethulia does. But after the Assyrians come, I won't have anyplace to practice. I tried in Grandmother's garden on the rooftop earlier, but she said I beheaded too many flowers."

"Perhaps you'd better conserve your shot until it's really needed." When the boy's expression lighted again, Judith frowned at the goat hair tent. "If your father and Naomi agree, I suppose you can help me." If they approved, it meant she would keep watch after all.

Ezra was already leaping for the stairs. "I'll go ask!"

"Wait, we need to—" The young man had already crossed the courtyard. *So eager. So eager for war to come.*

Then, from the kitchen doorway came a giggle, quickly hushed. "Good evening, M-master Ezra."

The magistrate's son paused with one sandal on, the other dangling from his hand. "What? Oh, hello—uhm. Dorcas?"

"Yes, that's me. I mean, is there anything I can do for you? Are you staying for supper? It's very good tonight, soup with lentils. I made the bread for the sop myself."

Judith listened to her little maidservant's rapid speech and frowned. She had never heard Dorcas speak so eagerly before. She sounded like someone else Judith had heard recently. Who?

Abra. Abra, out on the street with Sol.

"That's kind, but I'm on my way home. Be back soon—" A shuffling sound as Ezra fastened on his second sandal. Then he was gone.

On the roof Judith propped one hip on the wall and hid her face in her hands. She should go downstairs and talk with the girl at once. At once. She stayed where she was.

A moment later, her little kitchen maid's breathy laughter

sounded an arm span away. "Mistress?"

Judith jumped. *Oh, yes, I'll make a fine watchman.* "Yes, Dorcas, what is it?"

"I'm sorry, I didn't mean to listen, but I was in the kitchen and I—I heard Master Ezra. I wondered all day why you wanted the tent, and then I couldn't help overhearing you talk with him, and oh, please, I want to help, too."

Here was an opportunity Huldah would approve, a chance for Judith to deal coolly with a servant. "You have so many duties already, dear. Gathering fuel for the cook fire, grinding flour—you know that's an endless task. And you run errands for Huldah and for me. I need you to do that."

Dorcas teetered on her bare toes. "I promise to do them all first. I promise!"

The girl was so slender she barely cast a shadow. Would she be strong enough to keep that promise?

As Judith studied her little maidservant, she remembered the market day when she first fell in love with Manasseh. While she had helped Merari arrange the newest wares in his booth, her hand brushed against a beaker of precious, perfumed oil. The oil rolled toward the edge of a shelf, and Manasseh, busy in his own father's larger booth next door, reached through, caught and held the tiny vessel out for her. And smiled.

He smiled down at her, and Judith realized that, tall as she had grown, Manasseh was still taller. Over the bolts of fabric in her arms she smiled up into the sweetness in his eyes. And wanted that sweetness for herself.

Such a simple beginning to so much love. So much loss.

But both Merari and Manasseh's father had been merchants, even if hers did not succeed as well as his. Not all servants lived out their lives in servitude, but a far wider gulf divided Dorcas from Ezra.

"Mistress, can I help Master Ezra? And you?"

When she took this girl in, Judith hadn't given a thought to Dorcas's future. Love and marriage seemed years away for such a wisp of a thing.

"Very well." *I will make sure they never stand watch together.* Not to punish Dorcas, to protect her heart. Judith spoke quickly, over the girl's gasp of delight. "As long as you fulfill your other duties first. As long as Huldah agrees."

Judith hoped the old cook didn't shatter her crutch pounding it on the ground when she heard the news. "Now go, sleep." Before Ezra came back.

Moonlight glimmered on the girl's dark curls, lighting them with blue as she skipped closer. "But I want to keep watch tonight. I rested after we carried water, I'm not tired."

"No," Judith cut in. "We have more water to fetch tomorrow, and the day after." If they were fortunate.

Dorcas let out a huff of breath. "Very well, mistress. Peaceful night to you."

"And to you." Judith waited until the cadence of the girl's feet faded, then settled on the wall to watch the distant mountains vanish in the dark.

Chapter Eleven

JUDITH SEALED THE EARTHENWARE JAR, then hefted it onto the highest shelf built into the storeroom wall. The only one with any space left. Out on the hillside, the women of Bethulia carried ever-smaller pots from spring to storerooms in their race to supply the town. Ruth, Sol and the other potters went without sleep as they rushed to finish jugs unadorned with designs or color. Kilns burned every day except Sabbath.

"Did you go to bed at all?" Huldah's wiry fingers gripped Judith's wrist. "Stop, mistress. Rest. We've done much in just two days." A pause. "You've done much."

When Judith tried to move away the cook tightened her hold.

"You said we shouldn't squabble among ourselves with what's coming." Huldah jerked her head toward the wall, and the mountains beyond. "I don't agree with letting Dorcas waste time on the roof." She sniffed. "But I want to thank you for working to keep us safe and fed."

"I'm only doing my duty." As mistress of the household. Mistress of a wealthy household.

"Chut, I only do my duty, mistress." Huldah raised her wispy eyebrows, then caught Judith in a hard embrace. "Why is it so difficult for you to accept gratitude?" With one last squeeze, the older woman let go and limped toward the kitchen. "Time to cook if we're to eat today. That girl needs to mind the fire while I mix the bread."

Up on the rooftop, Dorcas's laughter trilled out.

Huldah shook both fists in the air. "That giggle! Worse than a branch scratching brick. Let the child stay where she is, I'd rather work in quiet than listen to her silliness."

"She's just a youngster." And Ezra must have arrived.

A glower from the hooded eyes. "At least the mite's started to round out a little. She was nothing but eyes, hair and elbows when she first came."

Blessed Lord, the old woman was twistier than an olive branch. "Hair, elbows and giggle?"

Huldah humphed. As she stomped away to the kitchen, Judith wondered if the cook really believed no one noticed how she heaped Dorcas's bowl with extra cheese. She waited until she heard twigs rattle on the hearth, then tiptoed into the kitchen doorway. After Huldah coaxed the first tiny quiver of flame from the sticks, Judith strolled in and nudged some dried dung into the fire.

"I'm glad you think Dorcas has started to fill out. It's hard for me to tell since she's growing taller, too." Judith watched the cook slap flour, salt and water into dough, then pat it along the curves of a bowl nested in the fire. As the surface heated, the unleavened bread would bake. "Well, I'll be upstairs—"

"Good. Bethulia can use every pair of eyes." Achior's voice, quiet as always, came from the gate into the courtyard. He slid off his sandals, noticed her watching him, and spread his hands. "Everyone in Uzziah's household removes their shoes at the threshold, so now I do it, too."

He tried to learn her people's ways, to blend in. "That's good," Judith said, and led the way to the roof. She touched Dorcas's shoulder and bent to whisper in the girl's ear. "Huldah just used the last of the flour. I need you to go grind more."

"But I—I mean yes, mistress." Dorcas eased around Achior with a respectful nod. A moment later the grate of the grinding stones rose from the courtyard.

Judith perched on one of the low stools she had carried to the tent that morning. "I suppose Ezra told you about my plan?"

Achior took the other seat across from hers, his eyes already on the mountain pass, and did his best to tuck his bare feet beneath the too-short robe. "I was there when he asked Uzziah's permission to help. I'm surprised the boy isn't here before me."

So was she. But Judith studied Achior's skimpy garment from the tail of her eye. She must find out if Naomi planned to weave a better fitting robe for Bethulia's visitor. If not, then perhaps she could—

No, he was Naomi's guest. Bethulia's guest, not hers. Judith shifted in place and bent forward to study the horizon in silence. Perhaps she could convince some of the village's women to make a simple garment or two. "How much longer do you think we have?"

"Days, maybe less." Achior shrugged, still focused on the pass. "Hours, perhaps."

He no longer tried to soften his words to protect her. If Achior spoke more openly to her, she could do him the same honor. Some of the time. "I feel them coming. A crackle in the air, like lightning just before it strikes."

"An apt description." He inclined his head.

Ezra bounded onto the roof. "Sorry I'm late. Have I missed anything?" The young man shaded his eyes to scan the distant slopes, as well.

"Not yet." Achior started to stand, then settled down again with a shake of his head when Ezra bounced to the wall and leaned across it toward the pass.

The boy flapped one hand, left then right, toward either end of town. "I stopped on the way to visit the other watchmen. Chabris seems calm as someone on his own rooftop. Gothoniel's sweating from more than the sun, I think." He grinned.

In the kitchen below their feet, Huldah shouted. "Where do you think you're going, you haven't ground enough flour to feed a single person for one meal, never mind the whole household—Where are you going, girl? Come back here at once!"

Scampering as if the old woman might give chase, stick and all, Dorcas whisked onto the roof. "Mistress, will your guests join you for breakfast? I need to know how much wheat to—oh!" The dimple flared beside her mouth. "Master Ezra, hello."

Judith caught the way Achior's pale eyes flicked from Dorcas to Ezra and back again. What would happen to an Assyrian serving maid who fell in love with a man above her station? Judith didn't want to know.

"Thank you, I already ate." Ezra did not even turn his head. Achior nodded agreement, and Dorcas wilted like a bud in high summer.

"Oh. Oh, I see. Well, I'll go tell Hul—tell—" The little maid raised one wobbly arm and pointed.

Judith's seat skittered backward. This time the tower of dust churning above the pass was not a cloud.

The women! *Blessed Lord, the women at the spring!* Even as shouts arose from the men farther along the wall, Judith clutched Dorcas's hand. "Run. Tell the women to hurry inside at once. At once!"

"No need for alarm. Not yet." But Achior angled his head toward the center of town. "Better go get your father, Ezra." He stood when the girl and boy sprinted away, their cries echoing across the courtyard and out into the street.

Judith watched the dust column spread wider. Was it her imagination, or could she hear the far-off lowing of cattle and the relentless beat of horses' hooves?

"You asked me when they would come, Judith. The answer is now." Achior gestured at the murk above the horizon. "It shocks me, how much I want to survive."

She jerked round to face him. "You're afraid? But—" But he had survived so many battles.

"All those years riding into combat, I accepted death." The former commander's mouth tugged into the familiar half-smile. "But here?" He spread palms calloused from years spent wrapped around a sword hilt. "I can't fight to defend myself. I can't attack. All I can do is wait to see if I—if we—survive."

If. Judith longed for water, for sheep's milk, for anything to ease her dry mouth. To her shock, Achior laughed.

"I've never felt so free. You're part of that, Judith. Part of why I'm grateful for every breath." He eased closer.

She stepped back. "Stop."

Dorcas had erupted from the gate and was leaping, slithering downhill. Abra, the nearest water bearer, spun toward the pass. The jug she carried sailed out of her hands and shattered on the rough ground. As the girl's cries faded into the distance, women's screams flooded the hillside.

Achior did not even glance toward the noise. "And Naomi treats me with a grandmother's warmth." He spoke quickly, as if to patch a dangerous opening. "Before you—both of you—I never had the chance to enjoy women's company. Since my mother died, concubines were all I knew."

He swerved away to stare down at the village women stumbling toward the gate.

Judith leaned over the wall, hands cupped around her mouth. "Don't panic, they are just coming through the pass." She was proud to see that every woman on the flight uphill clutched at least one water vessel, and that Abra took several from a girl staggering under the weight of an arm full of small jugs.

76

Best to focus on what was really happening than to give way to foolish imagination. Surely she was imagining things, from the sword she had dreamed in the grove to Achior's remarks a moment ago. Even Huldah and Abra, with all their wild talk about men, would not credit the crazy idea that Achior—

Yes, the idea would surely make even Huldah laugh.

Part Two
The Siege

Chapter Twelve
Judith

JUDITH GRABBED THE TEMPORARY FENCE with one hand when the old ewe shoved against her legs. "I know, little mother." She struggled to keep her balance in the straw. "I need to make sure your baby's perfect."

While the ewe bawled to her lamb and he bleated back to her, Judith checked the young creature's back and limbs for straightness. Her fingertips rubbed a rough spot just below one tiny knee. Scar tissue.

She stooped to release the lamb at once. Only flawless creatures could serve as sacrifice for the One. Judith dodged the ewe's rush and hopped out of the pen. The sheep glared at her through the rails, stamped one foot, then turned to nuzzle her baby. He thrust his nose under her belly and began to nurse, fat tail whisking.

Before Judith entered the next enclosure, she glanced at Dorcas. Her maid stood in a narrow walkway between the pens now crowding the village square. The lamb Judith had already selected from her herds nestled in the girl's arms.

"I know he's awkward to carry. I promise to find the other one soon, dear." Judith shouted to be heard over the chorus of baaing sheep, then climbed into a makeshift corral full of older lambs.

She stooped and caught the fleece of the nearest one. A female. Priests accepted male sacrifices only. Judith opened her fingers to let the ewe lamb escape, then dug both hands into another fleece before its owner could leap away. The young male reared up, bucked and squirmed while she tried to keep hold of him and check his straight back and sturdy legs at the same time.

Judith held the lamb close until he quieted, then eased over the fence. With him tucked under one arm, she did her best to right her tumbled garments, then nodded to Dorcas. "Let's go."

They wove between what seemed like countless pens. A cow lay peacefully in one, her calf curled at her side. From the next a bunch of goats watched Judith pass by, yellow eyes wild in spite of their motionless stance. One cried out loudly, as if annoyed by Dorcas's nearness, and the girl nearly dropped her lamb.

By the time Judith reached the line of village men snaked from the foot of the High Place to the edge of the square, her own lamb's hooves had scraped her thighs through the tough sackcloth. She turned toward Dorcas, panting in her wake. "I'm sorry, dear, I should have asked Abra to help me."

"We're fine." Her little maid squatted to set the lamb on his feet. She crooned and stroked him until the young beast sagged against her blissfully, tail flipping in rhythm with every pat.

She's forgotten why we're here. Judith opened her mouth to remind the girl, only to realize she was stroking her own lamb's ears. He slept, head propped on her shoulder, legs lax, eyes shut in dreams or bliss. Judith tucked both arms around the little animal, and stared at the black-clad back of the man in front of her in line. The lamb's heartbeat pattered against her breast.

At last she and Dorcas reached the High Place. "Bring the other lamb to me when I give you the signal." Judith started up the steps.

As head of a household, she selected the animals to be slain on the Lord's altar. It was her responsibility to watch the sacrifice give its life to the One.

The lamb bleated when she stood it before Sirach in front of the altar. The priest touched the animal's curly head. "Thanks and blessings to you, creature without flaw." The priest steadied the lamb with one gentle hand. He lifted the knife with the other.

Now his voice echoed off the stones of the platform. "Blessed art though, oh Lord. Accept this sacrifice. Heed your people's plea for mercy." With a smooth, practiced stroke, Sirach sliced the lamb's throat.

The metallic odor of blood mingled with the scent of sandalwood as he sprinkled the scarlet drops around the stone altar, then used the knife to divide the body and give the choicest parts to the flames. To the Lord.

"I have one more. A private offering." When Sirach nodded his permission, Judith crossed to the edge of the High Place. She gestured for Dorcas, only to find the girl already on the top step, tears trickling down her cheeks.

Dorcas kept her lips pressed together as Judith stooped for the lamb. The girl hurried down the steps, along the side of the square and into the mouth of the street that led home. Away from the High Place. Judith watched her go, and then carried the lamb to Sirach and the altar.

How many animals had her people sacrificed since the Assyrians appeared on the horizon this morning? A hundred? More? Judith made herself focus on the rest of the ceremony, on Sirach's prayers and the sacred odor of incense and blood.

Blessed art thou— She stopped herself. Private prayers did not belong on the High Place. After the priest burnt Judith's second offering, she descended to the square. Joakim, the next man in line, strutted up the steps with a servant boy at his heels holding a caged dove.

Bethulia was in danger. Why had the elder chosen the smallest possible creature for his sacrifice? Judith shook her head. It was not her business. Let it be between Joakim, the priest, and the One.

Eyes down, she eased between the men waiting in line. Most nodded, or murmured her name in greeting. At last she left the square behind, but the streets between her and home were crowded, mainly with women and children. Judith had to take strides half as long as usual.

At one narrowing in the street, where two neighbors had built porches outside their doorways, a group of serving women filled the road from side to side. Judith kept still with difficulty, tapping one foot. When another young woman tried to squeeze past her through the throng, only to trip over Judith's feet, Judith caught and steadied her. The girl wiggled her way past without a backward glance. Or a thank you.

Judith started through the ragged gap the other had temporarily cut through the crowd, only to recognize the clay-spattered garments of a woman on one of the porches. She stood on tip-toe and shouted. "Ruth! What's happened, do you know?"

The potter, arms stained brown with clay, half-turned toward her. Usually Ruth greeted Judith cheerfully. Now she just stared. "Everyone wants to get to the wall. To the rooftops, to see our enemy. To watch them make camp." She gathered her skirts to hop into a clear spot on the street.

Judith dodged around the jam of loitering servants, cut across the porch and jumped after the other widow. "You're welcome to come watch from my house."

The artisan looked as if she had not slept for days. She was only a dozen years older than Judith, but right now she moved like a woman older than Naomi.

"Please, come, share the evening meal—" But Ruth had already started off again, each footstep uncertain. "Ruth? Ruth, wait."

The potter did not seem to hear. Judith tried to catch up with her until Ruth disappeared in a group of artisans outside Sol's shop. Blushing, Judith ducked her head and did her best to hurry past.

By the time she neared her own house daylight was fading. A group of screaming adolescents clotted the street in front of the gate of her courtyard. She wanted to scream as well. She wanted the cool quiet of home. Even the reeking solitude of the goat hair tent would be better than this press of bodies. *Blessed art thou, oh Lord. Blessed art thou—*

Judith squirmed the last few paces through her gateway. Half a step inside she kicked off her sandals almost at a run and fled to the roof. Abra and Huldah were already there, crouched by the town wall. "Mistress!" The cook grabbed Judith's skirts and tried to tug her down beside them.

But Judith sidled away to stare. On every roof in sight women, men and children stood silhouetted by the last rays of sun. On her neighbor's rooftop, the shepherds who had helped Achior the day he arrived huddled with Gothoniel.

And out on the plain, the noise of carts and oxen shattered the twilight. The plain swarmed with soldiers, horses and livestock. Cattle bellowed. From their pens in the village square, Bethulia's rams and goats returned the challenge.

Judith started to sink to her heels, but then the warm smell of burning olive oil and a fan of light spread around her feet. "No!" She leapt to the staircase where Dorcas approached, each step slow and careful as she steadied the pottery lamp in her slender hands. Judith snatched it away and extinguished the light.

Dorcas's voice quivered. "I lit it so we can see, mistress."

"We're not the only ones with eyes, not anymore." Judith slipped one arm around the girl's shoulders and drew her down with the other two women.

"Use your head, girl." Huldah thrust her chin at the campfires.

Dorcas whimpered. "What—what are they d-doing?" Hand wavering, she gestured at a gang of naked men near the closest edge of the encampment. Their bodies gleamed with sweat in the light of torches held aloft by other naked men. Slaves.

"I don't know, dear one." Slaves, as her people had been slaves not so long ago. "I imagine they are hard at work building something for their Assyrian masters." Achior had numbered the foot soldiers for her, the archers and charioteers, even the beasts used to feed them all.

How many slaves lived in the camp? How long had they been slaves? Judith wondered if any had ever been rich, like her, and shivered. *Blessed art thou, oh Lord. Keep us safe from that fate again—*

Abra covered her ears. "So loud. So many. Why aren't the treetops shaking?"

"It s-s-sounds like thunder c-c-come down from the s-sky." Dorcas crouched by Judith's feet, a fold of sackcloth robe clutched in both hands.

Judith covered the child's cold fingers with her own. "Why don't you go inside?"

When Dorcas shook her head and pressed closer, Huldah grunted. "They're here. So be it." But even she spoke quietly, as if an Assyrian bowman might hear and take aim. "An army on the doorstep's not going to keep me from my rest." She hobbled down the first few stairs, paused. "You coming, girl?" Another grunt. "Oh, stay here. You'd just cry and keep me awake."

Abra made a harsh sound in her throat. "Old woman, if you don't—"

At the same moment Dorcas shivered upright. "I'm fine, Abra. And don't worry, Huldah, I won't make a sound." She slid one hand under the cook's elbow. Together the old woman and the child retreated to the servant's quarters.

"I wondered if anything would make Dorcas stop giggling." Abra rubbed both hands through her hair until it flared around her face. "It only took an army."

On the plain, the campfires already outnumbered the stars.

"'Countless as the dust of the earth,'" Judith murmured.

Abra jolted beside her. "What?"

"That's how Achior described them to me." Even with the former commander's warnings, Judith felt stunned. So many men, all armed. So many against so few.

"They scared me at first." Abra made a sound that might have been a laugh. "All right, they still do. But if we stay true to the Lord's law, won't we be safe no matter how many there are?"

Yes. "I'm only a woman, not a priest. But yes, I think so." Maybe now she could tell Abra what had happened near Manasseh's tomb? Ask if her friend thought it a vision, a dream, or the result of too little sleep—

A whip snapped out. A shriek cut the night. In the distance, one of the naked men toiling just opposite the spring had failed to move fast enough. Abra pressed both hands over her ears again as the lash struck over and over and over.

Judith closed her eyes, closed out the flicker of the campfires. But her memory of the sword of light shone against her eyelids, brighter than the flames spreading from horizon to horizon. She slipped one arm around her friend's waist. The moment for sharing her dream or vision was lost.

The slave's screams stopped long before the last blow fell. "Thank the One you sent Dorcas to bed." Abra wiped her eyes.

Judith nodded, her cheek in the notch of her friend's shoulder. Together they listened to the Assyrians seize the world outside the wall.

Chapter Thirteen
Holofernes

HOLOFERNES STALKED ACROSS the trampled grass toward his body slave, and Bagoas dropped to all fours and pressed his beardless face to the ground. "Your tent is ready, master. I've arranged everything as you prefer it."

"We shall see." If he found a single item out of place—Well, Bagoas knew the consequences better than any other slave in camp. Any living slave. Holofernes strode past the prostrate eunuch, who rolled to his feet and scrambled backward.

For a slave to turn away from his master guaranteed a beating, or worse, but Bagoas must open the flap before Holofernes reached the entrance. His slave scrabbled like a crab and managed to yank the fabric aside just in time.

Holofernes swept inside and pivoted at the pavilion's center to assure himself Bagoas had forgotten nothing. Rugs layered the floor—woven carpets from conquered domains, simpler rugs of dyed ram's wool.

His soldiers slept on plain mats, fleeces, or the bare earth.

Holofernes dreamed in a bed so large it required an ox cart to carry the frame from one siege camp to the next. Cushions and blankets heaped the bed, fabrics in every texture and weight.

A chair and table faced the entrance. Bowls and platters in half a dozen different styles covered the polished surface. Like the rugs, the cushions and blankets, each piece of pottery came from a culture now under Assyrian rule. Fresh bread, roasted lamb, olives and herbed olive oil filled the pavilion with welcoming odors.

The general narrowed his eyes and pivoted again, faster. Where was it? If that cur Bagoas had forgotten it again, his hide would festoon the walls of Babylon! Holofernes took a quick step nearer the bed, then dropped flat-footed to the carpets. Behind him, Bagoas shuddered.

The altar stood against the pavilion wall. Out of sight of the soldiers who would visit the pavilion on military matters, but positioned where Holofernes could pay homage in his few private moments. The general pressed one fist to his chest.

Tonight, honored Lady, he swore. Tonight he would complete the shrine himself, as his Lady Goddess desired.

The general finished examining every detail of his quarters, from the angle of the chair to the height of the oil lamps on their chains. He turned toward his belated meal, to find Bagoas on his knees again. The eunuch held a wine vessel in both hands.

Holofernes grunted. "Drink."

Bagoas tipped a mouthful of wine into one narrow palm and swallowed. The general watched the slave's elongated face for convulsion or sudden sweat, then waved him toward the table. Bagoas positioned the wine within easy reach of the chair, broke off a bite of bread and another of lamb. He sampled each, dipping the bread in the oil.

One leg thrust out, Holofernes waited again. Only when he was certain the eunuch suffered no ill effects did he snap his fingers. "Armor."

While his body slave removed Holofernes's pointed helmet and scale mail shirt, the general propped his sword against the chair, careful as always to stand between the slave and the weapon. He held his arms out from his sides. "Bagoas. How long have I owned you?"

"Five years, master." The eunuch eased the patterned robe down over Holofernes's head, careful not to disturb the elaborate curls and ripples of beard or oiled hair. Down on all fours again, Bagoas crawled around to smooth the fringed hem.

When each strand lay perfectly, Holofernes dropped into his chair and took his first mouthful of wine. "Tell me again, Bagoas. When did your priests decide you should join their number? When did they cut you?"

"On my sixth birthday, master." Bagoas lifted the shoulder-high fan, ready to stir the heavy air.

Six years old. A lifetime spent without women. Holofernes almost pushed his food away, then rapped his knuckles on the table. "Stop fanning me. I don't want the distraction."

"As you will, my lord." The eunuch straightened for the next demand.

While he ate, Holofernes studied the dishes before him. Bethulian potters had a reputation for creating beauty joined with utility. When the town fell he might add some local work to his collection. At least he would order the army's supply restocked.

From every direction he heard the sounds of construction. The clatter of cartwheels mixed with the thud of oxen hooves, shouted orders, the snap of whips as slaves leveled the road or built animal pens.

Assyrians organized all siege camps to one plan. Divided by a central road, with beasts and slaves kept apart from the soldiers. And the commander's quarters at the center. *Where I belong.*

Holofernes rarely noticed the noise any more. But at the start of a siege he liked to tune in. In the distance, a whip cracked again and again. "Pure music." He drained his wine.

"Master?" Bagoas stepped forward.

"Nothing. Send runners to the commanders. I expect them immediately I finish my meal." They would eat with the men, of course.

"Yes, my lord." The eunuch hunched his way out, facing Holofernes until the tent flap dropped between them.

"Bagoas!"

The lamp flames shivered when his body slave darted inside and dropped face first on the floor. "W-what did I leave un-d-done, master?"

"Leave the door open, I want to see."

"Yes, my lord. Apologies, my lord." The eunuch hastened to secure the woven flap and sped into the darkness.

A goat bleated nearby, cry abruptly silenced when the high priest cut its throat on the king's altar. Nebuchadnezzar, the god-king, only left Babylon once a year, on ceremonial progress to a token battle. The rest of the time Nebuchadnezzar sat on a throne as big as a bed, his palace shadowed by a ziggurat taller than every other temple in the world.

"The tower of Babylon." Words famous across the face of civilization. Holofernes pushed out his lower lip and left his half-finished meal to prowl the pavilion.

How did the king bear it, hearing reports of battles won by other men? Victory meant nothing without sight of the enemy's face—the victim's face—the instant before the fatal blow. The spoils of victory, from gold to necklaces, bracelets and rings, jingled delightfully. But the screams of the newly enslaved, the wails of the tortured, the weeping of captured women who would bear more slaves in nine short months? Only a commander on the field could savor those delightful sounds.

Holofernes sent an empty dish spinning across the table with one fingertip. The dish fell and broke on the edge of his chair.

Laughing, he crushed the fragments underfoot. Every slave in this camp lived or died by his order. Each soldier served the king, but the commands they obeyed came from him. Holofernes.

He sprawled in his chair and took another bite of lamb. A breeze stirred the walls. Through the open door Holofernes studied the town silhouetted against the sky on the hillside opposite his camp.

Did the sheep inside really believe their god kept them safe? Already, every sun-baked brick, every beast, every person belonged to him.

Holofernes crossed to his private altar and knelt. Fingers clumsy as a boy first brushing the warm curve of a breast, he opened the carved box that held Her image. His Goddess.

Chapter Fourteen
Judith

JUDITH JOLTED AWAKE AND NEARLY FELL off the stool. The din of screaming horses and shouting men from the Assyrian camp stormed over her. She had grown used to it, even woven it into her dream about a visit to the marketplace in a big city.

"You cannot sleep well on that seat. Let someone else keep watch while you go to bed." Naomi's familiar voice, breathless but laughing, came from the shadows of Judith's tent.

Judith scrambled up to embrace her old friend, then stood back and frowned. "What are you doing here?" Naomi had not left her own household for months.

"I wanted to see what you and my grandson are doing. I wanted to see the Assyrians for myself." Naomi dropped onto the empty stool beside Judith's.

"You walked all the way here?" Judith poured water from the jug she always kept nearby. "You must be thirsty."

Her friend waved the jug away. "Abra brought us water before

Ezra and I could remove our sandals." But she accepted the cup Judith poured.

Judith supported Naomi's fragile wrist when she lifted the drink to her lips. "Why did you come during the heat of the day?"

"We stopped to rest several times on the way." Naomi fanned her bare feet with the hem of her garment.

"If you had to come now, why didn't you ride?" Uzziah kept one donkey, ancient and gentle, just for his mother.

Naomi pursed her lips. "There are so many shepherds in the village, I feared the streets would be too crowded for me to ride."

"She was right." Ezra plodded onto the roof to join them, and collapsed at Naomi's feet. He rested his head against his grandmother's knee. She smoothed his dusty hair.

Judith had sent him home less than an hour before, for a meal and some rest. "Have you eaten?" She noticed the young man's drooping eyelids and half stood to call down to the courtyard. "Abra? Bring bread and butter for our guests."

"Thank you, dear one, I'm not hungry." Naomi leaned toward the plain, crowded with black tents across the eastern portion, and with fenced pens full of fine horses, sheep and goats to the west. She jabbed a knobby finger at the flock of slaves toiling painfully up toward the center of the camp. "What are they doing?"

"Building a road, I think." Judith looked away from the naked bodies. Beyond the eastern-most tents, phalanxes of soldiers marched and maneuvered, training for the day when they planned to murder her people.

Beneath the homely smell of smoke, from Bethulia's kitchens and Assyrian campfires alike, she caught the river-mud scent of equine sweat. To one side of the foot soldiers' training ground, mounted men galloped, halted and sparred. Farther away still, Judith glimpsed tiny chariots wheeling near the horizon. The teams of horses looked like ants, the glint of sun on helmets and spearheads insignificant as sparks from a cookfire.

"When did the last of the army arrive?" Naomi's voice sounded small.

"I told you, Grandmother." Ezra lifted his head and yawned. "They marched in just before I came home." He yawned again. "It's why you wanted to visit Judith, remember?"

"Oh. Oh yes, that's right." Naomi sipped more water.

Judith touched the boy's shoulder. "Why don't you go lie down in the reception room? I'll send for you when your grandmother's ready to leave." From the waxy look of Naomi's face, that might not be before nightfall.

"I think I will." Exhaustion thickened his voice. "Thank you, Judith. You'll be all right, Grandmother?" As soon as Naomi nodded, the young man plodded away.

Before he could stumble halfway across the courtyard, Judith heard Dorcas call to him. No giggle. Very demure. "Master Ezra, I brought you some bread and butter. I ground the flour and baked the bread myself, and Huldah let me help her make the sheep's butter."

"I'm too sleepy to eat yet—"

"There's a bench and some cushions in the reception room. Would you like a blanket?"

Ezra laughed. "I could probably fall asleep right here in the dirt." Their voices grew fainter as the boy and girl entered the chamber below Judith's feet.

She waited until the reception room door groaned around on its socket, then took the cup dangling from Naomi's hand. "I am always happy to see you, but why did you come all this way in such heat?"

"I can't see the invaders from our roof." Naomi peered past her. "You live by the village wall. Even if I only do it this once, I want to see them. I want to know what the Lord has in store for us."

Before Judith could answer Abra appeared, a platter laden with olives, sheep's butter and flat rounds of bread on her hip. "I found this on the bench in the courtyard where Dorcas forgot it. She's busy hopping between Ezra and the kitchen like a mother bird feeding the first nestling she ever hatched."

Abra helped Naomi balance the platter on her knees, then turned toward the encampment, one eyebrow raised. "It's taking the Assyrian dust longer to settle than we thought it would."

How long would it take? Weeks, months? The rest of their lives? "Can you convince Dorcas to leave Ezra alone? He's tired."

"Of course." After a last glance at the camp, Abra returned downstairs.

In the silence—no, Bethulia was no longer a place of silence. In the growling drone of noise, Judith smiled at her old friend. "Please, eat. You need your strength."

Naomi plucked up an olive, but only turned it in her bent fingers. "I've frightened you with my show of age. I'm sorry."

"I know your age as well as my own. Until today I never saw you look—" Judith's voice failed on the last word.

"Old?"

Weak. Judith only nodded.

Naomi ate the olive. "We all grow old sooner or later." She chuckled. "Sooner on my part, later on yours. I hope and pray."

Mother of my heart, don't leave me! Not yet. "Naomi, don't. I couldn't bear it if anything happened. If you—"

"Die? Death comes for us all." Naomi tilted her head toward the Assyrian camp. "There it is. Death with a sword in its hand."

Judith pushed the water jug aside and knelt at Naomi's feet. "They have nothing to do with us. Our Lord has promised—"

"Judith. Look at them." Naomi waited a moment in the noisy non-silence. "These people will devour our whole country. What if the Lord keeps us safe inside our walls, but Holofernes destroys everything outside?"

"The One won't let that happen. Keeping us safe means saving what we love. What we need." Didn't it?

Naomi clasped her hands, leaf-light, around Judith's. "Now I've frightened you even more." She leaned back and shut her eyes. "And neglected my grandson into the bargain. Not long ago, I would never have forgotten to make sure Ezra ate and rested before I demanded he take me somewhere."

"These are unusual times—"

A bellow of male voices across the valley jerked both women to their feet. "What're they saying?" Judith gasped. "Naomi. It's him."

"Holofernes." Naomi swayed, but lifted a hand to shade her eyes.

All across the plain they saw an orderly wave of motion as every soldier fell into ranks, even the few men at ease by their tents rushing into line. "Holofernes. Holofernes. Holofernes!"

The slaves at work on the road fell to the ground, human stones paving the way. Between them rode several men on horseback, sunlight flaming off helmets, swords and scale mail. A half dozen stallions, black, gray, brown and red, cantered toward the spring. Toward Bethulia.

"Holofernes, Holofernes, Holofernes!"

The leader of the horsemen swung his mount in a circle, near enough now that Judith glimpsed the flicker of the sword he held aloft. The soldiers' shouts erupted into cheers as the general's gray horse reared. He sawed the animal's mouth and forced it into a gallop, his commanders streaming behind him. Then the Assyrian general and his mounted retinue vanished behind the trees at the base of the hill.

"Did you see what he did?" Judith's hands fisted. The Lord of her people expected kindness to animals, even to sharing an over-laden beast's load. "How could Holofernes treat such a handsome horse so cruelly?"

"You expect him to be gentler with creatures than he is with humans?" Naomi hobbled across to peer over the wall. "I think they're coming up our hill."

Judith hurried forward to look as well, one hand on Naomi's elbow ready to tug her friend out of danger. "Do you think they'll find the—the tombs? Desecrate them?"

"Certainly not." But Naomi strained a bit farther over the wall. "I think they're headed for the spring."

"Do you think they'll pollute it?" *These people will devour our whole country.*

"That would be imprudent. It's their water source too, for now." Naomi spoke calmly, but her chin shook. "I wish Achior were here. He would know."

"We need to move away from the wall. If the general himself rides so close, an archer might as well." Judith led her friend to the shelter of the tent and bent to drag the tray of food closer. "Come, let's eat. More water?"

But though the butter shone, fresh and tempting, neither woman ate a bite.

Chapter Fifteen
Holofernes

THE SHOUTS OF HIS ARMY FADED only after Holofernes and his commanders rode into the trees. He halted his gray stallion at the edge of the stream. Yellow acacia petals spattered the ribbon of gurgling water, and he glanced into the branches above his head.

He would send Bagoas here later, to collect the flowers and bring them to his pavilion. He would have his finest vase ready on the altar, filled with the freshest water.

Now Holofernes focused on his officers. They sat tall on their horses, awaiting his command. To his right rode Melchior, leader of the troops from Esau. To the left was Sendal, the Ammonite who had replaced the coward Achior. Worse than a coward. A traitor.

The gray lashed out with one hind leg when Holofernes's knees clamped its sides. A bit chimed as Sendal's bay stallion sidestepped away. Holofernes tightened the reins until the gray stallion kept still, though every muscle beneath the glossy hide twitched. He glared as the creature's delicate ears swiveled back and forth.

I exiled Achior too soon. He should have whittled the Ammonite's flesh from his bones, should have left Achior's bloody carcass impaled on a stake outside Bethulia's tiny gate.

Holofernes kicked his mount forward a stride and spun it in place until the heavy hooves churned the pure stream to mud and foam. He swept one arm high to point at the village. "Those useless donkeys think their single, paltry god keeps them safe."

Melchior leaned over his stallion's shoulder to spit into the stream. "One god! A god for people meant to be slaves. Not a god of power like Marduk, or a warrior-priest like our king, Nebuchadnezzar!"

"Or even better, Ishtar, goddess of war and passion." Holofernes swung his mount around and pointed his sword at the mountains. "The truth is simple. The Bethulians rely on that narrow pass to keep them safe. Their safety ended when our first soldier stepped onto their lands." *Our lands. Mine.*

His commanders shouted agreement. When Holofernes thrust his sword back into place, they hushed at once. "We've taken this spring. Their only source of water."

Sendal smiled, a slow curve of lips. "Thirst will destroy them."

"Yes." Holofernes spoke quietly. "We will keep them under siege until they plead for surrender. Too late. From the moment they chose not to submit to Nebuchadnezzar, it was too late. We will guard the neighboring summits so not a single villager escapes."

"Which they'll try to do when thirst and hunger strike them." Melchior sat his horse at ease, legs long against the beast's springing ribs, reins loose in one hand.

Melchior knew the rhythm of victory nearly as well as Holofernes did. Thirst. Hunger. Fear that ripened into terror.

Holofernes nodded, smiling. "Tomorrow I will order the torturer's wagons on their first circuit around the village—"

"Tomorrow? But tomorrow is the seventh." Sendal spoke quickly, then blushed like a maiden and shut his mouth.

The seventh. One of the unlucky days. Holofernes swore to himself. Tomorrow he could do nothing. *By Ishtar, I want to get to work!* Siege and torment were as much part of an enemy's defeat as the instant a gate splintered and gave way.

"A wager, general." Melchior smoothed his horse's wind-blown mane. "How long before a messenger crawls out to us, begging for mercy?"

Anticipation was torture for victim and tormentor alike. "A week. Two at most."

Eyes nearly shut, Holofernes pictured his stallion cantering through the maze of village streets, hooves skidding in blood. He rode through the doorway into a house, lowering himself along the beast's neck. Inside, a woman crouched in a darkened corner, eyes bright with tears—

Once again, Sendal broke his reverie. "Their dying moans will be our call to attack."

He's eager, that one, thought Holofernes. With the shame of Achior as a predecessor, who could blame him? Holofernes jerked his chin at Sendal. "Camp here with your men. Guard the water supply."

He shifted in the saddle before the Ammonite could respond, and the gray stallion dug at the water, splashing cool drops over Holofernes's legs. "Melchior, the Esuans will make camp in the hills east and west of the town."

Melchior raised one clenched fist to his chest. "As you will it, General. I faithfully obey your smallest instruction, as you know."

Always so full of himself. This is a campaign, not a palace entertainment. "The rest of the army will stay in the camp." Now Holofernes let his voice rise with every word, so the sheep in their hilltop village had no choice but to hear him. "We'll starve them out."

"Starve them out!" Each commander shouted his own battle cry, the same cries their predecessors used when they rode into battle against the Assyrians. And lost. Black mane tossing, Sendal's bay spurted forward, confused into bolting as if into combat. More mud-darkened water flew into the air. The other men jeered, as the Ammonite struggled with his charger, spun and forced it back downhill.

Holofernes glared, his own stallion on such a tight rein the gray's chin touched its sweaty chest.

Melchior leaned toward him. "What now, General?"

"Now we wait." Holofernes whipped his mount up the trail to the new road. His road, built by his slaves. Beside the body of one of them—an old man lashed to death, judging by the marks on his naked back—Holofernes halted his stallion so sharply it snorted.

He ignored the creature's pinned ears and angrily clamped tail. He ignored the curses of his commanders when they yanked their horses to a halt to avoid colliding with him. Before he shot into a gallop once more, Holofernes surveyed the village's walls, gold in the sun.

He would have to wait. But not for long.

Chapter Sixteen
Judith

FOR SEVEN DAYS THE ASSYRIANS had occupied the plain, a dark, milling stain around Bethulia. Most soldiers kept away from the walls, but Judith began to recognize a few individuals. Every evening one huge soldier stood guard just downhill from the place of judgment. His helmet perched on his skull, and his height and broad body almost made his spear look like a child's toy. Almost.

On the eighth evening, Achior kept watch with her on the rooftop. Hoofbeats thudded nearby and a bay horse cantered up the path, long tail streaming. The rider yanked it to a ragged halt, and the lovely creature shook his head, ears flattened.

Achior jumped to his feet. "Desert!"

"You know him?" Judith could not see the rider's face beneath his pointed helmet. Achior did not answer her.

The bay stallion snuffled the air, then skipped and skidded sideways when the burly foot soldier lumbered into view. The mounted man nearly went over the horse's sleek shoulder, cursed and tugged himself back into the saddle with the reins.

"You there! Disturb my stallion again and I'll whip you myself."
The rider booted his mount down the trail and out of sight.

Achior stood at the edge of the wall, in plain sight of the big sentry. Judith raised one hand to motion him back, then let her arm sag at her side. The Assyrians did not mean to spill blood. Not yet. The enemy wanted their sweat, their thirst. Perhaps Holofernes intended to parch her people until no blood could flow.

"Did you know that man? Desert does not sound like an Assyrian name—" Desert. Not a person's name at all. "The horse?"

"Sendal was my second-in-command." Achior gave a short laugh. "Not second any more. It looks like Holofernes has ordered my men—my former men—to guard the hillside, or perhaps the spring."

Judith rubbed her arms. "Will they desecrate the graves?" Achior would know. He would tell her the truth.

"They plan to destroy you." He wiped one hand across his mouth. "Us. Defiling tombs serves no purpose, and Assyrians are always purposeful. If the graves were in sight of the wall, then maybe—"

Judith wilted a moment, then straightened with a frown. "Sendal, you said. He's the one who—who sat on your legs when Holofernes—" She swallowed.

"When Holofernes beat me. Yes. Now please forgive me." Achior bowed without meeting her eyes. "I must go." By the time his footsteps reached the courtyard, he was running.

"Achior!" Judith peered through the withered palm fronds into the courtyard.

Achior fled without stopping to pick up his sandals, never mind put them on.

Slowly, she returned to her seat.

"They have us surrounded. They have surrounded us for a week. Why do you continue to watch them?" Just the other side of the low wall that divided their rooftops, Rebekah glared at her, arms folded across her chest.

"Because I want to understand them." Judith forced a smile. "How's Nathanael?"

"Dirty, and I have no water to bathe him or myself."

Judith winced at the smell of her own body. Maybe she should ask Abra to rub peppermint into her robes again. It would ease her fear of offending other people. "None of us has bathed in a week."

"I finally got my baby to sleep a moment ago—" Rebekah tautened as if listening. "No, not again. Not now." Her voice climbed into a shriek. "I can't bear it."

Judith heard it as well, the creak and grind of heavy wagons pulled by slow-footed oxen. Sobs and screaming like obscene music.

The torturers and their wagon. Judith stood, ready to scrabble downstairs and inside, then dropped onto her stool again. *Blessed Lord, please.* But please, what? The Assyrian prisoners would receive mercy only in death.

She dreamed at night of the wailing, and the wet, heavy noises the torturers made while they worked. The wagon's stench crept over her and, fists clamped over her mouth, Judith fought down sickness. How many of the tormented hung, already dead in their chains? "Do the Assyrian torturers never sleep, even during the heat of the day?"

"How dare you?" Rebekah gathered her skirts, as if ready to leap the rooftop wall between their homes. "How dare you compare those swine with my son?"

"I did not." Judith moaned as the cries of the tortured grew closer. Grew louder. "I feel the same way about them that you do."

Rebekah snarled at her. "Liar. Friend of the Assyrian spy."

Spy? The word bit deeper than a spear point. "He's no spy, he's given us much useful information."

"Uzziah may believe that. He's a worn-out old man. Otherwise he'd do something about those filthy vermin." Rebekah's skirts lashed as she jabbed a trembling hand at the wagon creeping past outside the wall.

Judith realized she was standing an arm span away from her neighbor, and had no memory of standing, never mind stalking across to face her. "What do you expect him to do, go out and demand they stop?"

Her neighbor stamped one foot. "He could send someone to poison the spring."

"After the Assyrians leave we would have poisoned water forever." Judith's insides burned as if she had drunk that poison.

"*Oh.*" Rebekah's voice rose, piercing as the screams of the tortured. "I hate the way you pretend to stay calm. Though maybe you don't pretend. Maybe the Ammonite dog has promised you safety when the army breaches our walls."

"What are you talking about?" Achior could not promise her safety. "He is in as much danger as we are—"

Rebekah laughed, a jagged, ugly noise. "You almost sound like you believe that! I remember when you were only a poor merchant's daughter. Now you sell yourself instead of rotten cloth and ill-tanned leather."

"Sell myself?" The thought of lying with a man for money made Judith gag.

"That's what I said. Whore. You'll lie with the Ammonite spy, lie with Holofernes himself, while the rest of us bleed our last in the torturer's wagon!"

"Rebekah. How can you say—you know I'd never—"

"Hide what you are under that sackcloth, fool everyone into thinking you're so devout. You can't fool me. I won't be civil to you another minute." In a blur of scarlet, Rebekah plunged down the steps of her house.

"You've been civil? Tell me when, I don't remember it," Judith shouted after her.

Her neighbor's door slammed.

Judith

Like an old woman, Judith tottered down through the courtyard and along the passage into the room she had shared with Manasseh. Her breath snagged in her chest. She longed to cry, but could only lie curled tight at the center of the empty bed.

Chapter Seventeen
Judith

JUDITH'S BACK AND SHOULDERS ACHED from bending, from lifting the heavy water urn again and again. But using the dipper to fill vessels for so many people took too long. She tilted the urn so water spilled into the enormous bowl. "There, Lila, that should last you a while."

"Perhaps." Lila paced out of the courtyard, upright and graceful. Her hair, dark with a flash of silver, swung down to her waist as she left the courtyard.

Judith squatted to set down the heavy urn, hooked the dipper on one handle, then stood and stretched with her fists pressed into the small of her back.

"You've been doling out water all day. How long since you took a drink?" Abra grabbed the dipper and dunked it into the next urn in the row.

Judith held out her cup. The water tasted warm and earthy. She drank deeply, hesitated, and tilted the cup for Abra to give her more. "Was Lila the last person in line? No one else is waiting?"

"No one." Her friend sniffed. "And Lila will be first in line tomorrow, begging for more."

"There's no need for her to beg. We're neighbors."

Abra pointed the empty dipper toward the Assyrian camp. "They've been here two weeks. Lila ran low on water after four days, and acts like she's doing you a favor every time she asks for more."

"She's a widow with no children." And old.

For the first time that day, Judith focused on the drone from the encampment. She rarely noticed the Assyrians' noise any more, now the torturers' wagons had ceased rounding the walls. Perhaps all the victims had died? *Blessed Lord, they're not your chosen people.* But they were people all the same.

Abra rolled the empty urn away from its still-full neighbors and let it thud into place. "Did you notice the size of Lila's bowl? It holds enough water to last several days, but she's back almost every morning to fill it."

The taste of water turned to ash on Judith's tongue. "What are you saying?"

"Only that Lila looks and smells a lot cleaner than I do. Cleaner than anyone in our household, including you."

Judith's pulse quickened. Would one of the chosen risk losing the Lord's favor, just for clean skin? Though the One expected his people to stay clean as well. "She's a widow. Perhaps she comes here for the company."

"Not all widows are like you. Lila's husband died a dozen years ago." Abra lowered her voice. "I've heard it's a rare night when her house doesn't hold more than one heartbeat. Never the same, two nights running. Lila keeps plenty of company, believe me."

It took Judith a moment to understand. "Prostitution is forbidden." Judith pushed her empty cup into Abra's hands. "What Lila does is between her and the One."

Pottery scraped when Abra set the cup on the nearest bench.

"Maybe the One knows how Lila paid for that bowl you just filled with water. It's new, like the rug I saw her shake free of dust outside her door."

"Stop. Stop, Abra." Judith sagged onto the bench, remembering her argument with Rebekah the week before. They had passed each other on the street a dozen times since, but her neighbor had not acknowledged Judith's greetings. It should have made life simpler. Instead it hurt. "Water and food are growing short. Let's keep our tempers from doing the same."

"As you say, mistress." Abra snatched up the cup and stomped into the kitchen.

Judith stood to follow her, just as something crashed inside and Huldah began to curse. "Another one broken! Why fear Holofernes when we've got you around? It's a wonder there's still a roof over our heads."

Abra broke in, voice harsher than usual. "Can't you see the child's worn out? Go, Dorcas, I'll clean up the mess. I said I'll clean it, old woman!"

The little kitchen maid fled up to the roof while Abra and Huldah shouted at each other. Judith shut her eyes as the argument boiled out through the door. She imagined striding out of the courtyard, which seemed small and cramped right now. She pictured herself on the street, out on the hill. In her mind she shivered at the coolness beneath the trees as she sank down outside her husband's tomb.

How could love go on, vital as ever, when the heart of her beloved no longer beat? Judith opened her eyes to stare at the sky through the palm branches that roofed the courtyard. The fronds were so withered they no longer offered any shade.

"I apologize." Abra stood before her, hands gripped together. "I'm sorry I was rude. I'm just—"

"Hot. Tired." Judith leaned forward to haul her friend onto the bench beside her. "We all are."

Huldah lost her temper at the best of times. Since the siege began, she simmered over insults, genuine or imagined, longer than soup simmered over her fire.

"No more work for the rest of the day. For any of us." Judith tried to smile. "That's an order."

"Really?" Abra bounced to her feet, only to snort out a frustrated laugh when a hank of her hair tumbled into her eyes. "I'll go tell Dorcas and Huldah." She took a step toward the kitchen, then swerved upstairs instead. "Dorcas first. Huldah can wait."

"I'll tell Huldah myself."

"Thank you!" Abra stooped to kiss Judith's cheek, and then darted up to the roof. A quick murmur of voices, then a girlish squeal. Dorcas pattered past, tears forgotten, and skipped out onto the street. Abra followed more slowly to pause beside the bench. "I'm going to take a nap." She retreated to the servant's quarters.

The courtyard seemed spacious again. When Judith stepped into the kitchen, Huldah did not even glance up from her cookfire. "I heard what you said, mistress. I'm well enough where I am." Her wrinkled lips twisted into a smile. "No one will bother me if I stay here. That's rest enough for me."

"Are you sure, Hul—"

The cook straightened, hands on bony hips. "Go. Take your own advice. Rest, mistress."

Shaking her head, Judith climbed to the roof. She peeked over the dividing wall between her home and Gothoniel's and sighed. Rebekah was nowhere in sight.

Judith unbound her girdle, and then draped the woven belt over the nearest seat. Robes loosened, she unrolled a sleeping mat in the shade and stretched out on it.

She had not slept through the night since the Assyrians came. Now her eyelids closed, fluttered, and closed again. She would rest until time for evening prayers—

Then she was standing in the small room where she stored her garments. Not her widow's black, but the fine clothes she had not worn for two years. Her favorite robe, red and cream fabric with a pattern of stars, unfolded and drifted off the shelf. Skirts spread wide, the gown floated in the air before her.

The gold bracelets and necklace Manasseh had given her spiraled up to glint against the red fabric. Light flared off the precious metal, brilliant and blinding. The radiance intensified until garment and jewelry vanished. Only light remained.

Judith scrambled upright and scrubbed one arm across her face. She shook out the sackcloth twisted around her legs. Why had she dreamed about her best robes? It must be a dream. What else could it be?

Down in the courtyard Huldah called out. "Dorcas? Abra! Help! Someone help me, she's fainted!"

Fainted? Judith lurched down to the courtyard, trying to refasten her girdle as she went. Huldah was staggering through the gate from the street, one scrawny shoulder jammed under the armpit of a taller woman. Shoshana, Chabris's wife, her once-willowy frame shrunken, the soft contours of her lovely face tight against her skull.

Judith caught the fainting woman and half-supported, half-dragged the limp figure to the bench against the wall just as Abra hurried out of the servant's quarters.

"Water, Abra. She needs water."

"And chop some figs." Huldah left her crutch propped against the wall and bent to chafe Shoshana's fragile wrists. "Fruit slips down a dry throat easier than bread."

"No." Shoshana's voice came in a cracked whisper. "Just—a sip—of water—"

A sharp sound escaped the old cook. "Is that how you've come to such a state, lady? I warrant you've not eaten a bite for days, nor drunk enough water to keep a mouse alive. Do you wish to die before the Assyrians can get you? Do you want your wise husband to put you in your grave?"

Shoshana shook her head feebly, lids crinkled as if she wanted to cry and could not. "Others need food. And water. More. Than I do."

Judith dug the water dipper into the nearest water urn. "Here. Drink, slowly." While Abra bathed Shoshana's hands, face and feet, despite her protests, Judith tipped water between the dry lips. "How did this happen? Your family is well-supplied."

The elder's wife did not answer, just shook her head so strands of her dull hair snagged on the brick at her back.

"Huldah, stay with her. I'll help Abra with the fruit, then brew some reviving tea. Yes, I will," Judith said when Shoshana tried to stand up. "It will do you good." Huldah nodded and gently toweled the limp fingers dry.

Judith joined Abra in the kitchen. Her friend looked up from the plate of minced fruit. "I can tell you what happened. Chabris's wife shares what she has with the poor. Like you. She denies herself to give to neighbor children and her own slaves."

"Why doesn't Chabris stop her?" As protector of a family, the husband should recognize his wife's weakness.

Abra shrugged. "Shoshana is before his eyes every day. Perhaps he does not notice the change in her."

"How do you know all this?" Judith stopped, her hands full of dried herb leaves.

Her friend's mouth curved. "Really, mistress. Servants talk. Servants know everything."

Huldah's shout cracked the stillness. "Is the food on the way or have you gone to beg from the Assyrians?"

Abra sped out with the plate, but Judith sat for a moment in the clear space beside the hearth where her servants took their meals. She studied the mud-brick shelves built out from the wall, all crammed with pots of olive oil or grain. The single container of precious salt stood in a place of honor at one end. How many kitchens in Bethulia had shelves that stood empty?

Judith edged to the doorway to watch the others tend Shoshana, whose eyes burned as if with fever. Did she see things, too? Did a sword seem to flash out of nowhere, a favorite garment appear to dance in midair?

Like you, Chabris's wife shares what she has with the poor. Were Judith's dream-visions caused by too little rest? At least she had not told anyone, not Naomi or Abra or Achior.

Not that she had had the opportunity to tell the former commander anything. Judith whipped around to heat water for tea. She had not seen Achior for many days, ever since he left the rooftop so abruptly—

A slow sob from her ailing neighbor dragged her back to the present. Achior was not here. Shoshana was. Vowing to take better care of herself, Judith crushed the dried leaves into a mug and waited for the water to heat.

Chapter Eighteen
Judith

THE FIRST RAYS OF SUNLIGHT POURED through the reception room door and stretched Dorcas's shadow across the floor. "More olive oil, mistress?" The girl tipped the bottle over Judith's plate.

"Thank you, no." Judith dipped a morsel of bread in the smudge of oil already on her dish. "I have enough already."

"But the bread's not very good today." Dorcas whispered it like a shameful secret. "Huldah wouldn't let me use any seeds, and hardly any salt."

The old cook must want to make their stores last out the siege, now in its third week. Judith eyed the scrap of flat bread on her plate. "Huldah bakes so well her bread doesn't need salt, or oil for dipping." Usually it was true. "I'm lucky to have such an excellent cook in my kitchen, and your thoughtful service at my table."

"Thank you, mistress." Dorcas laughed, sweet as petals falling.

"If the siege lasts much longer—" Judith's fingers tightened on the bread.

Dorcas finished the sentence matter-of-factly. "We will go without salt altogether."

Judith nodded and bent over her breakfast. She had gone without salt before, but even during her deepest mourning she had not forced privation on her servants. But Dorcas did not know that. The girl joined the household after Manasseh's death—

Footsteps echoed across the courtyard, and Judith half-rose to her feet. "Achior?" She had not seen her friend for ten days.

Dorcas lit up brighter than an Assyrian's campfire. Dimple flashing in her thin cheek, she hurried to the doorway and leaned out. "The mistress is in here, Master Ezra."

Judith sank down again. She would allow the girl a glimpse of the magistrate's son. Forbid her all sight of him, and Dorcas would hunger even more.

Ezra skidded into the room, breath ragged. "Judith—my grandmother—she needs—needs you to come." He had not stopped to take off his shoes.

"Naomi?" The low table screeched when she shoved it aside. "What's wrong?"

Tears slid down his face to gather under his chin. "Grandmother?" Ezra choked and shook his head. "She's fine, it's the people. A crowd, in the square. On our doorstep. Shouting at—at my father."

Now she heard it. An ugly rumble from the center of town, woven through the constant noise from the Assyrian camp.

Ezra dragged her after him. "Grandmother sent me for you. Please hurry."

Sweaty hand clasped in sweaty hand, they sped outside. Judith paused to poke her feet into her sandals, stunned to find the top of Ezra's head past her shoulder. How did he keep growing on less and less food? "Dorcas, tell the others there's trouble in town. I'm going to help." *If I can.*

The girl scuttled after them into the courtyard. "M-Master Ezra? Mistress? What's happening?"

"Stay here, do you understand? Stay here until I return."

"Mistress!" The girl wailed, and a mourning dove nested on a nearby wall whistled into the sky.

Judith waved her back inside. "It will be all right. Let's go, Ezra." They set out at a trot. "Tell me what happened."

"I heard shouting and thought something had gone wrong with the sheep. I ran out into our courtyard and—" The young man's lips trembled, firmed, trembled again.

As they approached the square, Judith understood why he had thought first of trouble with the flocks. She heard men yelling, bleating goats and baaing sheep.

"In our courtyard. They rushed at me, our neighbors. Our neighbors! Red-faced, shouting. I ran inside and found Grandmother on the roof. She was staring down at them. She told me to cross the roofs to the tree at the corner of the square, to wait until no one was looking, climb down and run get you."

Why? What can I do?

Ezra dragged Judith around the corner and into the marketplace.

Chapter Nineteen
Judith

JUDITH STUMBLED AT SIGHT OF THE MOB. These were her neighbors? For a stunned moment she did not recognize a single face. If an Assyrian bowman had appeared, arrow notched, she would have died where she stood.

The knot of people surged and roared like a single being. Only Uzziah, his back against the front wall of his house, looked human. "My friends, I beg you. The Assyrians want fear to destroy us. Please, stay calm—"

Someone in the crowd hissed. Others joined in.

Ezra clutched her waist—to steady himself or her, she couldn't tell. "It's worse, there are more people than when Grandmother sent me to you."

Though he was shouting, Judith could barely hear him. Now she recognized individuals in the whirlpool of people. Rebekah stood near the front, her husband half a step behind her. Sol shook both fists under Uzziah's chin.

The magistrate motioned for quiet. "It is not our place to

understand the One's motives. They unfold in ways we will comprehend later—"

More hisses from the mob. Ezra turned his face against her shoulder. "Oh, Judith."

Her stomach clutched. Why had Naomi sent for her? What could she do when even the magistrate could not calm them? And where were Chabris and Joakim? The magistrate needed the elders' support.

A voice rich as a lyre rang out from the top of the High Place. "Listen to Uzziah." At a pace even slower than usual, Sirach descended the steps. "The Lord of our people is testing us."

Judith shuddered. Surely the priest would contain her neighbors. Calm them.

"Yes." Uzziah stood taller. "Our Lord favors us above all. Now, please, disperse and return to your homes—"

"Favors us with what?" An older woman fought closer to the magistrate, shoving a little girl out of her path. "Starvation? Death?"

Splayed in the dust, the child wailed. No one moved to help her. Judith squeezed Ezra's hand so hard he grunted. "Go back to my house, you'll be safe there."

Without waiting to see if he obeyed, Judith waded into the throng. She elbowed her way between two menservants at the edge of the rabble, rammed Sol aside like a palm frond. The child sprawled on the ground, weeping.

She scooped the little girl into her arms. "I'm here, little one, I'm here." Hot, trembling little body cuddled close, Judith rocked on her heels. "You're safe. I promise to keep you safe."

Rebekah's screech pierced the buzz in Judith's ears. "You have plenty of food and water, all you rich ones. You mean to sell us to the Assyrians as soon as we're too weak to fight! You'll let them roast our children on spits for their dinner."

The little girl writhed and tried to crawl out of Judith's lap.

Judith held tight to the quivering toddler and struggled to her feet, fury inside her hot as milk from a pan. "Stop!" She glowered at Rebekah, only a few paces away.

The young mother was a wraith of her former self. Her hair shredded around her face like burial rags, her scarlet dress stained and torn. Her son wept, a knot of misery at her feet.

Judith's breath whistled. "Look at this girl. She's hurt, frightened—and Holofernes didn't do it. You did."

A figure in black, long silver and dark hair smooth and shining down her back, started to sidle away from the front of the crowd. Lila. Eyes slitted, Judith watched Lila edge toward her house. The older widow had been the one who pushed the child, she felt sure.

Judith raised her voice. Lila would not escape without hearing this. "Look what the Assyrians can do to us. What we've already let them do. If we've forgotten to care for each other, we should open the gates and let them in because they have already destroyed us."

The girl hiccupped. Judith smoothed the child's damp curls, her own hand unsteady. *Who am I to shout at them? I squabbled with Rebekah on the rooftop, I have snapped at my dear friend Abra.*

"Don't listen to her, she's—" Rebekah's accusation cut off as if sliced with a knife. Thick arms clamped the young mother's waist, a hand sealed her mouth.

Gothoniel's hand. Rebekah flailed to free herself, but her husband scooped her up and carried her toward their house. One of her sandals fell, lost under the feet of the crowd.

She hammered her husband's legs with fists and feet, twisted her head to shout again. "How dare you grab me like some beast in a field? Put me down now!"

Her husband held her more firmly, his voice clear for the first time in Judith's memory. "You are frightening our son. Come, Nathanael, we will take your mother home."

"Y-yes, Papa."

"Good boy." With Rebekah's infuriated howls muffled against the shoulder of Gothoniel's sheepskin tunic, the family wove away out of the square.

People shifted. One or two meandered toward the animal pens, others wandered away down the nearest street. Most hurried out of the square. On the steps of the High Place, Sirach watched them go, his face dark above the white-on-white embroidery of his priestly clothes.

Judith lowered her head. She had not behaved discreetly, as a woman should. Then she sat up again, the dozing child held close. As a widow with no man to speak for her, what choice did she have?

Only Sol and a few other men remained in the square. One by one they slouched off in different directions. It was over.

She touched the girl's sticky cheek. "What's your name? I'll take you home."

"Elizabeth." Uzziah spoke from close behind her, his voice mumbling and uncertain. "Her name's Elizabeth."

"Elizabeth?" Naomi shuffled out of the house. "Did you find her?"

Heart's mother, you're all right! Judith pushed to her feet, and studied the heavy-eyed little face. "Your cook's daughter. I remember now."

"Put me down, Chudith. Want Mama. Want Naomi." Elizabeth squirmed and held her arms out to Naomi, who shook her head.

"I can't hold you now, dear, I'm a little tired today. Here's Ezra, he'll take you inside." Naomi held out her arms as her grandson darted up. "Thank you, my boy. You did just as I asked."

"Grandmother. Oh, grandmother." He hurled himself into Naomi's embrace, long arms wrapped around her, his narrow shoulders shaking.

Naomi wiped away his tears, then her own. "All is well, thanks to your swift feet and Judith's swift tongue. Now take Elizabeth in to her mother. We searched the house three times, I can't imagine how she got out."

The little girl skimmed down Judith's leg to the ground. "Can walk by myself." The toddler pattered inside. After another hug from his grandmother, Ezra followed her into the house.

"We should go in as well." Uzziah took an unsteady step to his mother and put one arm around her. He extended his other hand to Judith. "Will you join us?"

"I had better go home. My household's probably in chaos." Who knew what frantic tale Dorcas had told the others.

"This evening, then." Naomi closed her eyes and leaned against her son. "I know Achior wants to see you as much as I do."

Achior. "How is he? Where is he?"

"I insisted he stay inside when I recognized the mood of our people." Uzziah rubbed his face with one hand. "He warned me this might happen, but I didn't believe we could ever—and in so short a time—" Uzziah stared at Judith, but she knew he did not see her. "How have I failed my townspeople so completely?"

"Nonsense, my son." Naomi stood on tiptoe to kiss his grizzled cheek. "Bethulia has its share of malcontents. What place does not? Our Lord asks much of us, expects much. But we are human. If everyone was as upright and devout as Judith, we would have no need of a magistrate."

Judith blushed. "Indeed, I am not—"

"When I saw you in the crowd I was confused. What were you doing here, a woman among so many men, a pure believer among these—these wastrels?"

Devout? Pure? Judith's neck prickled. Had Uzziah not heard her scream like some city slattern?

"Thanks to Judith, peace returns to Bethulia. I will see you tonight, dear one." Naomi nodded to her. "Come, my son. Help me inside." Shakily, as if neither could move very far or fast, Uzziah and Naomi retreated inside.

The heavy door thudded shut behind them. For the first time in Judith's memory, she heard the wooden key scrape in the lock.

She left the courtyard, only to lean against the nearest livestock pen. The dust, kicked up by so many feet moments ago, settled around her. The reek of dung smelled heavy in the hot air. Gothoniel and the other goat- and shepherds usually cleaned the pens morning and night. Would it get done at all today?

The filth at the center of Bethulia symbolized the doubt that grew here as well. *Blessed art thou, oh Lord. Give us faith.*

She heard only the bawl of animals meant for sacrifice.

Chapter Twenty
Judith

BRA MET HER AT THE ENTRANCE to the courtyard and gripped Judith by the shoulders. "Has it begun?"

"What?" Judith's throat ached. *I want a drink of water. I want a bath.*

"Are they here? Are we under attack?"

Even shaking her head seemed like too much effort. "Didn't Dorcas explain?"

"Huldah gave her no chance. She started raving about what the soldiers would do to us. Dorcas ran off and hid. Blessed Lord, what happened?"

"There was a—disturbance in the square." Judith kicked off her sandals and plodded into the reception room. "Some of our neighbors gathered outside Uzziah's house and—" She had no word to describe what Gothoniel, Sol and the others had done. "Shouted."

"How ugly." Abra flopped down on the bench to hug her. "You took care of it, though."

Judith hitched sideways and stared at her. "Why would I have anything to do with it? Uzziah and Sirach were there." *And I'm only a woman.*

"But Ezra came to you for help, and you wouldn't have come back unless things had quieted down. Besides—" Abra scrubbed both hands through her hair and grinned. "Gothoniel carried Rebekah past just before you came home. That was more than their usual fight, wasn't it?"

Judith closed her eyes and slumped against the wall. "Yes." She tucked her arms around herself. "I don't understand. Why did Naomi send for me? I'm not brave. I'm exhausted."

"We all are. Look at me, tangled as a thorn bush, and too tired to care." Abra smoothed a hand down Judith's back, only to hop up. "You must be thirsty." She crossed to the water pitcher near the door. Water glugged. "You were gone a long time."

Judith wriggled upright. "I am thirsty." *Manasseh.* She wanted to cry, for her husband, and for what happened in the square, but no tears came. She took the cup Abra offered and sipped slowly. "I wish I could pour the rest of the pitcher over my head."

"Someday we will have water for the outside of our bodies as well as the inside." Abra spun away from her, pitcher held loosely in one hand. The contents splashed Judith's face and shoulders.

"Abra!" Judith sputtered. She started to mop herself off with the hem of her sackcloth garment, then stopped as the water saturated her robes and cooled the flesh beneath.

"How could I be so clumsy?" Abra winked. "I'll fetch you a towel." She whisked out the door.

Judith laughed.

But Abra hurried back in, empty-handed. "Huldah can't find Dorcas. We haven't seen her since she ran off to hide."

Judith sprang up, robes dripping. "You and Huldah search the servant's quarters and storerooms again, I'll take the rest of the house."

"What if we can't find her?"

Blessed Lord, had the girl followed her and Ezra to the square? "We'll hunt through the village until we find her."

Abra hurried out. "Huldah? Huldah, come with me—" A moment later Judith heard both women calling Dorcas's name.

She spun in a slow circle. The reception room's solid bench, the rugs on the floor didn't offer cover for a mouse, let alone an eleven-year-old girl. Judith stepped out into the courtyard, shafts of sunlight striking through the withered remains of palm fronds overhead. "Dorcas?"

First she checked behind the oversized urns, both those that still held water and the emptied ones. Now there were nearly as many empty as full containers. Judith hurried along the narrow passage to her private courtyard. Empty of everything except the derelict fountain.

"Dorcas!" Inside the bedchamber, she stooped to peer under the bed frame. Nothing. "Oh, Dorcas, where are you?" *Where are you?*

Judith gathered her skirts, ready to race back along the streets to the village square, when a faint rustle came from the small chamber where she stored the fine clothes from her married life.

"I'm—I'm here, mistress." The little girl rose from a nest of rumpled garments in the closet's darkest corner. "Am I in trouble?"

"Of course not." Judith clasped the weeping child in both arms, and Dorcas wrapped both arms around her neck. *Lord, there have been too many frightened little girls in my day.*

"I'm sorry, mistress, I'm sorry. You left—you left us alone and Huldah said the soldiers were coming. I didn't know what to do, you weren't here to tell me." Dorcas smeared tears across her face. "So I hid."

"Huldah will always take care of you, dear one. Abra, too. Listen. Can you hear how frightened they are for you?" The voices of the two women sounded clearly, Huldah's crosser than ever.

Dorcas pressed her face into Judith's shoulder. "I heard them b-before. I thought soldiers h-had them and they were screaming for me. For me to save them."

"Did you hear me call as well?" Judith waited until the girl nodded. "Why didn't you answer me?"

"I didn't want you to know I ran away like a baby." Dorcas crouched, hands over her face. "I will never be tall and strong and beautiful, like you, but I want to be brave. That's why I help keep watch." Even in the murky light of the closet, Judith saw her blush. "Mainly."

"You're a big help." Whether she did it to help, or just spend time with Ezra, did not matter.

"Thank you, mistress." Dorcas sagged against a shelf. "I can think in the tent. I never had time to think when Mama was alive, or—or after. I like it."

Judith brushed a fingertip down the girl's slender nose. "I do it too, though I didn't start to learn how until—" Until Manasseh died. "Until I was older. You have a head start on me. But you mustn't think I'm so very brave, Dorcas. I just do what I have to do with no man left to help me."

Dorcas knelt at her feet. "That's not true, mistress. You took me in when everyone else feared I carried the sickness that killed Mama." She pressed one cheek to Judith's foot. "I'm here because of you. Alive because you weren't afraid to give me a home. "

"Someone would have taken you in." Sooner or later. Would it have been soon enough?

"I had been alone for a week, and you came down from your tent, out of mourning, to save me. I never thanked you before. Thank you, mistress."

Judith stared. The girl's sobs had wakened her on what became her last night in seclusion, immersed in Manasseh's loss. On that night she had stayed in the musty tent a long time, certain someone would go to the child, comfort and quiet her. The hopeless grizzle went on and on. At last Judith rolled off her pallet and stepped out into the night air for the first time in more than a year. Bare feet whispering on the street, she followed the cries to the crumbled house Dorcas had shared with her mother, dead of contagion more than a week.

Judith picked up the girl, fragile as an armful of twigs. By the time she fed Dorcas a hastily pressed together cake of raisins and figs, then tucked her into a wooly pile of sheepskins in the servant's quarters, the night had gone—and her withdrawal from the world had gone with it.

Now her voice came out strangled. "Give your gratitude to our Lord, Dorcas."

"I am." Dorcas rocked onto her haunches and smiled up at her. "You are our Lord's hands. The Lord feeds me, clothes me, and gives me a home through you." She stood to hug Judith. "I'm all right now. I'll go tell the others you found me."

Stiffly, Judith bent to pile the rumpled garments on the shelves again. On top lay the starred gown, her favorite. She folded it and set it on top of the others.

Huldah's raspy calls for Dorcas broke off into a tirade of scolding. Judith tried to hurry, but could only plod slower with every step.

"How long do you think it would take soldiers to find you in that closet, girl? No time at all. They'd take their swords and—"

Judith made herself run the last few steps into the main court-yard, only to find Dorcas facing the old woman. "You and Abra couldn't find me."

"We don't have swords, either. Today it was our own people, not the Assyrians. But it will be. They won't call your name, your name won't matter to them. They'll take their swords, or worse, and they'll—"

"Dorcas, mix some dough for the evening meal."

"Yes, mistress." Dorcas swung away toward the kitchen.

When Huldah started after the girl, scowling, Judith stopped her. "Huldah, wait. I need to speak with you."

"No need. Abra already told me about the riot. Fools. Next time we won't be so fortunate. But if the Assyrians have plans for us, I have plans for them."

"Plans?" Judith put a hand to her aching head. "What are you talking about?"

"My sharp kitchen knife, some heavy pots and the roof." The wrinkled lips curved in an evil grin. "We'll drop pots over the edge, right on the solders' heads. Break a few skulls if we can. An old woman like me and a scared quail like Dorcas won't hold them long, but we'll do our best."

"If the Assyrians break in we'll all fight, not just you and Dorcas." Then Judith frowned. "Knife. You said 'knife.' What could you do with a knife against swords?"

"The knife's not for them, mistress. I would never spoil a good blade with pig's blood, but I won't leave that child for the soldiers to do what soldiers always do. When we run out of pots, I'll send Dorcas to our Lord. I'll make certain she dies as she lived. Pure."

Judith's legs gave way. Huldah pushed one bony shoulder under her armpit, the way she had supported Shoshana the other day. "You'd do that? To Dorcas?"

"I won't leave her at the mercy of those filthy dogs. You and Abra can make your own choices. The Assyrians have male slaves out there. We've seen them. They're bound to have women, too, but not enough to go around. Let the first soldier set foot in our gates and none of us is safe. Not sweet tidbits like Dorcas, not even a wrinkled, bitter old bird like me."

A cold knife seemed to slip into Judith's heart. "But if you'd acted today, it would have been for nothing." The words came out in a dry whisper. "Please, if you—if it happens, make sure the Assyrians are really here before you—"

A cackle. "Don't worry, mistress. I'm not going to waste all those pots."

Chapter Twenty-one
Holofernes

HOLOFERNES REMOVED A FALLEN ACACIA PETAL from his altar. "I will bring more blossoms for you, Lady. Tonight, I promise." He would send Bagoas on a search for flowers this afternoon, then select the best of them himself—

A hint of steam wafted through the air. Water splashed. Holofernes straightened away from the altar as his body slave staggered through the pavilion door, a wide basin in his arms. The eunuch eased down to place the basin at the foot of the bathing stool, already centered on a grass mat. "Your bath is ready, master."

"So I see." Holofernes flung his robe on the bed, settled on the bathing seat, and scrubbed his feet over the mat's rough texture. Bagoas scooped a pitcher into the warm water, which he poured carefully across the general's shoulders. As the stream flooded down Holofernes's chest and back, he curled his toes in the mat's brief puddle. "Again."

"Yes, sire." A gurgle of water, a grunt when Bagoas hefted the container at a different angle. Another gush of warmth swirled over the general's head, and down his body and legs.

"Again." The bathing mat grew soggy as the eunuch washed him. At last Holofernes raked both calloused hands through his dripping hair. "Enough." He stepped onto the carpets, arms extended. Bagoas hurried to dry him with soft cloths.

When only a pleasant dampness cooled his flesh, Holofernes batted the slave away. "Fresh robes."

"At once, my lord." Bagoas retrieved a fringed garment from the basket that held the general's clothing. "Does this one please you?"

A breath of cinnamon wafted from the fabric. Holofernes stroked the patterned sleeve. "It will do." The long, soft robe slithered over his head and down.

Outside the tent a sentry called, "Melchior to see you, General."

The Esuan commander wanted tomorrow's orders, no doubt. The same orders Holofernes had given each evening of the siege. "Tomorrow, we wait."

In memory, he heard Achior, always so quiet compared to his other commanders. *"Only if the people of Bethulia break faith with their god can we defeat them."* Holofernes kicked the lustrous fringe out from under his feet. "I should have killed him when I had the chance."

"Master?" Bagoas raised his head

"Bring my shoes." The instant the eunuch slid the decorated leather over his feet Holofernes stomped to his chair. "Melchior! Enter."

The Esuan strode into the pavilion. "General. Yesterday I stopped a scuffle between several men. Today I broke up half a dozen brawls."

"Our men grow restless." *So do I.* "It happens at this point in a siege."

"Exactly, sir. Daily drills no longer hold their interest." Melchior folded his arms across his chest. "What distraction can we offer them?"

"Distraction." A lion hunt? No, they had killed the last captive lion during the previous siege. Drumming his fingers on the table, Holofernes eyed Bethulia, still untouched on the opposite hillside. He banged the table with one fist and sat up.

Bagoas fell to the floor, forehead on his bunched fists.

"Melchior, order a circle of torches lit north of camp, out on the open plain. Have the men form ranks there before sunset."

"Sir?" Melchior's lids drooped even as his mouth curled upward. "And in the circle, you will have—what?" His smile deepened. "Or should I say, 'who?'"

Holofernes stretched out his legs. "There's delight in anticipation, don't you agree?"

"As you say, sir." Still smirking, the Esuan commander withdrew.

Holofernes stroked and stroked one palm down the smooth fabric over his belly. "Bagoas. The female slaves."

"What about them, master?" The eunuch kept his forehead on the carpets.

"Tell the slave masters I want the youngest and best women brought to the clearing outside my pavilion. Now. Strip them naked, those that still have clothing." He would personally select the two most tender, and offer one of them as a prize for the soldier who—

Holofernes slumped in his chair. Like the lion hunt, he had provided this amusement for his men before. Where was the joy in a familiar diversion?

Bagoas gazed up at him, jaw slack. "Master?"

What would entertain his men, while leaving them roused and still hungry for blood? "All the women. All the women are to go to the torch circle. Send the slave masters to me for further instructions."

First the women would dance for the pleasure of his troops. For his pleasure. His robes grew sticky with sweat as Holofernes pictured the women, breasts and hips swaying, torchlight setting bodies aglow. Dark eyes wide with fear, rapid heartbeats speeding the blood beneath their skin.

Already he imagined the roars of his men, tens of thousands of them, at sight of that vulnerable female flesh. Holofernes swallowed.

Bagoas swallowed, too. "You will have them d-dance, master? Dance only?"

"It is clear you have been a eunuch all your life! The women will dance to begin." His soldiers would draw lots for the youngest, the lushest or most lovely. They would draw lots for every woman in camp until all the women, old and young, lovely or worn, were taken. "The men who lose will take their turns later."

Bagoas came to his feet. "So many soldiers and so few women. Sire, the slaves will die long before—"

"Slaves die. Do you understand me? All slaves. Now take my message to the slave masters." He wanted to be alone, to envision the drama about to unfold.

But still the eunuch hesitated. "Master, the women will die long before a tenth of the men—have their chance. Who will cook when they are gone? Who will serve your army's lust?"

"There are always more slaves. Soon enough, the women of Bethulia will replace those who die tonight."

Tonight he would choose the youngest, most luscious girl for himself. Holofernes ground his knuckles into the table while he imagined the pulse of drums, imagined the circle of trembling women. His men would cheer his name while he stroked a fingertip down a bare breast here, moved on to pinch another woman's nipple, already hard with cold and fear. The soldier's chants would rise to a roar when Holofernes slid his hand between thighs already lax with terror.

Would he take her there in the circle, while his men watched, or draw out her suffering by bringing his choice to his pavilion? How long before she understood that to lie with him was to lie down with her death?

He would use her until her flesh broke, until her blood flowed hot around him. She would die screaming.

Unsteady, Holofernes wiped his mouth with the back of one wrist. How long had he waited for screams, for blood? How long since he rode into battle? Tonight he would ride. As his choice gurgled her last, he would bellow his triumph for every woman in Bethulia to hear.

"Master?" The whisper came from his feet.

Holofernes bent over the eunuch, who tried to crawl backwards away from him. "You have my permission to watch tonight, or hide somewhere and cover your ears. Now go."

The tent flap danced a long time after Bagoas ran out.

Holofernes contemplated his plans for after the revel. Should he have the women's bodies scattered before the village gate, or hammer their flayed skins to the walls? Either way, he wanted the people of Bethulia to recognize the fate awaiting them. Especially the women.

Holofernes focused on his altar to Ishtar. In his rush to set the night's entertainment in motion, he had forgotten to tell Bagoas to search for fresh flowers.

"I will find them myself, Goddess of War. I will bring you only the best." He raised his voice. "Bagoas? My armor. And send for my horse!"

Chapter Twenty-two
Judith

IN THE FLICKERING SHADOWS of her rooftop garden, Naomi lifted a small pottery lantern and called out, "Hilkiah? Bring me a touch of fire from the kitchen."

Judith stood, one hand extended. "He may be abed. Give me the lantern, I'll take it downstairs and light it myself." Though it seemed wrong to disturb the cool mystery of the moonlit roof—

"Stop." From his place under one of the potted trees, Achior held up one hand. "You've both grown used to siege conditions. The longer the Assyrians are out there the greater our danger, not less." He gestured for Judith to sit again. "Leave the lamp unlit."

Naomi set the lamp on the floor by her feet as Judith sank onto the bench beside her. A faint rancid smell wafted from the lamp, and she wrinkled her nose. Not so long ago, dirty oil would have been replaced with new.

Now every drop counted. Judith nudged the pot under the bench, where no one might accidentally knock it over.

As if the odor bothered him as well, Achior picked a sprig of anise and twirled it between his fingers. Even in the moonlight, Judith could see how the beard he had started to grow since she last saw him roughened his jaw. It made him look like a stranger—

She blinked. Achior was a stranger. A foreign warrior.

Naomi rubbed her knobbed hands up and down her arms. "My bones ache. If only I could soak away this soreness—" She stopped to listen. "What's that noise?"

Outside the walls, far in the distance, came a roar of shouts mixed with wild laughter. And—surely Judith imagined it—screams as well. All the tortured ones had died, hadn't they?

"What's that noise?" Naomi's voice quavered, a thing Judith had never heard before.

She scooted closer, one arm around her friend's bent shoulders. "They're even louder than the mob this afternoon." And sounded jubilant. Why would soldiers be happy in the middle of a siege?

Achior let the sprig of anise fall. "Holofernes sometimes arranges—entertainment for the men."

Entertainment? Judith expected Achior to explain. He did not.

Naomi crouched forward on the bench to squint at the former commander's face. "Animal fights?"

"Something like that." He snapped off another spray of anise.

Achior knew what the Assyrians were doing, Judith felt certain of it. As the roar from the camp escalated, punctuated now by rhythmic clapping, he spun the delicate stem between his fingers in time with the applause.

The distant beat hammered inside Judith like pain. Had Achior taken part in Holofernes's entertainments? Even the thought felt unclean. And yet Achior had spent a lifetime with a sword in his hand. He had killed hundreds of men, maybe more. And women. Had he—killed women, too?

Naomi's shoulders rose toward her ears. The moon cast her wrinkles in relief until she seemed a stranger, too, hunched and frail. "I hate to feel so helpless. It frightens me worst of all."

Achior's fist closed on the herb, crushing it. "And I feel like the eunuch Holofernes wanted me to be. When the mob gathered outside this house today, I wanted to stand at Uzziah's side and quiet them. Quell them, as I long to silence that rabble now!"

The shouting surged and dispersed, surged again. Judith stood to pace the rooftop, but could not escape the noise. Even from this place so close to the center of town, she could see the circle of torches beyond the encampment. Tiny in the distance, the lights flared and sputtered just past the farthest line of tents.

The "entertainment" must be happening there—

At last the awful cadence rose to a crescendo, faded into a rumble and broke apart. Judith drooped beside Naomi again, and Achior's fingers loosened on the anise. The flattened leaves fluttered to the roof, a smear of green and the ghost of scent.

He looked at Judith for the first time all evening. "Today you did what I could not. You saved the child and ended the riot."

"I did what I could." Cold inside, Judith turned to Naomi. "Why did you send Ezra for me?"

"When I heard our people—" Naomi's voice wobbled. "When I saw them coming across my courtyard, I couldn't breathe or think of a single prayer. I couldn't even raise my voice to call for Ezra! He had to find me." Her thin arms closed around Judith. "I wanted you here, soul's daughter. Young and strong, like I used to be."

"You're still strong." Judith waited for Naomi to agree. *All she needs—all any of us needs is more water, more food. For the Assyrians to admit we'll never surrender and leave us in peace.*

Her old friend nestled her head against Judith's shoulder. "Don't lie, my darling. I want to survive, to live to see Ezra wed. To hold his child, my great-grandson or -granddaughter. To look into the eyes of innocence again." Naomi's voice climbed, but grew higher and weaker instead of more certain. "I want what I will never have, the Assyrians gone from our horizon."

"You will have all those things." *Blessed Lord. Make it so!* Judith

136

recalled the din from the soldiers' revelry spewing across the plain, invasive as the stench of death.

Naomi shook her head. "I expect to die. I am old woman enough to hope death comes while I sleep."

Blessed Lord, no. "No, Naomi."

Her friend scooted away to rest her fingertips on the shoulder of Achior's robe. "You understand, don't you? Death is already here. I feel it in the chill seeping through me, no matter how hot the air. I taste it in what remains of our water, staler and flatter every day."

He dipped his head. "I should have known it would end like this. When I sprawled in the dust at Chabris's feet, perhaps I should have told him, 'We are already defeated. Surrender now.'"

"No." Judith leapt up, fists knotted.

Achior inclined his head again, this time to her, and spoke as if she had not moved. "Instead I lied, to Chabris, to Uzziah. To you, Naomi, and you, Judith. To everyone in Bethulia. Especially myself."

"We will not suffer defeat!" Could Rebekah have sensed the truth for once? Had Achior come not to help, but to rasp away Bethulia's courage and faith from inside the village walls? "We will not surrender." *We cannot.*

Achior rose onto one knee. "I'm sorry, Judith. I offered hope— the hope that hope exists, and that one god, your god, can protect you." He covered his face with both hands. "I'm afraid. Afraid most of all that I was wrong."

Blessed art thou, oh Lord. Blessed art thou—

The distant shouting and applause started over again, louder and more urgent. Judith squirmed away from Naomi. "I won't give up. I won't."

But images poured through her. Inside her, where she could not look away. Of Lila as she pushed the little girl into the dirt. Of Gothoniel as he hauled his writhing wife from the square. Her people had already broken faith.

JUDITH

"Heart's daughter, listen to me—"

"No!" Judith lashed out and sent the oil lamp skittering across the roof. While Naomi and Achior called her name, she fled the rooftop and down into the street. Into the darkness, alone.

Chapter Twenty-three
Judith

"**J**UDITH.**" **THOUGH ACHIOR** did not shout, his voice carried clearly. "Wait, please. I want to explain."

She tried to run faster, but the maze of small pens full of doe goats and their kids, sheep and lambs, rams or bucks forced her to pick her way. Moon-cast shadows made it hard to tell where fence lines ended and shadows began.

Achior's long, steady strides brought him closer. Like his clean-shaven face, his lameness was gone. Judith dodged between two more pens, and a startled lamb skipped to its feet. A goat bleated as if irked at this midnight awakening. She stood still.

If only the women of her people wore veils, like Assyrian women! Whether or not Achior was a spy, Judith longed to hide her face from him. "You must think me very silly."

"Silly?" He halted the other side of the sheep pen from her. "Why would I?"

"You and Naomi both speak of defeat as if we have already lost. You are both more experienced than I am, Naomi in years and you in war. But I—"

Achior circled the pen toward her, pale light washing over him. "Yes?"

Let him think her silly. "I still believe our Lord will show us what to do. How to save ourselves."

"I hope you are right." Achior's mouth twisted inside its dark frame of beard. "But the time for help, human or divine, grows short."

She stared at him, this foreigner. If he was here to destroy her people from within, nothing she said would change his mind. "The One sees farther than you can, or I. The One knows how much time we really have."

The lamb in the pen beside them folded its slender legs, curled against its mother on the scanty remains of clean bedding, gave a sleepy whimper and grew silent.

Achior's lips curved into the first real smile she had ever seen on his face. "I hope you are right. Will you come back to Naomi's roof? I want to explain why I've stayed away from your house all this time."

Judith edged away. "You have no need to explain yourself to me." The two of them were not family, not clan.

"I want to tell you anyway. Desert, the warhorse we saw from your roof, once belonged to me."

The sorrow in his voice made her pause. Achior had lost his people, his homeland, his place in society. Until now she had not heard him grieve. "You stopped keeping watch from my roof because of a horse?"

"My horse. Named for the light that races across the sands at sunrise, trained for battle before he came into my hands, and quick to obey heel or rein. Quick because the men who schooled him punish any horse who hesitates to obey."

Achior's hand fisted on the top of the fence. "Do you remember how Sendal, my replacement, wrenched the bit in Desert's mouth that day? I wanted to jump off the wall—no, fly off it, and drag the worthless cur out of the saddle."

"But Assyrians—" She stopped. Assyrians treated their beasts with the same cruelty they doled out to the world. Achior, native of the land of Ammon, long beaten and controlled by Assyria, must know that. "You were saying?"

"None of my men understood why I groomed Desert myself, no matter how stained with sweat and blood we both were. I often took him on long rides by ourselves, far from the practice field."

Though Judith had ridden only on donkeys, and those only during her marriage, she could picture it easily. The man and horse cantering across a plain, attended only by the wind and the drum of hoof beats. "You made him your friend."

Achior dipped his head. When he turned away to walk toward Uzziah's house, she accompanied him without thinking.

"In battle I want—" He caught himself. "I wanted a mount who obeyed out of friendship, not fear. I trusted Desert to carry me safely out of danger, even if I were too badly injured to guide him."

"Desert kept you safe." *Our Lord keeps us safe.* If only she could explain that to him! But if Sirach the priest could not do it, or Uzziah with all his wisdom, what chance had she? Achior had chosen a horse as the center of his faith, no matter what gods or goddesses he claimed to worship.

They reached the entrance to the magistrate's house, and Achior leaned against the wall. "Sendal has hands like anchors on the reins, and the balance of a year-old child in the saddle. He mocked me for making a pet of my charger. I should have known he would seize Desert the moment Holofernes exiled me."

"You ran from my roof that day because he was hurting your horse." Judith released a long breath.

The Lord asked his people to treat animals with kindness. Achior might understand little or nothing of her faith, but he cared for living creatures in a similar way. He was impure, bloodstained now and forever. But she refused to believe that someone with such compassion could be a spy.

"I couldn't bear to stand by, helpless, and watch my beautiful Desert, my friend, tortured by that bumbling hound." The former commander shook his head. "Until that moment I had not realized how powerless I have become! Seeing Desert flooded me with my past, the times I ordered my men to kill. The times I killed." He made a sound deep in his chest. "I was a soldier, a commander in the army. That makes no difference to me now. Countless lives ended because of me, just as countless lives will end here—"

"Stop saying that." Judith retreated half a step.

Achior stood away from the wall, hands held out, palms up. "Why didn't I defy Holofernes the last time I saw him? If I had challenged him he might have fought me."

"Your death would have done us no good—"

"I might have killed him and saved us all this pain. I might have convinced Nebuchadnezzar to attack some other place instead of Bethulia."

The sheep and goats were quiet now, in the depths of night. "You would still be living your own life. Do you want it back?"

"No." He flinched. "Though I do miss my homeland, and my old friends."

"Is that why you've begun to grow a beard again?" It made sense. "As a reminder of your own country?"

Achior scraped one palm across his chin. "In part. I know your men folk keep clean-shaven. It's not my way."

So he meant to mark himself as a stranger. He understood he could never be anything else. "Thank you for explaining to me. Now I want to bid Naomi goodnight." Wanted to ask her old friend's forgiveness for running off like a petulant child. Judith started to cross the courtyard, so much wider than her own.

Achior stopped partway across and bowed. "I'll leave you to say your farewells alone. Good night."

"Good night." She hurried up the steps to the rooftop garden. "Naomi—"

Stretched out on several layers of rug and fur, her old friend was already asleep in the starlight. Judith stood over her a long time, listening to Naomi's shallow breaths and the long pauses in between. At last she found her way down the steps again, across the courtyard and out to weave between the animal pens.

Though they had run out of fresh bedding days before, the shepherds still cleaned up after the beasts twice a day, and dumped the waste over a sheltered corner of the wall. They would clean the area later, after the siege ended—

A figure crept along the edge of the square across from her. A sleepless neighbor? Or one of the day's protestors up to fresh mischief?

Judith's steps wavered, even as she drew breath to call out. "Who are you?"

When the figure broke into a run, Judith glanced back. Achior had gone.

She caught up the skirt of her robe and sped after the fleeing shadow.

Chapter Twenty-four
Judith

"STOP!" JUDITH LENGTHENED HER STRIDE. She gained on the petite figure just ahead, garments billowing as she ran. She stretched out one hand ready to clasp the fine fabric, and then faltered. "Chana?"

"J-Judith?" Joakim's young wife swayed to a halt and turned to face her, eyes dilated in the moonlight. "What are you doing here?"

"That's what I asked you." Judith drew level with the panting girl. "Why did you run away from me?"

Chana crumpled against her. "Please don't tell my husband. Please don't—"

"Don't tell him what?" Before Judith finished the question, Chana lurched away to vomit against the nearest wall. *Blessed Lord, help us.* "You're with child?" Judith stooped to support Chana, one palm against the girl's sweaty forehead.

Chana moaned and tried to squirm away, only to retch some more.

"You are. Oh, Chana." Judith stroked the heaving shoulders.

"Why don't you want Joakim to know?"

The young bride scooted away from the mess she had made. And from Judith. She hugged herself, shivering in the hot darkness. "He's an elder—important. I can't dis-disturb him with—this— until after the siege."

Disturb him? "You're doing what a wife is meant to do." *Manasseh—the sons and daughters we never had.* Lips tight, Judith patted Chana's slender back. "Here, let's move somewhere more pleasant."

She helped Chana to her feet, and guided the younger woman to the display bench in front of Ruth's house, empty now the potter could no longer dig for clay. She nudged the girl down on the lowest shelf.

"How do you expect to hide this from him? Hasn't he noticed you lose your breakfast?" Even self-absorbed Joakim should notice such obvious signs.

"I don't always—I'm not always sick—in the morning." As if to prove it, Chana twisted off the bench and crawled away to vomit again. Judith steadied her and tried to take shallow breaths.

When Chana finished she slumped against Judith's shoulder. "Sometimes it happens in the morning, but it can happen any time." She gestured at the puddle behind them. "Like now."

All the more reason Joakim should take notice. "You're sick night and day, but your husband let you come out alone after dark?" Judith slipped one arm around the shaking girl. "It's your job to create and nurture a family. It's his to keep you safe."

"Joakim sleeps deeply. I tiptoed out when he began to sn—" Even in the moonlight, Judith saw her blush. "I left after he was sound asleep."

Had the elder slept through the disturbance this afternoon, as well? "Where did you plan to go?"

"Your house. For help with—" Once more, Chana gestured at the mess.

"My house? But I—" *I have no children. Oh, Manasseh, the sons and daughters we did not have.* "Why would you come to me?"

"I can't go to my mother. Joakim and I wed months ago, but she acts as if he may yet change his mind. 'Be sure that babe's a son,' she says." Chana pushed up onto her knees, eyes fierce, mouth trembling. "What can I do but pray our Lord sends me a healthy boy? My mother would never stop fussing if she knew I vomited at your feet."

Blessed Lord, how could such cruelty exist in the name of love? "Never mind about that. What about Joakim's mother?" A dutiful mother-in-law would guide a son's young wife.

Chana sagged against Judith again. "All she talks about is how things will be when I bear my first son," she said, her voice mouse-quiet. "And how long she spent birthing Joakim." The girl shuddered. "Judith, I'm so afraid."

Outside the walls, the last ragged shouts from the soldiers finally ceased. Judith lifted the girl's face with one fist under Chana's chin. "You came out alone in a town under siege?"

"For my baby? Yes." The last word hissed, vehement in the darkness.

Judith chuckled. "Then you're the best kind of brave, Chana. You do not let your fear keep you from doing what needs to be done." Perhaps Naomi's description of the girl had not been so accurate after all.

"Then you'll help me?"

"There are plenty of women who have been mothers in town—" Naomi! Helping Chana would give her old friend something happy to think about, and give Chana a source of wise guidance. "Why don't you go to Naomi?"

Chana wriggled her shoulders. "How can such an old woman help me? I know Naomi's your friend, but I can't believe Uzziah was ever a baby."

Judith choked down a laugh that would surely wake everyone in

Bethulia. "She raised a son wisely and well enough that he became magistrate." The laugh no longer tempted her. "And I have no children at all."

"But you're sensible. So kind, like a mother. No—an older sister." Chana clasped her hands at her breast. "Everyone in your household is a woman, and Abra knows so much about herbs."

Yes, Abra's herbs might be of use. Judith stood and shook out her skirts. "Come. Let's see what remedies my household has for you and your babe."

Cold, slender fingers slid into hers. "Thank you." Chana gave a tiny skip, only to clutch Judith's arm and wobble the next few steps. "Strange. I don't feel as scared."

"Neither do I." Perhaps the day's events had burnt fear out of them both, the way flames burnt a sacrifice to ash.

Chapter Twenty-five
Judith

A SHADOW, WINGS WIDESPREAD, floated across Judith's rooftop. Instinctively, she edged deeper inside her tent, then half stood to squint up at the sky. Another vulture? She had never seen so many of the unclean birds above the village before.

"Judith?" Achior called to her from the courtyard.

She watched a Grier eagle spiral into view. Another eater of the dead. "Up here."

The former commander reached the rooftop and hesitated. How long his hair had grown. It covered the tops of his ears, reached halfway down his neck.

Neither spoke. Only now that their ease together was gone did Judith see how comfortable she had become with him before.

"Good morning." Achior started to bow to her, only to straighten. His pale eyes followed the Grier eagle's slow spiral overhead.

Judith jerked her chin toward the encampment. "They seem to be having trouble waking up this morning." From the nearest row of tents, one or two soldiers stumbled into the cool light of the new day.

"Yes." Achior did not sink onto the stool beside hers, but tracked the flight of yet another vulture.

The wind changed direction and Judith covered her nose with one hand. "I don't know which smells worse, the Assyrians' livestock or us." And yet this stink lacked the earthiness of the stable.

"Don't blame the beasts for what they can't help." But Achior sniffed the air. His slanted brows arrowed down over his nose. "I would like to complement you on your courage yesterday." He took a step or two nearer the parapet. "I meant to say so last night, but other things distracted me—"

Judith squirmed. "I'm not so brave. Anyone would have done the same."

"Yet no one else did." Achior peered over the outer wall. His long back stiffened. "Judith. You have good sense as well as courage. You will need that good sense, that courage now."

He whipped around to face her, the mesh of lines around his eyes deepening. "Go inside, to the reception room or your own chamber. Stay there until I return. Keep your household within as well."

"Are the Assyrians preparing to attack?" Over his shoulder the encampment appeared the same, with less activity than usual, not more.

Only that clinging odor was different, that and the shadow of another vulture. As the bird glided lower, Judith rushed to the wall and looked down.

"Don't!" Achior lunged to stop her, too late.

Sickness clawed up from her belly to her throat. She reeled away from the sight of bodies scattered across Bethulia's place of judgment. Naked bodies. Female bodies half-hidden by the flap and rustle of black wings, the dart of beaks.

When Judith opened her eyes again, she was inside the goat-hair tent. Achior squatted beside her, a cup of wine held ready. "Drink."

Judith pushed the cup away. "No. Water—"

"You need spirits. Please, Judith. Take it." The instant her fingers curled around the cool pottery, he raised the tent walls. All except the one nearest the rampart.

Air moved through the shelter. Tainted air. Judith put her back to the hillside and gulped her wine.

"Here." Achior placed the jug within easy reach. "When you regain your strength, do as I asked. Stay indoors the rest of the day. All of you together in the reception room."

The largest room, with the stoutest door.

"Those poor women." Judith surveyed him over the cup. "Is that how Holofernes entertains his troops? The torches we saw last night. The cheers and applause. And all the time the soldiers were—"

"Don't." Swifter than any of the birds outside, Achior swooped to bend close to her. "Don't think about it. I will come back later tonight."

Judith rolled to her knees. "Where are you going?" Even on his first day in Bethulia Achior had not looked so pale.

"To clean up that shameful mess." He strode away.

THROUGH THE LONG DAY her household carried on as normal, though Judith couldn't find it in her heart to restrict them to the reception room. Not so close to the wall and what lay strewn across the hillside beyond.

So Dorcas ground flour. Huldah mixed the flour and baked bread. In hushed tones, she sent the little maid from storeroom to kitchen to courtyard on one errand after another. Abra mended torn garments, head bent low so her wild hair hid her face.

Only Judith could not settle to a task. She stood at her loom for the first time since Manasseh's death, but her fingers refused to move in rhythm. Some rows tightened toward one end or another, while others gaped loosely.

As time for the evening meal approached, she tore out all she had done. While she yanked out the last thread, Abra darted across the courtyard from the gate. "Abra?" Judith hurried out of the reception room. "Where have you been?"

"Out seeking news."

"Achior told us to stay home—did you hear word of him?" All day she had wondered how he meant to clean the hillside of its abomination.

Abra shook her frazzled head. "Nothing. I don't think anyone even knows he's gone, except us."

And perhaps the magistrate. "I'm going out." Judith brushed the last snippet of wool off her skirts.

"Where?"

"To the High Place, to make a sacrifice." As head of the household, she should have done so the instant she saw those women. She could not think of them only as bodies.

Judith had the streets to herself. The sweet stink grew fainter the farther she walked. Had Uzziah ordered everyone to stay inside their homes? Judith doubted it. *My people want to stay out of this air, soiled by the stench of death and the flap of dark wings.*

In the market square Judith selected a calf from a pen that held some of the choicest animals from her herds. The creature's coat lacked the gloss of a beast fresh from the fields. But his curved forehead was perfectly shaped, his back straight, his haunches firm. She led him to the steps of the High Place, only to pause. Would Sirach be on duty, or secreted inside his small dwelling, like everyone else?

The young creature bawled for its mother while Judith hesitated. A moment later, Sirach's shadow stretched, long and thin, down the steps. Usually the priest waited while townspeople brought their beasts up to him. Now he met Judith at the bottom and helped her bring the calf all the way up to the altar.

Quietly Sirach murmured the traditional questions, and listened to her replies. The priest scattered the blood, then offered the choicest parts of the calf to the Lord. To the flames.

Uncomforted by the ritual, Judith trudged away. *Blessed Lord. Blessed Lord. Blessed Lord.* All the way home she sought relief in prayer, but could repeat only those two words. Even they failed her once she reached her house. "Has Achior returned?"

Abra shook her head.

Where was he? Judith swallowed a screech of frustration. "I'm going up to the roof."

"But mistress." Quick steps behind, then in front of her. Dorcas held out one delicate arm, as if to block Judith's way. "You know what Achior said—"

Huldah hissed. "Quiet, girl. If our mistress chooses to put herself at risk—well, that's her right. Come, you may as well move our sleeping mats into the reception room." She snapped her fingers.

On the rooftop, Judith stretched out on her back. Had the sky ever taken so long to darken? She held one arm across her face in an attempt to escape the odor that now permeated the village. Bethulia had never seemed so empty of life.

Light, muted footsteps crept close, a sleeping mat whispered across the floor, and Dorcas tucked one small hand into hers. "I want to be up here with you, mistress."

"Thank you, Dorcas." She should send the girl downstairs. But— "I'm glad of your company, too." As sunset stained the sky, the little maid's breaths grew more regular. Soon Judith followed her into sleep.

SHE WOKE TO THE CRACKLE OF FIRE and the smell of burning oil and greenery. Judith plunged upright. *Fire.* Had the Assyrians set the gate alight?

Beside her Dorcas rolled up into a crouch and trundled backward so fast she nearly pulled down the tent. "Mistress?"

"Shh. Downstairs, Dorcas. Now. I just want to see—" As Judith crawled toward the wall, the patter of feet told her the girl had retreated.

A flicker of radiance to the south confused Judith. Beneath the odd scent of herbal-infused smoke, she caught a whiff of flesh. Then a sheet of flame roared up toward the stars. Smoke swelled, blown by the wind back across the plain and the Assyrian encampment.

And a long arm reached over the parapet.

Judith screamed.

With a kick and a twist, Achior hauled himself across the wall and flopped onto the roof beside her. Soot smeared his face and garments, and broken leaves clung to the fabric and his hair.

Judith crushed both hands to her lips to smother another shriek. "Where have you been?" She crept nearer. "What have you done?"

"I—know—" He coughed. "I know your people—bury their dead. I couldn't do that, so I—Fire cleanses, Judith. It's more decent than letting them rot."

"How did you—" Her tongue fumbled. "Were you out there all this time?"

Panting, Achior squirmed upright, back to the parapet, legs extended. "I went out the same way I came back in." He smiled. She had never seen anything as wicked as the flash of teeth against his smudged skin. "I've always liked climbing."

"But—" Judith worked some saliva into her mouth. "But what about the soldiers?"

"Any soldier I met had no chance of raising an alarm." He tossed a knife, ringing, onto the roof. "It took longer to gather enough brush than I expected. I hope Uzziah and Naomi don't blame me for using so much oil."

"They won't." Judith crumpled against the wall at his side. Her people did believe in burial. Yet what funeral other than this would those dead women ever receive? "Thank you."

Achior grunted and stood. "I did it for all of us. Now I'm going to bed."

"Sleep well." *My friend.*

Judith began the prayer for the dead as he plodded away. While she prayed, she listened to the fire. It burned long after dawn.

Chapter Twenty-six
Judith

"**E**ZRA, WHAT ARE YOU DOING BACK HERE?** You barely had time to reach home—" Judith's voice trailed away as the young man plodded up to her across the main courtyard. In the transparent light just before twilight, everything about Ezra drooped. His lank hair, his shoulders. His arms swung loose at his side like uncoiled rope, and his feet barely left the ground.

"We're surrendering to the Assyrians. At dawn," he mumbled. "Tomorrow morning at dawn." His mouth squared in a silent wail, but no tears fell.

"Surrender?" Judith rubbed the ache between her breasts, but the pain only deepened. "But—but the siege. It's only lasted thirty-four days." Thirty-four days. Was that all it took to break faith?

"Chabris told me when I reached the square. Before I could go in our house." The boy's breath hitched. His eyes squeezed shut, but still no tears came, as if everything inside him had gone dry.

Color bled across the sky as the sun slid lower. "Why? Why surrender now? We've held out so long. Why now?" Her shout rang off the courtyard walls. Surely the One had a plan to save His people, if only they gave Him time?

Face pinched, Ezra did not answer. His grubby wool garment bagged around him, holding the shape of his once-firm body.

She couldn't bear to see his fragility another moment. Judith lunged past him and up to the roof. The Assyrian campfires, scarlet and orange that matched the sky, blurred as her own eyes filled.

"This morning Father said we only have enough water to last five more days. I guess that's why." Ezra's voice sounded distant, and Judith realized he had stayed downstairs. Rooted by shock and exhaustion.

She knew how he felt, but made herself move back toward him. Before she reached the bottom step Ezra was stumbling out the gate. "Wait!"

He stopped without looking at her. "Grandmother always says you're devout. Will you pray? If you ask the One, maybe our enemies will show us—" Ezra swallowed, his whole body shaken with dry sobs. "—show us mercy."

"Of course. Of course I will." But he fled before she finished speaking.

Judith crawled up the last few steps to the roof. There she fell flat, arms extended, as her own tears rushed down. "Blessed art thou, our Lord. Show me! Show me how to save my people."

Naomi, weakening every day. Every hour. Abra, sturdy in body and soul. Tender Dorcas, and Huldah, sour and tough, with a kernel of fearlessness in her heart. And Achior. Achior and so many others.

Judith rocked in place. *Show me what to do. Show me and I'll do it, no matter what the cost.* The air shifted, cold and brilliant against her closed lids. When she opened her eyes, the sky was black. But silver mist drifted around her.

Mist at this time of year? Judith crouched against the roof beneath her. She clung as it seemed to spin. The silver light curved above and around her, a glowing orb brighter than the stars. Its blaze blotted out the enemy's campfires.

Judith tried to stand and couldn't, her bones vibrating. The radiance streamed through her. *Blessed Lord, stop—it's too much—* She flung up one arm to block the vision unfolding within her. As if anything she did could stop it.

She collapsed, unable to feel the rough surface of the roof. The light, the power, ebbed and vanished. But each step she must take remained clear. Her best gown. The sword. Abra's loyalty. All were part of the One's plan.

She sweated in the warm darkness. No mistaking this for a dream. The Lord had been giving her this message all along.

Judith lurched to her feet. The Assyrian camp spread out before her, all the way to the horizon. Hundreds of thousands of soldiers between her and her target. Holofernes. At the thought of what she must do, what the One expected of her, Judith's belly heaved. "I can't. I can't do it. Please, don't ask me."

You can. You will. The command echoed inside her, outside. She could not tell.

She rubbed her eyes with hands cold as raw meat. Who would believe her? And yet—Unsteadily, Judith circled the roof. Each step grew longer, faster. More sure. Who else could even try, if not a woman? A young woman, and strong. A widow, wealthy. Free to come and go.

"Judith?" Abra stood on the top step, fists at her hips. "Why are you up here? Did I hear Ezra right, that we're to surrender?"

"No." She heard the vehemence in her own voice and bowed her head to accept her fate. "Are the others awake? We have much to do."

She led the way to the servant's quarters, Abra close behind her. Dorcas and Huldah both sat on their bed furs, already dressed as if waiting. How had she not seen their beauty before? Dorcas, glowing with possibility, like the lamp she held. Even twisted old

Huldah burned from within.

"Dorcas, run to the magistrate's, then the homes of the elders. Ask them to come here at dawn. I need to show them something before we surrender. Before Uzziah tells our townspeople we plan to surrender. Do you understand?"

"At once, mistress." The girl hurried away while Huldah sputtered.

"How dare you summon those men? Have you lost your wits? I never—"

Judith spoke over her. "Heat water so I can bathe."

The older woman's jaw dropped until her chin nearly brushed her breastbone. "A bath? We barely drank enough water today to keep our tongues from cleaving to the roofs of our mouths."

"If only yours had done so! Do as she bids, or I'll thump you myself!" Abra and the cook glared at each other. Huldah twitched one shoulder and stomped out, grumbling. Only then did Abra face Judith. "What do you want me to do?"

"Come help me choose a fine robe."

"For you to wear when you address the magistrate and elders?" Abra chuckled. "It does sound strange."

"I already know what I will wear." The One had showed her weeks before. "These are for you." She touched Abra's dirt-smudged cheek. "You must take a bath as well." They would go before Holofernes like royalty deigning favor, not supplicants begging for life.

Her friend hesitated. "I?"

"Yes." In the storage space beside her room, Judith sorted through the garments from her married life. She set aside her favorite. "This needs to be aired. And—yes. This one, too." She held out an undyed garment embroidered with curlicues of black. "This will look well with your hair."

"My hair?" Abra edged away. "I don't understand."

What can I tell her, Lord? "You and I will be going outside the walls before nightfall tomorrow."

"How can we go anywhere with the Assyrians—" Abra tensed. "That's where we're going."

Judith lowered her head.

Abra swatted both garments to the floor. "I won't! Beat me if you will, but I won't do it. You're going to take word of our surrender to Holofernes yourself!"

"No! Abra, listen to me." Judith gripped her friend's shoulders. "I'm going to see to it that the Assyrians surrender to us. The Lord has a plan—" She collapsed against the nearest shelf. "I won't force you to come with me, though I'm—I'm not sure I can do it without your help."

A pause. "The One has a plan? How do you know?"

Here it was, and Judith still didn't know how to answer.

Then Abra embraced her, her tumbled hair shredding around both their faces. "If our Lord asks you to defeat our enemies, of course I'll help. Of course I will."

So easily? Judith held her shaking friend tight, then stepped away. "There will be blood. Murder. If they catch us we die."

"If you're going, I go too." Abra began to tidy her hair. "When do we leave?"

Huldah's crutch thwacked into the bedroom. "Your bath is ready, may the One forgive us." She goggled at the fine garments scattered across the floor. "What's this?"

"Judith is going to—"

"Stop, Abra, she doesn't know!"

"—to defeat Holofernes!"

The sizzle of the lamp sounded loud in the hush. Huldah leaned harder on her stick. "Really."

Should Huldah even know? Too late now. Reluctantly, Judith explained what they needed to do.

In the end, the old woman sniffed. "Madness." Then she cackled. "The Lord appeared to you, mistress? Yes, madness. But maybe I won't need the pots and my knife after all. Though I'll keep the blade close, just in case. Now you'd best bathe while the water's hot." She stumped out again.

Abra snuffled out a laugh. "At least she stopped yelling. Now, I think you should wear your lapis necklace and the gold earrings—"

The earrings Manasseh had given her their first year of marriage.

Her friend darted back and forth, trying on bracelets until she found a simple string of beads. "Here. These will suit me."

"Yes, they do." Judith pulled off her sackcloth robe and let it fall. So much to do, when she already felt exhausted. The women of her house accepted the news. Now to learn if the village leaders would, as well.

Chapter Twenty-seven
Judith

"**W**HY ARE WE HERE, UZZIAH?" Joakim's peevish voice broke the predawn stillness of her courtyard, and up on the roof Judith's palms dampened. Before the magistrate could answer, the elder hurried on. "I don't care how wealthy the woman is, she is a widow and childless. How dare she order us to come meet her?"

"Invite," Uzziah said. A faint rasp told her he had removed his sandals, polite even on what he thought was his last day as magistrate. His last day alive. "Judith did not order, she invited us, Joakim."

She wove her way past the tent, to the low balustrade that overlooked the main courtyard. "Welcome, sirs. Please, will you join me?"

"Of course." Uzziah headed toward her. With a grunt, the elder followed him.

Stumbling a little, Judith returned to the open portion of the roof, sank onto the low seat she had arranged with its back to the encampment, and smoothed her skirts over her thighs. The fine-woven wool felt weightless after all her years in sackcloth.

Joakim puffed into view on the top step. The stringy elder took one look at her and erupted. "Why are you dressed in finery?" Scowling, he sniffed the air. "Cleansed, too. You've bathed! And you're dripping with jewels. Do you want to start another riot, woman?"

What did he know of riots? He did not even know his wife bore his child—Judith gripped the edges of the stool with both hands. "I promise to explain as soon as the others arrive."

"Yes, give her a chance to explain." But Uzziah's keen glance took her in, from embroidered hem to the golden earrings that swung from her lobes. He stood still before folding onto the makeshift bench facing her.

Joakim continued to splutter. "I tell you she'll start another riot!"

"Only if your fuss draws enough people for one." Chabris strode across the roof. His garments, usually a warm gray that accented his gray-flecked beard, had stains old and new down the front. He perched on the wall between her roof and Rebekah's. "Now, Judith, what do you need to tell us before the surrender?" He sounded composed as ever, as if about to hear one side of a disagreement he must judge.

Blood coursed through Judith's body to pound in her fingertips and in her ears. All night she had tried to decide how to begin. How to explain. "You know the story of the evil men who attacked a maiden. The One struck them down—"

"I'll not listen to a woman preach." Joakim stomped away in a whirl of garments, only to hesitate a step away from the stairs. "Chabris? Uzziah?"

Chabris lifted one shoulder, still wide in spite of his loosened jowls. "The priest plans to spend our last day of freedom in prayer. I may as well find what comfort I may in Judith's words."

Uzziah said nothing at all, but his chin wobbled. Seeing it,

Judith ached. She had never seen the magistrate look so much like his mother.

"Pah." Joakim flung himself away. "When you're ready to do what we must do today, send me word." His footsteps thudded away across the courtyard below them.

Chabris angled his head. "Eager to surrender, is he?"

Uzziah rolled one hand toward her. "He just wants it done with, as do I. Please, Judith, say what you must. But quickly."

"The Lord—" Why hadn't she brought a cup of water with her? "The Lord has shown me how to stop Holofernes from defiling our town, the way he punished those evil men—" Judith broke off as Achior quietly joined them.

Chabris stroked his chin. "What are you saying, Judith? Surely you don't mean the One spoke to you, a woman?"

She had not expected any one to guess. She dipped her head. "Yes."

Uzziah's eyebrows tightened. "The law of Moses and our Lord is plain. Women are not to take part in the work of men, never mind the work of the One." For the first time in her memory, the magistrate studied her with mouth twisted and nostrils pinched, like a thief he must punish. He would relish punishing.

"I did not intend to do so. *I did not pursue this.* "But the One did come to me."

"Your people thirst." In his filthy, borrowed robe, Achior took a single step, one that aligned him with Judith. "Will it do such harm to hear what she says your god said?"

The remaining elder pursed his lips, but Uzziah nodded. "You are a good woman, Judith, pious and wise for your age. For a woman." He almost smiled at her. "And my mother loves you. I will listen."

"But be brief," Chabris said.

She stood, and prayed the skirts of her robe hid her shaky knees. She would tell the truth. All of it. "Our Lord came to me as a circle of light. He promises that the Assyrians will surrender to us in five days if I go to their general before sunset today."

"But what will you do there—no!" Uzziah bounded to his feet. "Judith, I forbid it. I won't allow you to sell yourself."

"Wait, Uzziah. It might work." Chabris propped his chin on one fist "What is the virtue of one woman against the safety of everyone else?"

Judith clenched her skirts until her fingernails poked through the cloth. "I am not going to give myself to Holofernes."

"Give, or be taken. It will come to the same thing," Achior growled. "Uzziah, you must forbid this. She will die. Eventually. Her sacrifice will save no one."

Was he remembering the dead bodies of the Assyrian slave women? "If I do as our Lord bids, no one will die." *Blessed Lord, please make it so.*

"As your Lord bids. What exactly is that?" Achior stalked toward her.

If she told them the details, none of the men would let her go. She stood, and the seat tipped over.

At the crash, a white dove burst out of its nest in the wall and flapped in a circle above Judith's head. The first light of sunrise edged the bird's wings with gold.

Chabris traced the bird's flight with one finger, only to slip off the wall and stare at Judith in wonder. "I'm no priest, but I call that a positive omen."

"A dove, a bird of sacrifice." Achior barked out the words. "Whatever Judith means to do, understand this. She is sacrificing herself. She won't make it a dozen paces through that encampment. She'll die." His eyes caught light from the sun as well. They gleamed at her like silver coins. "You'll die, do you understand?"

"I won't be alone. Abra will go with me." *And our Lord, too.*

"Two women? You think that makes you safer? Oh, gods!" Achior whipped away from her.

"I have to do this. Our Lord will protect me." At least until her task was done.

Beside her Uzziah wilted on his seat. "Our best efforts have brought Bethulia to this. Surrender. But who calmed the rioters? Judith did. Who does my mother turn to for support? Again, Judith." The magistrate sat straighter. "Achior, you are a foreigner, a former leader. Even you come to Judith at times."

For friendship, not guidance! But her mouth was too sticky for speech.

The sun rose higher. "We've done as we believed best, you and I." Chabris leaned toward the magistrate while more birds welcomed the growing light and warmth with a few notes of song.

Uzziah stood. In spite of his dirty face, draggled hair and dirty garments, his chin lifted with a touch of his former authority. "We have sought a solution, trusted the One to show us the way. Perhaps this is the chance we've awaited all along. Very well, Judith, we'll hold out another five days." He lowered his voice. "And I won't tell my mother you've gone until after you return."

"But I want—" Judith pressed her lips together. She longed to see Naomi before she left, whisper to the old lady of the miracle on this rooftop. Would Naomi believe in a divine light that blotted out stars and enemy campfires? Yes. Her old friend would. *Blessed art, thou, oh Lord. Help me live to share the tale with her later.*

"You won't tell Naomi." Achior's fingers clamped the edge of the parapet. "What do you plan to say to your people?"

Uzziah faced the Ammonite commander. "The truth. The One has sent a sign."

Achior shoved away from the wall. Judith expected him to fling himself away down the steps. Instead he prowled the perimeter of the roof, much as she had done the night before.

"Our Lord asks us to study his laws. Only an imbecile believes there can be only one solution to a problem." Chabris's dark, intelligent face was somber. "Judith, I will pray you are our best solution, and that the Lord guides you safely through your task."

"We all will." Uzziah tucked her in his arms for an instant, pressed his sunken cheek against hers. "For my mother," he murmured, and then let her go.

Her eyes stung. "Thank you."

"Even if you fail—forgive me saying it, Judith!" Chabris smiled. "You're the one taking the risk. Five more sunsets won't make much difference to our fates. Now I must go to my wife, tell her we have a small time left together." He trailed away down the steps.

A tear traced one of the furrows in Uzziah's cheek. "Safe journey, my dear." Footsteps quick and unsteady, he followed the elder out and away.

The burning orb of the sun lifted above the horizon. Only Achior remained on the roof with her.

Part Three
The Encampment

Chapter Twenty-eight
Judith

ACHIOR KEPT HIS BACK TO HER, head low, fists on the parapet once more.

Judith swallowed. "Achior. Speak to me, please."

"How can I? I feel like I've fallen from my horse onto hard ground." He lifted his head to observe the encampment before he turned to examine her. "I feel I've never truly seen your power until now."

"Not mine," she whispered. "The Lord's."

A corner of his mouth curled upward. "If you say so. Certainly there's no other way for us to escape death, not that I can see. I've survived to play the role few military men live to play. Advisor to a woman. Very well, Judith, you've convinced me. You or your god." He dropped to his heels in front of her. "How will you arm yourself?"

Did she dare tell him? She needed to trust someone with all the truth. Someone who would remain behind. Who better than this man, this former commander? The bracelets clasped around her wrists clinked against each other, a feminine mimicry of clashing blades. "A sword."

His head shot up. "Is there such a weapon in Bethulia?" When she didn't reply at once, his brows gathered.

"No," Judith said. "But there is in Holofernes's tent. His sword."

"How do you know where he keeps his weapon?"

"Our Lord showed it to me." Her fingers curled against her palm. "I have already felt the shape of its hilt."

Sweat shone on Achior's forehead. "It's real. Your god really has sent you a vision. Shown you what to do."

"Yes. Abra and I will leave soon before sunset."

"You will leave—" The sun curved higher in the sky. Its light shone in his wan face. "Before sunset. Yes, that will be safest." He spread his hands. "As safe as you're likely to be."

She laced her fingers together. "I know your faith is—different." In six days, perhaps she would ask him who, or what, he worshipped. If he loved a deity, or just his horse. "Will you pray for me while I'm gone?"

Now sunlight spilled across the land, spreading a glow across the treetops and the top edge of Bethulia's wall. "I hope you know I pray for you, always." Still on his knees, he leaned forward and embraced her, his lean arms tight around her waist.

For a moment Judith stayed there, his head a warm weight against her hip. Then quietly she leaned back.

Achior's clasp tensed an instant. Then his arms slid down her hips and away. He stood and bowed. "Is it because I'm a foreigner? Because I'm not an Israelite?"

"In part." Across the valley a sentry called. Over Achior's shoulder, Judith watched the Assyrian guards change place.

"In part? Your god's laws are strict, but—" He released a quick breath. "You're still the wife of Manasseh."

Her throat filled, then her eyes. "Most women would have remarried by now, especially if their husband left a brother, any male relative." A child born of such a union would have been considered Manasseh's. "My husband left no one."

"Only you." Achior's mouth twisted in the painful half-smile she remembered, from before his injuries healed. "You told me the first day we met. You said, 'Everyone knows I still love—'"

Judith's lips formed the name without sound.

"I should have known then. And I shouldn't worry you today, of all days. With your—adventure before you." Achior bowed so low Judith saw the top of his head. "Peace and thanks, my friend. You never need to ask for my prayers."

"You thank me?" The words choked her.

"Yes. Because of you I'm no longer sealed in by armor and duty. I'm alive inside because of you, Judith." Abruptly he straightened and looked in her eyes. "We never will be man and wife, but—do you feel this, too? We are one in spirit, like two sides of the same piece of cloth."

By all the laws of her people she must disagree. But she knew Achior spoke the truth. Silently, she and her friend watched the sun climb the blue arc of sky.

Chapter Twenty-nine
Judith

"**Y**OU'D BEST KEEP THOSE FANCY GARMENTS** hidden. Here." Huldah flung a length of sackcloth around Judith's shoulders, and tossed another piece to Abra. "Wear these until you're outside the gate. You don't want a fuss before you leave the village."

"We don't want a fuss at all." Fingers cold, Judith adjusted the rough fabric so it covered most of her from neck to hem, then did the same for Abra, who tilted her head at the old cook. "Well? Are we disguised enough to suit you?"

Huldah reached out to twitch each makeshift cloak one final time. "It's not me I'm thinking of. If you want an argument with Rebekah between here and the gate, that's your affair." Her mouth quivered. "Our blessed Lord be with you, mistress," she said more gently. "I pray he keeps watch over you both."

She hitched away toward the kitchen without a backward glance, only to stumble when Dorcas flew past her like a shooting star. "Careful, girl—"

"Please, mistress, don't do it." The little maid clutched Judith around the waist. "Don't go."

"You shame us all with your racket. Be quiet, girl." When Dorcas ignored her, Huldah pounded her stick on the ground. "Go back to bed."

"No, it's all right." Judith smoothed one hand over Dorcas's hair. "I thought you understood. It's not my plan, it's the Lord's. Would you have me say 'no' to the One?"

The girl buried her face against Judith's breast. "N-no, mistress."

"Well then?' Judith peered into the tear-striped face. "Come, let's both keep our promises. I'll keep mine to our Lord. And you?"

Dorcas kept hold another moment before she let Judith go. "I'll keep b-busy and keep faith." She wiped her eyes and stood tall.

"I'm sure Huldah will find plenty for you to do." Abra winked.

"Now, bed. Unless you think it's time to get to work." Huldah snapped her fingers. She and the girl returned inside.

"You don't fool me, old fraud," Abra called out. "I know you'll miss us."

"Do you have everything?" Judith eyed the basket tucked under Abra's arm.

Abra jiggled it and pottery clinked. "Dishes, bread, wine, olives, some cheese. Everything you told me to bring."

Everything the Lord had showed her to bring. "Rags?" They would need those most of all.

Abra tapped the basket. "To cushion the dishes and keep the bread fresh."

Yes, for now the cloth would do that as well. "Let's go." Already the sun was a line of blood at the horizon.

As they crept past her neighbor's meager house, Judith heard Nathanael's dreary wails through the crumbling, high-set windows. "More, Mama, 'anael's hungry."

"I know, sweetheart. Here, have some of my bread." Rebekah sounded infinitely patient, even sweet.

Judith hurried on. She had no business hearing such a private moment. Yet she was glad she had overheard. Even on what might be her last day, Rebekah's tenderness for her son never failed. *Blessed art thou, oh Lord. Bless and keep them safe, mother and son.*

At the village gate, two figures stepped out of the shrine built into the wall. "Judith?" Ezra hurried to greet her. "I caught Achior leaving our house and made him tell me why. Such an adventure! I wish I could go with you."

Achior kept back, behind the young man. "I explained the task was risky enough for you and Abra."

"I'll do my best to help you from here." Ezra hopped in place alongside her. "I'll keep watch every day from your rooftop. If anything goes wrong in the camp, you can signal me."

How? And what could this boy—could anyone—do even if she managed it? Judith clasped his wrists. How thin he was. "Thank you, Ezra. That's a comfort."

Achior held up the stout wooden key to the village gate. "We brought this for you. You'd better go, you'll scarcely reach the encampment before dark as it is." He turned aside and fumbled with key and latch. Ezra pushed the gate open just wide enough for the two women to slip through.

"Thank you," Judith whispered.

Abra followed her outside with a nod, and the gate closed behind them. The groan of the wooden support in its stone socket sounded loud here outside the wall.

JUDITH RESISTED the urge to crouch against the wall. Fingers unsteady, she loosened her makeshift cloak and let it fall. "This thing itches. I'm leaving mine here."

Abra shrugged hers aside too. "Good idea."

Then, muffled by the mud bricks, they heard Ezra's voice. "My friend Ham says Judith's beautiful."

"He's not the only man to think so." Achior's reply came faintly, as if he was already moving away, back toward Uzziah's house.

"Oh, yes. At least—until the riot. Before then she'd walk by, and men would grin and whisper to each other." Ezra's voice grew more distant as well. "I think it's wrong to look at her that way. Not just because she's a widow. Because—"

"Because Judith is Judith," said Achior.

Through the barrier, Judith could not hear their footsteps fade. Or maybe it was the boom of blood in her head. She tidied her robe, and then looked up.

Abra's eyebrows had disappeared into her hair, already tumbled when she whisked off her sackcloth cloak.

"Well?" Judith had not expected to be in a hurry to go. "Let's be on our way." Dust stirred, cool and soft around her ankles.

Her friend adjusted the basket at her hip. "It feels strange to be outside again."

Judith nodded, eyes on the campfires that glimmered from horizon to horizon, but came closer at each step. She heard the flames spit and crackle, as loud as the splash of water from the spring.

A bowstring creaked in the gloom. "In the name of Nebuchadnezzar and his general, Holofernes, declare yourselves."

Chapter Thirty
Judith

BESIDE HER, ABRA YELPED and nearly dropped the basket. Judith's legs trembled inside her skirts, but she stretched to her full height. "I am Judith, a widow from Bethulia. I bring an important message for Holofernes. Take me to him at once."

The bowstring creaked again. "You're the messenger? You're a woman." The bowman called into the shadows. "Someone bring me a light."

"Did you say *woman?*" A rowdy voice answered the guard, so close behind the two women that Abra spun around. "Is she pretty?"

"What do her looks matter?" Footsteps approached from the darkness to Judith's right. The speaker gave a rough chuckle. "We can't see her face, it's night time!"

Judith locked her knees to keep from falling. If she fell, the soldiers would be on her. Across the hillside, moonlight shone on a helmet here, a mailed shirt there, as men pushed and shoved closer. *Blessed Lord, how many of them can I not see?* She reached out to find, then catch Abra's cold hand in hers.

A throaty bellow, louder than the rest. "Has Holofernes given us more slave women? Good, send one my way!"

Slave women. The memory of flesh-tainted smoke made Judith gag. Abra mewed. "Judith—"

She released her friend's shaking fingers and advanced one long step. "I carry an important message for General Holofernes. Who is in charge here? You will come forward at once."

A hiss of pitch, a sputter of sparks streamed from the nearest campfire. The torch cast its circle of light to reveal its bearer, a brawny man nearly a head taller than Judith herself. She recognized him as the big guard who sometimes stood watch nearest Bethulia's gate.

As the torchlight spread over Abra, then herself, Judith spoke in as commanding a tone as she could muster. "Take me to General Holofernes. At once."

More jeers and shouting erupted. "Not just any woman—a beautiful woman," shouted a soldier she could smell if not quite see. "Two of them!"

"I'll trade my week's meat ration for first choice!"

Judith heard Abra whimper again. She groped for her friend's hand, drew her close. "You will do no such thing. Your general has waited more than thirty days for my message. How will he repay anyone who dares prevent me from delivering it?"

"And telling your general what no one else knows." Abra's hand was colder than water in winter, but she flicked her head in fair imitation of her usual saucy manner.

If only the growing crowd could hear above their own lust-filled shouts.

Then the big sentry let out a roar. "Quiet! These women are the messengers we've waited for. They are here to meet Holofernes, not entertain a pack of dogs like you."

"Bethulians. Slaves. Amounts to the same thing." A soldier

strode into the circle of light and tugged his armored shirt over his head. He let it fall with a shimmer and a clink. "Come on, Ox, move the torch. Let's see their faces."

More footsteps crunched through the undergrowth at Judith's back. Another soldier shouted, "Faces don't matter, let's see the parts that do."

On a wordless roar of agreement, the bare-chested man lunged at Judith, arms outstretched. She smelled him, leather and sweat

"Shut your mouth." With a crackle of burning and the reek of pitch, Ox thrust the torch at the greasy mat of hair on the soldier's chest. "Now. Return to your tents, all of you! These women are messengers."

As the burnt man rolled out of the way, howling amongst the legs of his fellows, an older soldier in full armor stomped into the torchlight. "The men of Bethulia send women to acknowledge their defeat?"

"Cowards." A gobbet of spit sailed out of the darkness.

Judith sidestepped just in time and nearly gagged. Even after weeks without water to bathe herself, the reek of so many—how many?—unclean bodies made her ill.

"The cowards' messenger is on her way to the general," called a voice that sounded little older than Ezra.

"Messengers. There's two of them." A lean figure stepped onto the path near Ox.

"Two women for Holofernes." One short, stout shadow let out a raucous laugh. "I guess the general's due, after his generosity the other night!"

Ox crouched, a warrior's stance, and spun in place so the torch burned a wheel of fire around Judith, Abra and himself. "Quiet," he bellowed. He spun again, and the flames left a smear of orange against the darkness.

The afterglow revealed a nightmare of leering faces and crowding bodies, some still clad in armor, others wearing far less. Judith couldn't breathe for the stink of sweat-soaked leather and lust.

Still in battle stance, Ox rasped his long knife free and pointed it at the nearest men. "Go, or I give your names to the tartans. Will punishment improve your hearing? Maybe you'll obey faster tomorrow, when your flesh has no skin between it and your armor."

A hush as shocking as the rising shouts had been. Only when the cacophony ended and the ring of men drew back did Judith realize how hard she was shuddering. Beside her Abra's breath wheezed.

"We just wanted a look." The bare-chested soldier climbed to his feet. For a moment he scowled at Judith, rubbing his enflamed, soot-smeared torso. Then he stooped for his mail shirt and trudged away.

Feet scuffed in the dark as another, then another unseen figure withdrew. As the soldiers retreated, far slower than they had approached, Judith nearly vomited. Her fine wool robe clung to her back, her hair to her neck. Abra's fingers were colder than mountain snow in hers.

Blessed Lord, thank you thank you thank you thank you— Now that her eyes had adjusted to the torchlight, she could see the first edge of moonlight gleam on mail and helmets. A circle of men several hundred strong had surrounded them.

The torchbearer grunted. "I am Ox. Come with me." He set off at a brisk pace, down the last bit of path to the stream.

Judith pressed her lips together to hold back a sob. "By all means." Hand squeezed around Abra's so tightly her friend cried out and her own bones crunched, she hurried along in their guide's torch-cast shadow.

"What a civil welcome they're giving us." Abra sounded buoyant, but pottery rattled in the basket she clutched to her breast.

Ox halted. "I am seeing you safely into the general's charge. Would you rather find the way alone?"

"Of course not." Judith gestured for him to move on.

Their guard shook his head. "Remain silent. Word will spread quickly. The next group of men may fear the tartans less than they desire your flesh."

The next group. Judith fought not to whirl and run uphill again to Bethulia. She made herself continue toward the stream. Abra stumbled over a rut in the track.

By the time the guard helped them across the creek, Judith's teeth clacked together. The noise drowned the bubble of water against rock. She prayed it masked her voice from any men who lingered nearby. "I've seen you before, soldier. You act as sentry in the evenings."

He kept going. "I do."

Abra hopped onto the far bank after Judith. For a breath they leaned against each other. "Blessed Lord, I knew they filled the landscape. But I didn't know there were so many of them."

Judith nodded, then urged her friend after the guard.

As they paced along the smooth, slave-built road, the stinks of the encampment thickened. Ashes, urine and sweat. *How can soldiers live in such filth?* How could she—could Abra—for the time left to them?

As their guard led them farther and farther from the village, farther along the plain, more dim figures flitted in and out of the torchlight's edge. Keeping pace with the light, with Abra and with her. Judith choked on the reek of unseen, unkempt bodies.

By the time Ox guided them into an open space, a fine pavilion at its center, the tramp of footsteps sounded like thunder. "Women!" More and more male voices picked up the cry. "Two women in the camp!"

Ox tilted the torch so Judith could see his broad face. His lips barely moved. "Keep silent until you are inside Holofernes's pavilion." Then he shouted into the darkness. "Get back to your tents. I won't warn you curs again."

Judith took measured strides to keep from stumbling. Abra scurried after her. *If we run they'll be on us like hounds on a hare.*

And yet. *My people were not always the Lord's peaceful children. I am descended from David the warrior as well as Solomon the wise.* Her knees strengthened.

Ox halted a few paces from the pavilion entrance. Under his pointed helmet, their guard's skin gleamed greasily. He glared as first one man, then two, a handful, then more soldiers than Judith could count, edged into the clearing around the pavilion.

"I ordered you men to go. Do you want to learn at firsthand how General Holofernes deals with those who disobey an order?"

Judith's heart thumped even harder. *Blessed Lord*— Ox had not been sure he could escort them safely.

A grumble rippled through the crowd. At last the soldiers, some still in armor, some half-clad, slowly withdrew. When the last vanished in the darkness, Judith sagged into Abra's arms, only to stiffen her knees to keep them both from falling.

Their big guard pursed his thick lips. "When you stand before the general, have no fear. If you bear the news he wants, he will treat you well."

Judith let go of Abra and dipped her head. "I understand."

Then a tall, lean figure stepped into the glow from Ox's torch. The skin across the tops of Judith's breasts tightened. *No— Achior*—What was he doing here? The soldiers would drag him before Holofernes, torture him, kill—

"What's all this?" As soon as the newcomer spoke Judith realized her mistake. He was long-muscled like Achior, but wore a full beard. His carefully oiled hair twisted to his shoulders.

She took a breath. "I am Judith, a widow from Bethulia. I bring Holofernes news that guarantees his victory."

"That, madam, is already guaranteed." The newcomer took a step closer, and she recognized him. Sendal, the Ammonite who had taken Achior's horse. He glared down his long nose at Ox. "The Bethulians send word of their surrender with a woman?"

Judith's hands fisted in her robe. "My message is for the general's ears only." What if this traitor insisted she tell him everything?

"I command the Ammonites." Sendal's nostrils pinched. "I am in the general's confidence about all things."

"Even so, sir." Her fingernails pierced the fabric. Ox's torch sputtered in the silence.

"You, sentry." Sendal gestured the way they had come. "Aren't you guarding the perimeter? Return to your post."

"Yes. Sir." Ox shot a glance at her, then swung away down the slope.

When the last of his torchlight faded, Judith resisted shifting closer to Abra. Now they were truly alone in this camp filled with thousands of men.

"Come along, woman." Sendal strutted toward the pavilion, and left them to follow as best they could in the dark. "Your people have kept the general waiting thirty-five days."

Judith lifted her chin and spoke to the back of Sendal's narrow head. "He does not have much longer to wait." *Blessed Lord, help me make it so.*

Chapter Thirty-one
Judith

ABRA FOLLOWED HER SO CLOSELY their skirts tangled, and Judith tripped on one of the ruts scored into the earth. A month ago grass had rippled across this ground. Would it ever grow back?

The Ammonite commander tucked his helmet beneath one arm. "General, it is I, Sendal. I bring you good news."

After a pause, a beardless slave in a short tunic poked his head out of the pavilion entrance. "Holofernes has not finished his evening meal, commander. He says he will speak with you tomorrow—"

The slave's high-pitched voice distracted Judith for a single breath. A boy's voice, a beardless chin. This was not just a slave, but a eunuch. Abra hissed and edged away from him.

"Bagoas." Sendal snapped his fingers. "Tell Holofernes I have brought him the Bethulian messenger. A lady from the town."

She and Abra had brought themselves! Judith tried to work saliva into her dry mouth, but the slave had already withdrawn inside the pavilion again. She squared her shoulders and took one step in front of Abra. The Assyrians would see her friend as nothing but a servant. *I must play my part now. A lady of Bethulia.*

Abra clutched the basket close with both arms, and stayed that half-pace back.

The tent flap parted again. Lights from within silhouetted Bagoas. "Lady, the general bids you enter." When Sendal bustled forward, the eunuch stood his ground. "Commander. My master requests that you return to your own portion of camp."

"But I—" Sendal sputtered, then jerked his head. "Very well." He marched back into the darkness, backbone spear-stiff.

As Bagoas turned toward her, Judith thought she saw his lips twitch. "Your name, lady?" Again, the shrillness of his voice jolted her.

"Judith, widow of—" No, she would not give her beloved's name to anyone in the camp, would not think of him until she left it. If she did.

The slave withdrew. "The lady Judith of Bethulia, master."

Bagoas held the opening wide for her to pass through, and Judith nearly kicked off her shoes, but caught herself just in time. This was no pious household. She caught up her skirts and swept inside.

Silver lamps illuminated the fabric walls, layered carpets cushioned the floor. A table faced the entrance. Beyond it sat Holofernes, bowls and platters of food before him.

She glimpsed an altar against one wall of the pavilion. Holofernes worships a goddess? A man who thought nothing of torturing living women thought God was a woman! *How does he justify his acts?* she wondered. Maybe he simply reduced his goddess to her most bloodthirsty aspect to justify his own actions—

The general stood slowly as wind swirled through the open door, caught the lamps and made them sway. Shadows chased across his face so Judith couldn't quite see his expression. She had expected a sinewy man, whippy from long battles and longer marches. Though she stood taller than most men in Bethulia, she had expected to look up to meet a general's eyes, not down.

The breeze died, the lamps steadied. Holofernes's full mouth curved in a smile that warmed the longer they looked at each other. He stretched out his hands to her as if in welcome. "Lady. Judith. You are the Bethulian messenger?"

"I bring you a message. My lord." Judith dropped to her knees on the carpets. A muted clatter of dishes told her Abra had done the same.

"Your people send me a woman with word of your—surrender." He lingered on the final word, and the brilliant blue fringe at the hem of his robe slithered closer, closer to where her fingers burrowed into the dyed animal skin rug.

At first she didn't understand him over the thunder in her head. Then Judith pushed to her feet. "My lord, no one sent me. I come to you of my own accord."

His brows nearly met above his hooked nose, even as his smile broadened. "Oh?"

She bent her head, though it made her scalp itch not to see his face. "I have escaped Bethulia and its cursed inhabitants."

"Lady, you intrigue me." One hand, square and muscular, reached out as if to cup her chin.

Before he could touch her, Judith raised her head. His curled beard, his hair stiff with dressings, nauseated her more than the foul odor of meat cooked with milk.

"Do you fear me, my dear?" He ignored Abra, still prostrate on the floor. "Tell me the truth, Judith."

It would be the only time she did so. "Yes, my lord."

Holofernes laughed. "Don't. I never harm anyone who chooses to serve Nebuchadnezzar, king of the earth. If you are not here to surrender your village, why are you here?"

She longed to blurt her story, to keep this butcher away from her. From touching her. *Careful. Not too fast.* "I can no longer stay with my own people."

"You don't wish to starve any longer?" He sounded interested, almost gentle. But his eyes, black as stones at the bottom of a cold stream, stayed steady on hers.

"My people are half-crazed with thirst and hunger—" Judith hid her face with her hands. "I still can't believe they mean to do it!"

"What can a few shepherds do against an army that has defeated half the world?" One heavy eyebrow shot high. He leaned against the table at his back.

"They plan a great evil, general. When the last of the water is gone, they will drink the sacred wine, then roast and eat the animals meant for sacrifice." Judith observed him through her parted fingers. Would an Assyrian understand such a sin, or must she explain?

"So much for the godliness of Bethulia!" The general clicked his fingers at Bagoas. "Send for my commanders. We attack at dawn—"

No. Judith lurched toward him. "You mustn't do that."

Holofernes rounded on her. "You dare tell me what I must and mustn't do?"

For the first time Abra lifted her head and whimpered. Judith almost did, too. "Indeed not, sir. I only meant that my—that the people have not yet broken faith with the Lord. If you attack now you won't win. Not yet."

"Really." The full lips hardened. He studied her, a long, leisurely examination of her body from her hairline to her sandaled feet. "Your information appears of limited use, madam. How am I to know when to attack?"

"That's why I am here. I am devout. I serve our Lord truly. Every night I will go out to pray. When Bethulia breaks our Lord's law, I'll know."

"You are a seeress?" The general's voice hushed. "You—have

visions?"

Against the general's chair leaned the sword from her vision in the grove. Judith contented herself with a nod. "Yes, my lord. The moment my people—that is, the people of Bethulia—commit their sin, I will see it. I will know, and share my knowledge immediately with you."

"This is a fortunate day." Holofernes settled at the table and eased back in his chair. "Bagoas."

"Master?" The slave hurried forward.

"Prepare a tent for our guest. See that she has every comfort, and that both she and her servant—" He glanced at Abra, still motionless near Judith's feet. "—are well guarded. Establish them near my pavilion, to insure they remain undisturbed."

"My lord." Bagoas ducked out.

Holofernes poured wine into two cups. "And now, you will dine with me."

"Thank you, general." He believed her. Judith nearly wept. "I regret that I cannot join you at this time."

"Oh?" The thick hands stilled on wine jug and cups.

"If I'm to receive my Lord's message, I must keep faith with His laws. You do want me to receive the word we both long to hear?" Could Holofernes discern how the lie slowed her tongue?

He plucked a grape from a bowl, rolled it between his fingers. What had Achior told her? *"Holofernes can never keep quiet, even as he waits out a siege."*

"I accept your hospitality with gratitude," Judith said quickly. "But I'm quite tired. If you don't mind, I'd like to rest until the time for my contemplation—"

"When is that? What will you do then?" The general's words struck with the force of stones from a sling.

Judith prayed her expression remained calm. "In the quiet of the nighttime I will go out to—" *To Manasseh.* She stood tall. "To the trees above the spring, my lord."

"To the spring? Very well, to the spring." Holofernes popped the grape in his mouth. "But another time, when my cooks know your preferences, you will share a meal with me."

For the second time that night, her robe clung to her skin, beneath her hair and around the waist at her girdle. Judith lowered her lashes. "I look forward to it." *Yes, we will dine together, Holofernes. You and I and the Lord.* "Now, good night. Abra, get up." She tried to roughen her tone, as if her maidservant were less important than a broken sandal, and less valuable. "Bring the basket."

For the first time ever, Abra obeyed wordlessly.

"Good evening. Judith." The general lingered on her name.

Though he didn't move as she led Abra out, Judith felt his gaze even after the door swung shut between them. His presence filled the encampment like a fire hidden inside the luxurious pavilion.

Chapter Thirty-two
Holofernes

HOLOFERNES LISTENED TO JUDITH'S FOOTSTEPS die away. Only when they faded completely did he gulp the last of his wine.

She stood taller than most men, and as broad shouldered. Different from the type of woman he usually chose—broken-spirited before he even broke her.

He rounded the bed to squat before his private altar, where the wide-hipped figure of Ishtar knelt, hands curled around her perfect, round breasts as if offering them to him. Until now, Holofernes had imagined the goddess offered him the milk of success. Of victory.

Now he imagined Judith's breasts crushed against his chest, her legs locked around his waist. Hadn't Judith said she was a widow? She must be practiced in the ways to delight a man— But she offered him more than beauty or experience.

Sweating, Holofernes stooped to brush his fingertips through the dyed fur rugs where Judith had lain. Did she truly have visions? Yes, she had entered his encampment on one of the month's most fortunate days, but he required further proof. He must learn the day, the month and year of her birth, especially the phase of the moon. That would reveal much about her.

If she had the gift of prophecy. If she lied.

With a noise of disgust, he stooped before the altar again. Judith came from a lesser culture. Likely they kept no dates, no records at all. His country dominated the world not only because they defeated lesser beings, but because they understood the importance of recordkeeping. Holofernes studied the image of his goddess, sovereign of love and of war, only to scowl.

What if Judith's presence was a trap? Except no man would be fool enough to send a female on such a task. No woman could plan such a thing on her own, and no female, especially one from a weaker people, would dare lie to Holofernes, the god-king's general. Aside from that—

Every hair on his body tickled upright as he remembered Judith's face when she spoke of her god. All the light in the tent had seemed to flow from her, not the lamps.

Holofernes strode across to the entrance, hacked it aside. Every fiber in his body tautened when he stared at the newly raised tent across from his. Seeress or not, he would make Judith his. Soon. It seemed like years since the night of the entertainment, since he crushed the life from that slip of a slave girl.

Holofernes took one long step out into the night, one step toward Judith. Then he swung around with an oath and stomped back inside his own brightly lit pavilion. "Bagoas." A moment's delay made him shout. "Bagoas!"

"Yes, Master." The eunuch darted inside at last. "The women—"

The *women?* Oh, yes. Judith had a maidservant.

"—ate a simple meal and now they're quiet." His body slave bowed low. "You do want me to keep watch over them?"

"Over her. Indeed." The eunuch might have the wit to observe Judith's behavior, but not the strength or power to keep her safe.

"Listen carefully, there is much to do. First, take word to Sendal. The Ammonites must pull back from the spring." Judith needed to await her visions undisturbed.

Bagoas straightened. "But, Master—if she wanders through the camp unattended—"

Holofernes sent the slave to the ground with one swipe of his fist. "Did I not say you had much to do? Next, you will tell my commanders to send a selection of their most reliable soldiers to me. I must choose an escort who will protect her, and remain untempted by his own lust as well." Once selected, her guard would carry weapons that ensured Judith's safety.

He pivoted to stare at the pavilion wall between Judith and himself, and a smile tugged his lips. Would any of his soldiers dare stand between Judith and their general?

"Yes, my lord." The eunuch nursed his bruised cheek with both hands.

"Send messengers throughout the camp with this announcement. Any man who distresses Judith in any way won't live to see dawn."

"As you wish, Master."

"Now go." Holofernes flung himself into his chair and chose another grape, only to scowl and toss the fruit aside. "Bagoas! Discard these. Some of them are bruised."

Chapter Thirty-three
Judith

TWO SLAVES STRUGGLED WITH THE TENT Holofernes had ordered raised for her. In the unsteady flare of torches, Judith could see that the fabric walls were not as fine as the general's pavilion. But the structure dwarfed the basic shelters assigned to the soldiers.

A heap of rolled carpets, dyed rams' wool rugs and cushions sprawled across the ground between her and the two slaves. The general clearly intended for her to be comfortable, at least for now.

Off to one side, Abra watched the men struggle with the poles and heavy lengths of material. Unlike Bagoas, these slaves wore nothing but sweat. Each time one of them turned away from the tent, Abra shut her eyes. Judith reached out to slip one arm around her friend's waist. Abra yipped and jerked away.

"It's just me," Judith murmured. "Why are you watching them if their nakedness bothers you?"

"If I stare into the dark, I imagine soldiers creeping up on me. Us." Lips pressed together, Abra glanced around the dim encampment, then focused on the slaves and the tent again.

Judith turned away with a nod. Bethulia was a dark smudge on the hilltop opposite them. Her village, her home, looked so tiny seen from the center of this vast encampment. Though she studied the smudge from one end to the other, she could find no hint of light. Perhaps everyone in Bethulia slept. She hoped so.

Had Ezra kept watch from the rooftop, as he promised? Had he, and perhaps Achior, watched Ox's torch on its flaring journey across the plain, and known when the two women reached Holofernes's pavilion?

Hundreds of soldiers' tents stood between her and home. Did the men inside those tents sleep or lie awake and listening? For her.

"Your tent is ready, mistress." Abra's voice sounded so muted Judith almost did not recognize it.

Finally, shelter from the thousands of spying eyes. "Good. We will rest—" Except no "we" existed for them here in the Assyrian world, a world of owners and slaves. Only Judith, the mistress, mattered. "I must rest before I pray."

Abra shifted the basket under one arm. "Do you wish to direct me while I spread the rugs and cushions?"

"No." Bagoas scurried over from the general's pavilion. "Lady, I will arrange your things."

Poor creature, she would never get used to the penetrating quality of his voice. "Thank you, Bagoas—" As much as his startled frown, the fresh bruises on the eunuch's cheek told her not to express gratitude to a slave. "My maidservant understands my preferences."

"As you desire, lady." He backed away from her.

Here she was the lady, Abra nothing but a servant. It required all her self-control, but Judith left her friend to wrestle the rolled rugs and heaped cushions into the tent by herself. *Huldah would be pleased*, she thought. *I'm finally behaving as a wealthy widow should.*

At last Abra poked her tousled head through the doorway.

"Mistress." The instant Judith stepped inside, her friend fastened the door flap behind her.

One layer of cloth between themselves and all those foul men. She clung to Abra for a long time, swaying. Abra's tears trickled down Judith's neck. At last her friend drew away and wiped her eyes. "Shall we unroll the rugs first?"

Judith seized one from the pile and shook it open. There were more carpets here than in her house and Uzziah's together. Abra knelt to spread out a dyed rams' wool rug, only to stare when Judith tossed a third haphazard across it. "Let's follow the general's example and layer them."

"Layer them?" Abra considered the rest of the carpets. "They'll be ten deep."

Judith nodded. As they worked together to coat the ground with rugs, her neck and shoulders loosened. She could still feel the ruts carved into the earth by ox carts, marching feet and hooves, still smell the stink of impure combinations of food, yet the task soothed her like a prayer.

At last she and Abra sank down to rest, each on her own mound of cushions. When her friend opened her mouth to speak, Judith held a finger to her lips. *Later*, she mouthed. Abra's brows twisted, but she turned away. Judith did the same.

Perhaps her friend dozed. Judith twitched every time a sentry tramped past, every time a not-so-distant soldier snored or grumbled in his sleep. Unlike the black tent of her widowhood, the paler walls of this shelter let moonlight seep through.

When the moon glowed brightest, Judith rolled upright. "Abra? Waken, it's time." Abra sat up, and Judith gestured at the basket left beside the doorway. "Bring that, it has things I need."

Holofernes would certainly send spies after them. The spies must grow accustomed to seeing the basket in Abra's arms.

Judith smoothed her garments and hair, reached out to open the doorway for herself, only to hesitate when Abra hissed a warning.

Her maidservant opened the tent flap for her, but before either set foot outside a hulking figure with a torch blocked their way. Judith squinted against the flickering light. "Ox?

The sentry thumped his free fist to his chest. "Lady. The general ordered me to escort you where you need to go. I will stand watch while you pray."

Abra sprang out to face the big man, fists on her hips. "Why you, of all the men in camp?"

"Abra. What does it matter?" Judith inclined her head to their guard. "Thank you for your assistance."

Ox lumbered away from the tent and down the slave road. As Judith hurried after him, she noticed that in addition to the short sword at his hip, their guard now bore a spear more in proportion to his height than the one she had seen from her rooftop.

They passed between the lines of tents, back the way they had come after sundown. Even now the camp was far from silent. Soldiers snored or mumbled in their sleep. One dreaming groan sounded so close Abra nearly dropped the basket. Here and there, a man cried out in a dream.

How many of these men dreamed of wives long unseen, of children grown past recognition? Why, the soldiers were human beings— Judith tripped and caught herself at the edge of the stream, remembering how the men had crowded around her and Abra just a few hours before. Their humanity made the men more dangerous, not less.

Embers drifted from Ox's torch as he held it to light her way, then Abra's, across the stream. He started up the slope toward Bethulia, only to halt in the middle of the path. "I will tell you why the general chose me as your guard."

"Yes?" She waited for some tale of special bravery or bravado.

"Because I brought you safely to him before." His voice sounded flat, but Ox lifted his light to stare straight at Judith. "I will keep you safe. Tonight and every night. I have sworn it."

Judith set her lips to keep them steady. Close behind her, Abra whispered, "Thank you, Ox."

"Where do you need to go for your prayers, lady?"

She knew where she wanted, where she needed to be. Judith's long strides carried her past the guard, and Abra's footsteps pattered after her. Ox passed them both and stood in the path. "Where are you going? Back to your people?"

"There is a quiet place a little farther on." *Manasseh!* But before Judith reached the tree where she had so often sat these last few years, she tripped on trash strewn both on the path and around it.

A snapped off leather strap, a spearhead split from its shaft. Blackened circles from campfires. Propped against the entrance to Manasseh's tomb stood a rough target dotted with snapped off arrows. *Oh, Manasseh—* How was she to pray in the midst of this mess? And yet—the dread that had haunted her for weeks vanished. The tombs were unmolested.

As Judith scowled at the army's remnants, she realized what they meant. The soldiers who had camped closest to Bethulia's walls were gone. Holofernes believed her enough to withdraw part of his army away from her village.

Abra kicked dirt over the broken sandal. "Disgusting."

"What did you expect?" But Ox lowered his torch so it no longer highlighted the debris. "Where there are men, there will be mess."

"I must begin." Judith flicked a hand downhill, toward the spring. "You will pace a circle around us, far enough away that your light does not disturb me, near enough to keep me safe from your comrades."

Ox swayed, head thrust forward. "I am ordered to keep close to you."

"And I am ordered to deliver my Lord's vision of victory to Holofernes. I cannot do that with you constantly at my elbow. Do you want to explain the reason for my failure to the general or shall I?"

The big sentry swayed from foot to foot a little longer, then edged away. "No, lady." He marched away in a curve that led him first up, then down the hill.

Moonlight and tree shadows striped Abra's grin. "I had no idea you could speak so sharply to anyone."

"Nor I." Judith swooped to embrace her friend, only to back off hastily in case Ox, or a less visible spy, could see them. "I won't be able to focus with this thing here." She nudged the target away from the tomb entrance. *There, Mannaseh.*

"What if Ox comes back?" Abra's whisper came out of the dark.

"We'll hear him—or anyone else who approaches." Judith prayed it was true as she ducked behind a stout trunk to relieve her bladder.

With the water Abra had brought, she washed her hands, and then took the basket and removed the linen cloth within. Voice raised for the benefit of any Assyrian listeners, she spread the cloth on the ground at the foot of her favorite tree. "May the One know that today we have eaten only pure bread. We touch nothing unclean."

She sank down with her back against her tree. Abra sat opposite her, then leaned closer. "Aren't you afraid at all?"

Judith held up one quivering hand for Abra to see.

"In the general's tent you dropped to the ground so gracefully, like weaving cut free of the loom. Judith, be careful. He watches you the way a buck goat watches a doe."

"I know." She stretched her shoulders against the cedar, grateful for its solid presence between her and the encampment. "We must both be careful."

"Me, I'm nothing to him. A stick fallen in his path." Abra yawned.

"Holofernes is not the only man here. Remember our walk into camp?"

Her friend shuddered. "I'd rather not."

"Nonetheless." Judith curled her still-shaking hands in her lap. "I'll pray now."

Occasionally Ox's torch sputtered in and out of sight as he circled them. Abra's breathing softened toward sleep. After a while she toppled gently sideways, curled up on the ground. Judith watched the moon's imperceptible shift from overhead toward the horizon.

Blessed art thou, Oh Lord. Blessed art thou— The moon slid lower, and sank from the sky. The wind fluttered through the leaves. *Blessed art thou, oh Lord.* Abra snored, a woman's snores, so different from the snorts of the soldiers crowded into their tiny tents.

Blessed art thou— Judith repeated the phrase over and over. No image, no vision appeared. But she heard the wind, she watched the moon. Abra moved in her sleep again, one of her legs against Judith's ankle.

Even here surrounded by enemies, she was not alone.

Chapter Thirty-four
Judith

THE STARS WERE FADING. Judith stretched out her cramped legs with a groan. She rubbed her thighs, sore after a night spent squeezed tight. Without realizing it she had kept herself braced against rough hands reaching out of the darkness, or a brutal knee thrust between her legs.

Now she watched Ox approach, his torch burnt down to lingering sparks. Even with his new weapons, what could their guard do to stop a dozen or more molesters? "Abra, wake up." When her friend yawned and stretched, Judith pried herself upright with the support of the tree, only to sway when the earth dipped underfoot.

Abra scrabbled up to tuck one arm around her waist. "What's wrong?"

"Just a little dizzy." Grateful for her friend's warmth, Judith stamped life back into her numb feet.

"I'm sorry, I meant to stay awake." Abra frowned toward Ox. "Why do you suppose the general ordered only one soldier to keep us safe?"

"We're alive and unharmed, so it seems one is enough." *Only one that we can see.* She raised her voice as, armor creaking, Ox halted half a dozen paces away. "Escort me to our tent. We—I mean, I—must break my fast."

The sentry crushed the tip of the smoldering torch into the dirt. "First the general will want your report."

Report. "Do Assyrians consider prayer a military act?" Judith took an unsteady step, then another. Wisps of fog hovered above the stream. She felt as insubstantial as the vapor.

The sky grayed with dawn. Light dew coated the worn grass, cool against the edges of her feet. Just ahead of them, Judith noticed other footmarks, long and thin, dark on the damp, pale ground. Male footprints, bare footprints.

Judith raised her head in time to glimpse a whisk of pale fabric at the crest of the slope. Was it Bagoas, Holofernes's slave? *Holofernes's spy.*

Then two soldiers marched out from a line of tents a little farther up the hill. The men halted, grinning at sight of her and Abra. At once Ox moved to stand between the soldiers and Judith, one hand on his sword hilt. "Be about your business."

The shorter of the two men thrust out his jaw. "You must be Ox."

"I'm Ox." The big guard spread his feet wide and drew his sword. "Move."

"You've had all night to look your fill. We just want our chance." The lankier of the two soldiers winked. "So, Bethulian women are beautiful. Good. I have something to look forward to after all these weeks with nothing to do."

"Wait. We don't know they're beautiful, do we?" The short soldier leered at Abra. "Tell me the truth, girl. Do they all look like you?" He reached out to rub her cheek. She batted his hand away.

Judith braced herself to touch impure flesh, to kick and claw these men before more woke to join them. Before she could move,

Ox crowded between the short soldier and Abra. The tip of Ox's sword nicked the smaller man just below his chin. "You know my name, you know where the women come from. You've forgotten what matters most. Our general's warning."

The gangly soldier's face grayed. "No harm intended. No harm at all. He was only joking."

"That's right. Only a joke." The shorter man edged back from them.

His lanky companion shoved him away along the track toward the stream.

"Thanks for the warning, Ox. We won't forget again."

But the short soldier's voice carried clearly in the hush of the still-sleeping camp. "Don't understand what the fuss is about. They're not as wonderful as those dancers we had. Well, that some of us had." Both men laughed.

"Still, they're women and they're here." The tall soldier sounded wistful.

Colder than her night-damp clothes, Judith stared after them. The smaller man glanced over one shoulder at her, shot a look at Ox and then back at her. He waggled his tongue.

Ox took one hard stride after him, sword held ready. "Do you want me to slice that in half for you?"

Only when both men broke into a jog and finally vanished into the trees did the guard cram his weapon back through his belt. Red to the edges of his helmet, Ox gestured her toward Holofernes's pavilion. "Lady, pay no attention to those stupid curs." He marched close behind her and Abra, spear bobbing over one shoulder. "They were talking about an—an entertainment the general provided awhile ago."

Entertainment. Judith recalled the reek of burning flesh and clamped her teeth. Beside her Abra choked out a question. "Were you one of the lucky ones, Ox?"

Their guard glowered. "I did not—"

"Thank you, Ox." Whether their guardian had done nothing to the slave women, or simply had no chance with them, Judith did not want to know. "Abra, he just defended our honor." *Our lives.* "That's all that matters."

"It was my duty, lady." Movement sounded in a nearby tent. More soldiers awakening. Ox quickened his pace. "Hurry now. The general expects your report at first light."

"Indeed." Judith hurried to keep level with him, her body vulnerable flesh again instead of morning mist.

Chapter Thirty-five
Holofernes

HOLOFERNES STRETCHED OUT, belly down on his bed. The cushions beneath him gave like a willing maiden and he bit down on a wrinkle of fabric, working it into a point with his tongue and clamping down to suck hard—

Outside the pavilion sounded the slap of bare feet. Holofernes rolled off the bed as his body slave trotted into the tent. "Well?"

"The women are on their way, Master." The bruise shone, swollen and purple against the eunuch's dull skin. "Before they—I mean, before the lady Judith arrives I will tell you what I saw."

"Yes?" Had Judith's flesh shone from within, had she performed strange rites in the moonlight? Or had the woman crept close to the village walls and whispered a report of all she had seen inside the camp?

Bagoas gulped. "She did n-nothing, my lord."

"What do you mean?" Holofernes stalked toward his slave. "You saw nothing? Judith did nothing? Did she lie down and sleep? Explain yourself."

Bagoas fell to the carpets, arms extended. "I—I saw nothing because she did nothing, sire. There was nothing to see."

Nothing. Holofernes punched the nearest cushion, then whirled to vent his feelings on his slave. But more footsteps drew near, light ones mingled with a soldierly tread. Holofernes kicked Bagoas in the belly, then the head when the eunuch dared roll away from him. "What are you waiting for? Get out!"

As Bagoas crawled out under the bottom of the closest pavilion wall, Holofernes flung himself onto his bed again. He tossed a corner of the blanket across one shoulder, adjusted another over his lap. "Enter." Legs and the other shoulder bare, he leaned against the bed frame. Let the woman see what she would be getting. If Bagoas reported truly, Judith would get what was coming to her sooner rather than later.

With a rattle of scale mail, the guard lifted the flap for Judith to pass inside. Cool air stirred the pavilion. By Ishtar, she was enticing enough to tempt Nebuchadnezzar himself. Deep-breasted, wide-hipped. Holofernes studied her at his leisure. "What news, lady?"

Her voice came slow and thick. "I bring you the Lord's greeting."

The Lord. Sneering, Holofernes swung to his feet, tugging the blanket along with him. What kind of god had no name? Proper gods had proper names, like Ea, god of wisdom, or Marduk, the god of gods. Like Ishtar, goddess of love and war.

"His greeting." Holofernes clipped the word. "What does that mean? Nothing but this—your god didn't answer."

That brought her head up. Judith advanced, so close to him the hem of her robe brushed his bare feet. "General, the One did answer my prayer. We just did not receive the answer we want."

Holofernes pressed his toes deeper beneath the cloth. Dew chilled the hem, but higher up the fabric felt warmed by her body. One wrong word and she would be on her back with more than his toes inside that robe. "Explain."

"My people—" Judith's fingers curled against her breast. "I

mean, the people of Bethulia have not broken faith yet."

How did she know that? Vision, or whispers from some confederate still inside the town? "When will they do so?" And the god Shamash judge and condemn her, how dare this woman stand so tall before him? Holofernes wished he had kept her waiting outside the pavilion. Tomorrow he would order Bagoas to attire him in the full glory of fringed and embroidered robes before he let Judith step foot into his presence.

"Tonight I will pray again—"

"Prayer." Did she believe simple prayer sufficed? Not even supplications offered in a temple, but in silence in the wilderness. No incense. No sacrifices. Nothing, just as Bagoas said.

"General, I do not believe it will take longer than two or three more days. Even the worst profaners will not take sacred goods on Sabbath."

Holofernes twisted so he could gaze at the altar half-hidden beside his bed. He let Judith wait. Let her wonder and fear slowly build. But when he faced her again, the woman's expression revealed no anxiety.

"Very well. We wait." He ground out the words like bones in a mortar.

"Thank you, general." Judith drew away from him with slow grace. Her skirts slid across his skin, light as a fingertip tracing the arch of his foot.

How did she stay so composed? He was the one sweating. Holofernes followed her, one quiet step, two. He would allow her one more moment to believe she was escaping, that he believed her. Hands outstretched to close on the fullness of Judith's buttocks, he drew breath to shout for the guard. The poor dog could do whatever he wished to Judith's maidservant—

Then Holofernes froze, fingertips nearly brushing Judith's hips, sudden sweat chilling his flesh. What if Judith remained so tranquil because she told him nothing but the truth? He folded his arms just as that wooly sheep of a maid peered at him.

By Marduk, he must keep patience three more days. For victory. For Judith in his bed, willing and passionate, or fighting with all her exceptional strength.

He watched her hips sway with the slow exhaustion of her movements. Fighting or passionate did not matter. Either would satisfy Ishtar. As much, he hoped, as Judith would satisfy him.

Before the door swung shut behind her, Holofernes shouted for his body slave. "Armor." He held out one foot for Bagoas to bind on a sandal, only to stand with it on, foot still in mid-air.

What if he followed Judith himself tonight? He would learn firsthand if she lied or told the truth— Holofernes swore. He would not manage a dozen paces without half his men recognizing him, even after nightfall. Their shouts of adulation would spoil any chance he had to follow the woman before he even left the open space around his pavilion.

Holofernes ran one hand down the tiny plates of armor stitched to his shirt. What could a woman actually do, anyway? Priests were men of power. Men. Judith was nothing but a vessel, a body made to receive, not act.

The instant Bagoas fastened the second sandal Holofernes swiped the slave's legs out from under him, and planted one heel on his useless throat.

"M-m-master?"

"You witnessed nothing last night because nothing is all a woman can do." He waited until Bagoas gagged, then bent, snagged a fist in the slave's tunic and hauled the wretched creature to his feet. "Listen carefully. Tonight, you will follow her again. And this time you must watch for—"

Chapter Thirty-six
Judith

JUDITH HELD HERSELF CAREFULLY UPRIGHT on the walk between Holofernes's pavilion and her own. The instant the flap swung shut, she dropped onto her bed. Abra collapsed on the cushions beside her, curly head close on the same pillow.

"He was naked inside that blanket." The general's casual nudity chilled Judith. "I felt you cowering at my heels. You, cowering." She shifted to breathe the last of it in Abra's ear. "I could kill him for that alone." Then she bit down on her knuckles to keep from crying out. "Please forgive me. I should never have brought you here."

Her friend moaned. "You must not say that—if anyone hears us—Down by the spring, when those two soldiers said—what they said—when the little one touched me—I wanted to bolt uphill to the gate and scream for someone to let me in."

Judith pushed up on one elbow. "Why didn't you?"

"How far do you think I could get before one of them caught me? The short soldier, or Ox. Or some man we couldn't even see, but who was there. Watching us. Waiting." Abra gestured at the camp outside the tent walls. "Besides, I won't leave without you." She hugged Judith tight.

"And how do I repay your loyalty?" A tear dripped off Judith's chin onto the top cushion. Abra rolled upright to cuff her shoulder.

"We're still alive, aren't we?" Then she crouched again. "We should stop talking before someone hears us."

"No." Slowly, Judith sat up and hugged her knees. "It's only natural for us to talk." Besides, unless Bagoas could drift silently as a feather, they would hear the spy's footsteps on the dry, broken grass that surrounded their tent. Their prison.

Abra dragged her fingers through her hair. "What did the general do to you? In his pavilion just now?"

"He did nothing to me. You were there, you would have seen." Had Abra noticed the general slide his foot inside Judith's robes?

A gurgle of laughter, swiftly silenced. "I kept my eyes shut tight most of the time. But I saw him follow behind you when you turned to leave. Judith, he was so close to you, his hands outstretched."

"I didn't know." She was shaking again, and hugged her knees harder to hide it from Abra. "He tucked his toes under the edge of my robe." Judith felt sure that had she shown fear at that moment, both she and Abra would be dead now. Raped and dead. "I curled my toes inside my sandal as tightly as I could to keep him from touching me."

That startled another giggle out of her friend.

"He will never do to us what he ordered done to those slave women. I swore it to our Lord the day Achior and I discovered their desecrated bodies. I swear it to you now."

Abra's mouth squared in a silent howl. "How? How can you keep such a promise?" She did not wait for an answer. "I prayed this morning. All the way to the general's fancy tent I prayed for us to live through today. I prayed for the Lord to help me convince you to escape home tonight." She rested her forehead against Judith's.

"Did my prayers work?"

Judith said nothing, just smoothed Abra's hair, the curls springy under her touch.

Abra sank back on her heels. "There's my answer." Movements uneven, she dipped into their basket and tore off some bread. "Eat, you'll feel better. Stronger, anyway."

"Thank you." Judith chewed, swallowed. She did not taste a bite.

The sun was up by the time Abra tidied away their simple meal. "Did you ever watch Gothoniel separate a buck goat from the does after breeding season, to keep the buck's scent from sullying the milk?"

"Yes." Her neighbor had his failings, but he was gifted at handling his herd. "He's so bulky, but he moves like a hunter when he's among his beasts."

"One day on my way up from the spring, I watched Gothoniel with a buck that didn't want to be caught. The beast dodged this way, ducked that, but Gothoniel had him cornered in no time." Abra angled her head toward the general's pavilion. "You're doing the same with him, aren't you? Holofernes thinks he's in control, and all the time you're guiding him where you want him to go."

Time would tell. Silently, Judith stretched out again. She expected to watch daylight brighten and burn, as she had watched the moon cross the night sky. But the instant she shut her eyes, sleep closed over her like deep water.

Chapter Thirty-seven
Judith

JUDITH WOKE, SWEATING IN THE STUFFY HEAT. Over the subtle odor of the herbs Abra had rubbed into their clothes she smelled bread. She sat up to find her friend arranging bowls of food.

Abra nodded at her. "What will you have for—is it breakfast or supper?"

"Who knows? I'd like olives with the bread." This pavilion was far more spacious than her goat-hair tent at home. Judith longed to open the door and let wind freshen the space, but the breeze would blow the stink of sweat, urine, and worse inside with it.

Judith flopped onto her bed cushions. "I don't know which bothers me more, the stench or the noise." How had she managed to sleep through the racket of marching, shouting men, the din of horses and cattle?

"The smells are worse." Abra shuddered and slid a shallow bowl of bread and olives across to her.

Judith blinked. "Why do they upset you more?"

"They sicken me so I don't want to eat." Abra squatted, studied her own plate of olives. "Can we please change the subject?"

"Of course." Though now all Judith could think about was how filthy this place was. She made herself bless the meal. Gradually, the familiar taste of olives heartened her. By the time they finished eating the noises of the camp had quieted with the fading light. Abra wiped the dishes clean, then started to return them to the basket.

Judith caught her wrist. "Leave them here."

"But— oh, very well." Abra stacked the bowls in a corner. "Let me see to your hair and garments."

"I can do what needs to be done." Judith smoothed her hair, then shook out her crumpled robe. Usually she slept in her under robe, or naked. Not here.

Abra tidied her own clothing, and did her best with her unruly locks. "Now?"

"Not yet." Slowly the light that needled through the walls shifted color, from gold to pink, from pink to pale gray. When the last of the sunset glow vanished, Judith stood. They had left much later the previous night, but she could not bear to remain inside another instant. "Bring the basket."

Eyebrows lifted, Abra tucked the empty container under one arm.

Outside, Ox stood at the ready, torch freshly lit and sputtering. "Lady." As he had the night before, he escorted them toward the tomb.

All the way along the slave road, Judith felt the presence of unseen soldiers like a yoke across her neck. Armor gleamed here and there in the twilight, a thousand shining shadows against the low-slung tents. When Ox halted at the edge of the stream to light them across, a spare, upright figure stepped onto the path just beyond the flow. Abra squeaked, and Judith dunked a sandal in the chilly water. *Achior!*

The instant she gasped, Ox had one hand on his sword hilt. He raised the torch higher so its radiance spilled over the man. Sendal.

Judith's breath stuck, but she dipped her head. "Greetings, commander."

Lips closed tight, Sendal smiled. "Lady. How go your prayers?"

"Prayers aren't easily counted, sir." Unlike the people this man had murdered, or the lands he had taken by force.

"Unfortunate." Though he spoke to her, Sendal shifted to eye Abra. "And you, my pretty, tangle-haired wench? Do you enjoy your stay with us?"

Judith tasted the olives she'd eaten for dinner at the back of her throat. Would Ox dare defend Abra from Sendal, his superior? "Holofernes disagrees with you, sir." Cold as her sodden sandal, she stepped sideways, between her friend and the Ammonite.

"What?" Sendal flicked a brief, disinterested glance at her, then sidled closer to the stream. And Abra. "Tell me, lovely one, what is your name?" He held out one hand as if to assist her across.

Judith felt a tug at the waist of her robes when Abra gripped the fabric. "I said your leader disagrees about my prayers. Now let me pass, sir. I need to discover the answers Holofernes seeks."

At last the Ammonite focused on her, his nostrils pinched. "While you're about it, pray to find those answers quickly. Ox, get that torch away from me before I strangle on the smoke."

"Sir." The torchlight showed Ox's face, stoic as ever. But Judith thought she heard a rumble of amusement in their guard's voice. He escorted them uphill to the clearing, then departed to patrol slow circles around the area.

Judith sank down on the ground facing Manasseh's tomb, but Abra stayed on her feet, arms rigid, empty basket clamped against her body. She crumpled without warning, hands burrowed in Judith's skirts like a baby gripping its mother. "D-did you see how he g-gaped at me? What if he c-comes back and—and—"

"Then I'll yell for Ox. We both will. Or—" *Blessed Lord, guide me.* "You can slip away to Bethulia right now. I won't stop you."

"No." Jaw thrust out, Abra smeared her tears away with the edge of her robe. "You said you can't do this without me. We'll stay. And if that s-scrawny bully tries anything, I won't scream for Ox. I'll f-flatten him myself."

Scrawny bully? Judith almost laughed. "With my help." Together she and Abra would do what must be done. "Now we need to follow the same routine each night." She raised her voice for the benefit of the Assyrian spy. "Spread out the cloth."

When cloth and basket were in place, Judith leaned back against her tree and shut her eyes. *Blessed art thou, oh Lord—* She waited. Except for the muffled tread of Ox circling them, she heard nothing but distant snores from the encampment. *Blessed art thou, oh Lord—Blessed art thou—*

When she opened her eyes to peek at the sky, Judith expected dawn to stain the horizon. Instead, all was dark. Ox's endless marching only marked the drag of time.

Teeth gritted, she waited through the rest of the night. Not in prayer, or peace.

Just—waiting.

"Did you hear that?" Abra sprang to her feet.

Finger to her lips, Judith strained to listen. There—a hiss of leaves. Her hair tickled upright on Judith's neck. She peered this way and that. A branch became an extended arm, a boulder seemed a figure crouched to attack. The rustling noise did not come again.

At first Abra quivered, her head swinging left and right until her hair spread around her like a cloud. Eventually she slumped to the ground, worn out by fear. But Judith stayed rigid. Across from her, the blank stone of Manasseh's tomb shone white in the moonlight, then dimmed and darkened as the moon set.

When the sky turned ashy with dawn, Judith stood at last, her body heavy as a sack of stones. There was no sign of a spy, of anyone. Perhaps Bagoas had never been there either. "Rise, Abra.

We'll return to camp as soon as you're ready."

"I'm ready. I'll deal with this—" She tugged her matted locks, lower lip unsteady. "—when we're in—in the tent."

"Then let's go. Ox, where are you?" Too late, Judith realized she had just announced her isolation to any soldiers nearby. *I should have followed Huldah's example and brought a sharp knife with us.*

Brush crackled, not the stealthy sound of a spy or approaching rapist, but the honest tread of their guard. "Coming, lady." Dead torch over one shoulder, Ox shambled up to stand partway between her and Abra.

Judith fought not to weep as he led them toward the center of camp, exhausted as much by the emptiness of the night as by anxiety. Had she been wrong to believe the One wanted her here? Had it all been nothing but her imagination? She paused to glance back at Manasseh's tomb. *At least I got to visit one last time.* If she knew nothing else, she knew Manasseh had loved her. They had loved each other—

"Lady. What are you doing?" Ox's voice sounded gruff.

Judith rushed the last few steps to the tomb. Cheek pressed against the cool stone, she ignored Ox's demands that she return to camp at once.

She had just spent an entire night straining to hear the One's voice, when the message was in front of her the whole time. Manasseh's tomb. Her husband had died trying to feed everyone in Bethulia, just as she risked death and worse to save them now.

I understand, beloved. The One meant for her to die, too.

Chapter Thirty-eight
Judith

IN THE TENTS THAT LINED THE SLAVE ROAD, men coughed and swore themselves awake. Judith barely heard them. She barely felt the rutted earth beneath her feet.

As Ox escorted them up the gentle slope to the crest of the plain, Abra linked fingers with her. "What's wrong?"

I'm going to die. Judith opened her mouth, then shut it again and shook her head. Even if she and Abra were truly alone, how could she share this truth? In any case they had reached the open space around Holofernes's pavilion. The entrance was opening.

"Welcome, lady." Bagoas held the doorway wide, but the spy had the grace, or shame, not to meet her eyes.

Judith brushed past without a reply, took a single step inside and froze. Sweat sprang out between her breasts.

Each thumbnail-sized piece of metal stitched to Holofernes's shirt glistened, as if freshly scrubbed clean of an enemy's blood. His pointed helmet dangled from one hand.

"Good morning, lady." He fitted on the helmet. It cast just

enough shadow to hide his eyes. "You rush into my presence, but have nothing to say?"

Abra's fingers closed on the girdle around Judith's waist again. The touch steadied her. "I know you long to hear my news, general. I hurried to tell you and arrived out of breath." She was panting enough to make it seem true. "My people—the villagers still refrain."

"In other words, nothing has changed." He tapped his fingers against the scales of his armor. "Dine with me tonight."

Abra's hand fell away from Judith's gown. She pushed past Judith and stood in front of her. "Tonight is a sacred fast."

Holofernes did not even turn his head. "Lady. Your servant dared speak to me. Punish her."

"I will, sir. In private, as is the way of my people." Judith pressed her lips together. "She spoke the truth. Tomorrow is indeed a day of fasting."

His eyes narrowed, but Holofernes jerked a nod. "I see. My people understand the good or ill luck of certain dates. Tomorrow, then." He took one slow step closer. "Tomorrow evening we will dine together. We must."

"I will speak to you about that tomorrow." Judith wheeled, and Abra scrambled after her. "Hurry, wench." She did not slacken pace until she stood inside her own shelter. Neither did her friend.

Before Judith could open her mouth, Abra grabbed her by the shoulders and shook her. "You can't do this, I won't let you. I won't let you!"

Judith shoved herself free. "How do you expect to stop me? You knew the plan all along." Most of it. How had her friend guessed that the One demanded Judith die?

"I was there just now!" Abra spat the words. "You promised to give yourself to him tomorrow night."

Give—? "Scream," Judith hissed, then clapped her hands as hard as she could.

Abra gave an odd little hiccup. Judith struck her tingling palms together again. Abra squealed. At the next mock blow, tears sprang from Judith's eyes at the burning in her palms, and Abra finally loosed a scream loud enough to reach Bethulia.

"Perhaps that will teach you respect for your betters," Judith shouted, and shook her tingling hands. Under cover of her friend's half-genuine sobs, she whispered, "I promised to dine with him. To dine, that is all."

"But he—"

Another loud clap. "Silence!" A ridiculous thing to demand of someone she was supposed to be beating. Abra fell onto the cushions, wailing. Judith dropped to her knees to embrace her friend. Tears ran down her own face. "Please, forgive me." To save them both she must mimic the cruelty that surrounded them. "You will be there, too, remember? When the moment comes I will need your help."

Abra lifted her tear-stained face. "So you always say. But what am I to do?"

"You will pass me the sword." Judith set her teeth. "And hold him down."

Abra's eyes rounded behind the thicket of her hair. Judith tucked an errant curl behind her ear. "Together, we are stronger than he is." *We have to be.*

Chapter Thirty-nine
Holofernes

THE INSTANT JUDITH LEFT, HOLOFERNES caught Bagoas by the front of his tunic. The frayed cloth tore as he dragged the eunuch up onto his toes. "Tell me what happened last night? This time you will leave out nothing."

"I already told you everything, master, I swear it, master. First the lady Judith comforted her serving maid, and then—"

"Comforted?" Holofernes shook the eunuch so hard they both nearly fell. "Earlier you said only that they whispered together." And why would Judith, would anyone, comfort a slave?

Bagoas opened his mouth, closed it again. "I don't know, master."

"Silence, or I will remove your chattering tongue." Holofernes threw the slave to the floor and stalked away to stare at the other pavilion across the open space.

In his presence Judith treated her slave sensibly, like a creature. A convenience. But he once heard that certain Israelites regarded slaves as family members.

"Pah!" Holofernes tossed his helmet toward the bed. "You say

Judith talks with the slave. Here in camp?"

Bagoas's head bobbled. "Yes, sire. I cannot stand near enough the lady's tent to hear what they say."

Holofernes raised one hand, and his slave hushed his chatter at once. Judith might simply be giving orders to her slave. But what if it was more than that? "Tell me everything that occurred last night. Again."

"I did, sire, I did. I swear it!"

"Again. Everything Judith did from the moment she stepped out of her tent." Holofernes sat in his chair. "Begin."

Bagoas whimpered. "Master, you told me to focus on the light around her, if it changed and how. To listen for any voice or sound that came from the air. Nothing like that happened."

Holofernes stamped across the pavilion, set one foot against the cringing figure's chest, toppled him and dug his heel into Bagoas's exposed throat. "You. Will. Tell. Me. Again."

In broken phrases, the slave choked out a description of Judith's journey to the grove and her brief meeting with Sendal. When Bagoas described how Judith had embraced—embraced!—her maidservant, Holofernes nearly crushed the eunuch's worthless throat.

"Why? You are leaving something out." No real lady, whatever her heritage, would touch a worthless ewe like that fuzzy-haired maid. "What happened after?"

Bagoas gagged. "The lady—Judith—sat—eyes shut—the rest of—night. Sire—I saw no light. I heard—no voice or sound—" Tears leaked from his eyes. "The lady did not move again—until she called—called for the guard."

Holofernes stepped aside. "She came straight back here?" If only he could see Judith at prayer for himself, then he would know for sure.

The eunuch's fingers burrowed into the rugs. "Ye—no, master. I—I forgot. Just before she called for Ox, the lady crossed to a tomb."

A tomb? Holofernes reached for his chair, sat. "And?"

"She wept."

A tomb. A widow, weeping. "Your duties as a spy are ended." Useless, mutilated creature, less than half a man. How could Bagoas understand an ordinary woman, never mind one like—Holofernes turned his head to study his altar, then tugged on his helmet. "Don't lie there lazing, get back to work."

From now on he would handle things as he should have from the beginning.

Chapter Forty
Judith

JUDITH AND ABRA DID NOT SPEAK the rest of the day. When the air inside their pavilion finally cooled, Judith stood and her friend picked up the empty basket. They stepped outside into the starlight, where Ox waited, feet braced, shoulders set.

Even in the dimness Judith noticed the dark smudges below his eyes. "Ox, do you never rest?" And why, *why* did Holofernes trust them to a single guard, one who must grow more exhausted every day?

The big man did not answer her, just strode away down the now-familiar road. With a hiss, Abra sped after him and bounced into Ox's way. "Did you hear my mistress? She asked you a question."

"Abra—Ox—it doesn't matter." It was just one of a thousand things Judith would never have the chance to know.

Head low, Ox dodged Abra and hurried toward the spring. Judith caught her friend by the wrist and tugged her in the wake of their guardian's broad back. He crossed the stream in one easy leap, only to take a stand with the rivulet singing between them.

"Lady, I do not sleep well." The night air was cool by the water, but sweat dappled his forehead. "The noise of my brother soldiers and the light of day keep me awake. I am very tired."

Abra's fists closed on the empty basket. "Do you think we sleep easily, surrounded by thousands of stinking men?"

Ox wiped one hand across his mouth. The sword at his hip dipped and swung. "I am only a soldier. Words are not my tools—"

"We can tell!"

Judith stepped close to Abra and tucked one arm around her. Tightly, to quiet her. "Just tell us—me—what you mean, Ox."

"I fear I will fall asleep tonight. During my watch. If I sleep, someone could sneak past me." Ox dabbed his tongue over his lips. "Do you understand, lady? Anyone could sneak by and I would never know."

Abra jerked loose of Judith's grasp. "What are you saying?" The basket nearly fell out of her arms. "Soldiers will come for us tonight, rape us?"

Blessed Lord, no. She could not come so close to her goal, escape rape, torture and death for three days, only to fail now—

"No. No, lady, Abra, I promise you on the head of my baby son. Well. I picture him as a babe, but he is a boy now." Ox curled one arm against his chest as if to cradle the infant he had not seen for so long. "Do you understand me?"

He wants us to escape. For one sweet moment Judith let herself believe it could be so simple. She could sleep in her own room tonight, visit Naomi, hug Dorcas. Argue with Huldah and seek Achior's counsel one more time.

But for how long, one day? Two? Until the village elders unlocked Bethulia's gate and stood aside to let the Assyrians march through.

With a splash, Abra bounded across the stream and up to their guard. "You are warning us. Telling us to escape."

Ox nearly dropped his torch. "I am warning you to stay alert."

"Then you must do the same." Judith crossed the water in a

single stride and stood close to her guardian. "Do you hear? You must do the same."

"Yes, lady." Shoulders sagging, he marched them to the space beside Manasseh's tomb.

The instant Ox left to circle the area with his torch, Abra dropped the basket. "He thinks we should run away." She paced a smaller, tighter circle around Judith, like a fly caught and buzzing for freedom. "Maybe we should listen to him."

"Instead of the Lord?" The words flashed out of her like lightning.

Abra faced her, mouth quivering. "I am not like you, Judith. I am an ordinary woman. I can hear Ox, see him. The One does not appear to me in a burst of light. I heed the laws of Moses, but I do not hear the Lord's voice."

"I am no different. I am ordinary, too." Blinding light on her rooftop, and the memory of Mannaseh's love. A vision of the general's sword, and the warmth of her friendship with Abra, with Naomi. "I am ordinary, too."

"The Lord does not shine His light on ordinary women." Then Abra reared back and shook one fist at the stars. "If the One appeared to me I would ask only one question. Why, why did He give me such unruly hair!"

Judith laughed. She laughed, weeping. "I love you, Abra, unruly hair and all. You were my friend before Manasseh even learned my name." And now, years after Manasseh was gone. She fought to keep her voice to a whisper. "I've put you in grave danger. I'm sorry."

"The One put us both here." Abra shook her hair out of her eyes. "Since your widowhood, the Lord is your companion. Perhaps that is why you see visions. For me, for most of our people, the One is more teacher than friend."

"You're my friend. I want you to take Ox's advice. Go." Judith pointed uphill to Bethulia. "Save yourself."

Abra glared at her. "So I can grow too weak to crawl away when the Assyrians take the town? No, you need my help." A pause. "The one true Lord needs my help."

"So do I." Judith held out one hand until Abra sat beside her, then closed her eyes to prepare for her last full night in the Assyrian camp. Her last night anywhere.

Chapter Forty-one
Judith

SHE BREATHED THE RESINY SCENT of cedars. Their incense cleansed the air and made the grove a temple. Except for Ox's regular tramp, no footsteps disturbed her. Perhaps Holofernes's spy had given up.

When cool light shone against her lids, Judith peered through her lashes and staggered to her feet. She had expected moonlight. Dawn streamed, pink and scarlet along the horizon. How had the night passed so swiftly?

She stood to wander a few steps closer to Bethulia. How were the people inside those well-loved walls? Did Naomi still live? Had Chana's baby started to show—

Abra rose and joined her. "Are we going to sneak away after all?"

"I was just wondering how Naomi is. And Dorcas, Huldah." Everyone. A spear of morning light shafted through the branches. No blade formed of divine radiance, just a touch of sun that warmed her face.

"What now?" Abra stooped for the empty basket.

"Now I will tell Holofernes what he wants to hear." Judith gave one last glance to her husband's tomb, then one toward the village walls. No one would carry her body through the gate and home.

"Grief passes, and fear. Love endures." She started down slope for the Assyrian encampment.

"Judith?" Abra panted after her. "Aren't you going to shout for Ox?"

"Not today." Judith sped across the stream just as the guard pushed through the brush toward her, ponderous as a bull.

"Lady! What are you doing? You must wait for me."

She ran faster. "Our Lord has spoken at last." She spoke clearly, so everyone within range of her voice would hear. Halfway up the slave road to the general's pavilion, she paused and said it again. "The Lord has spoken!"

Abra caught up with her. Judith grabbed her friend's wrist and broke into a run. Ox paced and then passed them with a glare, his armor clattering at every stride.

His surly look did not slow her down. Not even the reek from the soldiers' latrine pits could do that. Tonight she would complete the Lord's task. And then?

I am coming, Manasseh—

Chapter Forty-two
Holofernes

HOLOFERNES FACED THE OPEN PAVILION DOOR. He had stood there since before dawn. Where was Judith? Surely she had arrived much earlier on the previous two days.

Long after dark last night, he had wrapped himself in a black cloak, crept barefoot along the slave road and across the stream, ready to watch her pray. To learn for himself if she lied, or described her powers truly.

He shuddered as he pictured her, eyes shut, breasts rising at every breath. That image had hung before him like a lamp on his stealthy journey down the hill, across the water and up to Judith's place inside the belt of trees. His blood pumped harder with every step. In the end he could not move in silence.

Halfway up the track to Bethulia Holofernes had plunged behind a tree just in time to avoid coming face to face with Ox. Eyes narrowed, the general watched his sentry circle past, torch held high. So, Ox did not remain in sight of Judith while she prayed—

A sudden, a horrible idea kept Holofernes hidden in the brush.

226

What if Judith had not received a vision from her god because she was not alone? Because of the presence of the spy Holofernes himself had set upon her?

Holofernes stood in the scrub and silently cursed. He swore aloud as he returned to his pavilion. As he retreated to it. He could not—would never—observe Judith's visionary experience for himself. Inside the pavilion he hurled the cloak into a corner and shouted for Bagoas.

"My bath." When the eunuch only stared, Holofernes shouted. "You will bathe me now."

"Master, the water is not heated. I—"

"Then go heat it. Now!" It no longer mattered if his roar woke every soldier in the camp.

After he was cleansed, Holofernes crossed to his altar and knelt before the image of Ishtar. "Guide me truly, oh goddess!" Would that She could show him the truth of what Judith did in the grove. But he had never experienced that kind of divine visitation. Why would he? Men of action rarely did.

Now Holofernes watched the stars dim. Where was Judith? She must come, and soon. Perhaps—yes. He stood, arms extended. "Bagoas. Armor." Today he would go out to meet her. He would go as far as the spring and wait.

The rustle of her skirts was his only warning.

"General, I bring good news." This time she spoke before she reached the open door of the pavilion, her full lips deliciously bowed. "Tonight, my people—" Her brisk pace faltered a little, her smile faded. "The people of Bethulia—"

Holofernes leaned closer. "Yes? Yes?"

"They will slaughter the goats intended for holy sacrifice. While the meat roasts, they will drink the sacred wine. Lead your army to the village gate at sunrise, and it will shatter at your touch. Every man, woman and child will be yours, perfect and unharmed."

Unharmed until my arrival. Eyes on the woman a bare step away from him, Holofernes snapped his fingers at his slave. "Bagoas, send the message to my commanders. We attack at this time tomorrow." And the instant his slave departed on his errand, he and Judith would finally—

But that instant she swooned halfway to the carpets, and Holofernes's heart battered inside his throat. "Lady, why do you faint? These people will betray your god. Betray you." He reached out to her. "Judith, let me comfort you. Not tonight. Now." By Ishtar, now.

Judith jerked back a step. "No, my lord."

"Why?" He stalked after her, pace by pace. "Tell me, do you grieve for those—those pathetic sheep?" He leveled one hand at the village on the hill.

"No." Judith stood tall and gazed down at him. Just so subtly down. "I am tired. These nights of prayer and waiting have exhausted me."

Holofernes scowled. It might be an excuse. But he wanted her awake and at full strength. He sank onto the edge of his bed, still tumbled from his own night of waiting. Waiting for her as much as the message she had finally given him. "Go, then. Rest."

"Thank you, general. Thank you, Holofernes." Another smile, smaller this time, her mouth a teasing curve. Judith swayed from the pavilion, maidservant at her heels as always.

As always. He had barely noted the presence of the tumble-haired shadow beyond Judith, but now Holofernes listened to the women's footsteps fade. "Bagoas. About tonight."

"Yes, master. The lady Judith cannot eat foods prepared against the laws of her god. I have spoken to an Israelite slave about the meal, master. The slave will bake bread fresh for the lady."

"Israelite men know how to grind flour? How to bake?" Proof of their weakness as a race.

Bagoas paled. "Not a man, master. An old woman, too dried and scrawny to—to be of use in your—your entertainment."

This creature had seen to it that a female slave remained alive? Holofernes flexed his fingers, only to relax his hands on his knees. He would whip Bagoas later, tonight or tomorrow. Perhaps he would wake the eunuch from sleep with the first lash. The first of however many it took for the insolent mongrel to die.

For now, Holofernes kept his tone silky. "You gave a food order in my name?"

"Judith's—the lady's—beliefs—" Bagoas's lips grayed. "I did only what I thought you would wish done."

Yes, he would enjoy removing the eunuch's skin one stroke at a time. Holofernes stood, arms loose at his sides. What difference did the food make? He chuckled. After all, most of it would go uneaten. "Armor."

While the slave attired him for his morning ride, Holofernes gazed through the still-open doorway at Judith's pavilion. Hidden inside there, she slept on the cushions he had provided. She slept, her body as full and powerful as the goddess Ishtar's.

And that fuzzy-headed ewe, her slave woman, slept there too. Holofernes shifted his weight and raised one foot for Bagoas to slip on his footwear. "Tonight you will welcome Judith's slave with wine. Not from my personal stock, do you understand?"

Bagoas went still. "Drugged wine?"

"Exactly." Holofernes watched the sunshine flow closer across the vibrant colors of the rugs at his feet.

"Sire. They will refuse any wine I offer as unclean. Even Abra will—"

Abra. Was that the slave woman's name? "After the wine has its effect, have her delivered to Sendal. A reward for moving his men from the spring. After he's done with her, tell the guard to take the second turn. He deserves it after these nights on duty."

"M-master." Bagoas sounded confused.

Holofernes toyed with the hilt of his sword. The flat of the blade would waken the slave to his duties. "What did you expect me to do with the slut, give her to you?"

"No, sire." Bagoas stuttered. "I thought—the men would draw lots, like they did for the slave women last time."

Holofernes laughed. "Easy to see that you have been a eunuch all your life! Why would I make a spectacle of such an ordinary female?" Of course Judith's maidservant would die. Eventually.

He strode into the sunlight, morning air fresh on his face. Slaves held his charger ready, and Holofernes sprang onto the beast's back, clamped his legs and galloped toward the mountains. It was good to feel the stallion's bounding strides, to test its strength against his own. Just as he would test Judith's strength tonight.

Chapter Forty-three
Judith

A PULSE AT THE BASE OF JUDITH'S SPINE beat fast, faster. "Abra, hurry." Her friend continued to root through their piled belongings in the corner. "The general is waiting."

Abra only grunted, and then flourished a bunch of limp herbs. "Here." She crawled over to Judith and pushed the fragile stems through her girdle.

Judith inhaled the soothing odor and left the plants in her belt. "No fear?"

"No fear," Abra whispered. She stood to open the tent entrance for Judith to pass through. Together they stepped out into the cobalt evening. The clear area around the pavilions seemed empty without Ox.

Framed by the spill of lamplight from Holofernes's pavilion, Bagoas held a cup of wine in each hand. "Welcome, lady." He offered the jewel-colored cup to Judith, a plainer one to Abra. "Welcome to you both."

Judith held up a hand, palm out in refusal. "Our Lord forbids us to drink wine made—" Uncleanly. "Wine we have not made ourselves. Come, Abra." As she continued into the pavilion, Judith heard the eunuch whimper.

"Please, lady. Abra. Drink. It is—it is a custom of my—of the general's people. In honor of a guest."

"I am no guest." Abra sounded demure enough to please even Huldah. "And my mistress will drink wine enough tonight with the meal." She opened the door flap into Holofernes's pavilion, then eased aside to let Judith enter.

Every fringe on the general's robe swayed as he stalked toward her. He gave her no chance to avoid his touch but sealed her fingers inside his calloused ones. "At last, my dear. Sit. Be at home." He marched her to a chair beside his own. Only when she was seated did he release Judith. His palm slid teasingly against hers.

"Thank you, sir." Under cover of the table, Judith scrubbed her contaminated flesh against her robe, though she knew it did no good. Blessed Lord, how would she bear it if he touched her again?

Holofernes stood over her, his nearness like a hot wind against Judith's skin, his face flushed. When Abra paced in, eyes focused on the carpets, he glowered, then gestured at a pitcher on the table. "Bagoas."

The slave poured wine into his own palm and drank, while the general watched with narrowed eyes. For signs of poison, Judith thought, as Bagoas filled an ornate cup, the match of the one she had refused outside.

Holofernes gestured at the laden table. "I ordered a cook from your own nation to prepare each dish you see. You may dine in perfect confidence. Every bite is in accordance with your god's law."

Judith bent her head as if in acknowledgment while she studied the meal. Glistening olives, freshly baked bread, a platter of roasted calf. Only another Israelite would choose this most savored of dishes. Assyrians preferred that abomination, meat cooked in milk—an insult to every mother animal.

At last, at last, Holofernes moved a little away from her. "Is anything the matter, my dear?" Each word came sharp and quick.

"There's so much to choose from, you overwhelm me." Judith almost heaved. What could she keep down? "The bread smells sweet and fresh. I'll start with that."

Just in time she remembered to motion for Abra to serve her, rather than simply pick up a piece for herself.

"Only bread? Well—it will do for a start. But you haven't sampled your wine." Holofernes twirled his own cup, watching her.

Even if the wine had been pure, Judith could not bear to touch the vessel. Assyrian tribute, stained with misery. Her life would likely end in this elaborate tent with its lingering odor of sandalwood, a profanation of everything sacred. But she would keep herself clean in the few ways left to her.

"My mistress enjoys water fresh from the spring." From her familiar basket, Abra lifted a pottery jug and cup. She poured out the last of the water and set the drink at Judith's elbow.

Holofernes grimaced. "Water?"

"We come from different lands, different peoples. We have much to learn about each other." Judith drank the stale water from the simple clay cup. Stale, but still the sweet water from the spring, from home.

"To knowing each other." His throat worked before he finally drank a single, testing sip of wine.

Wine. She stared at him over the rim of her cup. The wine outside had been for Abra as well as for her. Why did Holofernes want them both to drink?

He took another sip. "Bagoas. Withdraw. I will call if I have need of you."

"Master." The slave nearly fell through the doorway in his haste to be gone.

Holofernes set down his cup. No, she needed him to drink

more. She needed him drunk—

The general glanced at Abra. "Your maid may retire also. As soon as she feels sleepy." A corner of his mouth tweaked up for an instant.

Sleepy. The wine outside had been drugged! And he did not know neither of them had drunk a mouthful. As if Abra guessed the truth as well, her friend covered a yawn with one hand.

Judith set down her water. "General, I—"

"Use my name." His tone thickened. "I want to hear you say my name."

"Holofernes. Holofernes, I want you to understand. I am a widow—"

Abra yawned again. Quietly, as if to avoid attention, she drifted into the shadows between the bed and the table, then sank to the carpet. Rolling onto one side with her back to them, she gave another noisy yawn.

Holofernes shoved his plate and cup away. "Now we're truly alone." His chair tilted and fell when he stood. "I want you, woman. I'm sure you know it very well."

Judith stood to keep distance between them. *"I want you, woman?"* For an instant, she flashed back to her husband's wooing, always with words of love no matter how demanding his touch. Obviously the general was unpracticed at seduction. Slave women couldn't say no.

Holofernes stalked her around the table. Judith barely managed to skitter out of his reach. "You drugged Abra's wine?"

"You knew? Clever. Another time she might prove a lively distraction. But now?" He opened his arms. "Your god has given you the message I waited for. Pay your debt to me."

Judith stood still. "You speak like I am a creature you have bought."

Holofernes squared off, hands on hips, feet spread wide. "No more evasions. Tell me true, woman, are you willing? Or has this all been pretense, nothing but an attempt to save your skin?"

Blessed Lord, give me strength. He was not drunk, not nearly as helpless as she had hoped him to become. "I have never lain with a man other than my husband."

"Is that all?" Holofernes laughed. "Our passion will make you forget your husband ever lived."

Every fiber of her being hardened. Quickly, Judith backed away from him toward the bed and tripped where the edge of one rug overlapped another.

Holofernes lunged at her.

In a whirl of robes and hair, Abra leapt out of the shadows. Lamplight shone on the heavy helmet she swung with both hands. Holofernes's helmet. She clubbed him with it on the base of the skull, and the general plummeted without a groan.

Blessed Lord, had anyone heard that awful sound?

"Judith—" Abra dragged the sword from its place at the end of the table and shoved it at her. "Hurry—"

Holofernes had landed across a corner of the bed, head hanging over the edge. Perfect. Her numb fingers closed around the hilt Abra slid into her palm. Judith grasped Holofernes by his oiled hair. It slithered in her grip, but she set her teeth and lifted so his neck stretched taut.

His eyelids flickered. "Judith. What, what are you—"

"I am giving you my Lord's true message." She had planned to shut her eyes, but they were too dry. Teeth clenched, Judith dragged the blade across his throat.

Holofernes reared up and clawed the air as his blood spurted, its coppery scent horrible against the thick odor of sandalwood. His legs kicked beneath the patterned fabric of his robe. The fringes danced. And then one foot found purchase among the cushions and he almost shoved himself free.

"Abra. Quickly." Judith dug the edge deeper against his neck, rocking the blade back and forth. Abra threw herself flat across their enemy's thighs and pinned him down.

Her hands felt fused to the sword. Judith lifted it and hacked down blow after blow, panting. Sobbing. The blade ground against bone. With a horrible gurgle, Holofernes finally grew still.

Judith longed to escape those still-staring eyes, the fan of blood across the bedding, but she could not move. It took all her strength to toss the sword to the far side of the bed, where it crashed against a low table or bench with a sound like broken pottery.

Weeping, Abra hitched herself off the bed. She stood, tripped on Judith's hem, and they fell in a tangle of arms and legs.

"Get—get off me. Let me stand." Judith managed to wriggle upright, her teeth chattering. Abra stayed crouched by her feet.

No shouts came from outside. No sound but their own tattered breaths. Judith forced herself to look at the figure on the bed.

The head dangled, connected to the body only by strip of flesh and broken bone at the back of the neck. She swallowed a sourness that might never leave her mouth. Legs watery, she went to retrieve the sword. "We're not—not quite done. The basket. Put it under—put it under his—"

Judith stared at the smaller mess beyond the bed, a smashed figurine, a cracked bowl. Fallen flowers and spilled water, with Holofernes's bloodstained weapon in the middle of it all. An altar to some Assyrian war god? She would never know. Judith picked up the sword. "Put the basket on the floor."

Face turned to one side, Abra nudged the basket into place.

Lamplight flared like lightning along the edge of the blade. *One cut. Get it over.* Judith swept the sword down and the general's head parted from the neck, teetered on the lip of the bed for one horrible moment, and finally thumped into the basket. The sword slid from her fingers to quiver point down in the layered rugs on the floor.

"Help—" Her voice dried to nothing. "Help me."

Abra fumbled the cloths over the pallid face splashed with blood, stood and almost tripped over the corpse's legs. "We'd better cover it—him—up."

"Yes. Maybe. Maybe Bagoas will think he's sleeping." And maybe both of them would walk out of here alive after all, instead of Abra alone.

Together, she and her friend wrestled what was left of Holofernes into the middle of the bed. Abra's face looked green, and Judith twisted the bedclothes so she didn't have to touch the corpse. *Unclean. Unclean. I will never be clean again.*

At last they tidied the blankets over the remains. Grimacing, Abra tucked the basket against her hip. "I pray I packed in enough rags to—to soak up the—"

"You did." Judith brushed the pavilion door open. Nothing had ever felt as good as the hot night air. Perhaps she would survive to see the sun rise over Bethulia again, to know her people were free—

Torchlight flickered. Ox marched out of the darkness. "Lady? Where are you going?"

Chapter Forty-four

JUDITH YIPPED. Abra almost dropped the basket.

"Lady?" Ox lifted his torch high. His heavy eyebrows drew together. "I did not expect to see you tonight."

Judith spoke though numb lips. "It is time for my prayers. Prayers of—of thanksgiving."

The guard did not move.

She took a step along the slave road, then another. "Come, Ox. Guide us."

"Lady." Ox shifted the torch to one hand. "I am only a soldier."

In the swirl of light and shadow, Judith could not see if he was reaching for his sword. Was Ox the one who would send her spirit to join Manasseh? She must distract the guard long enough for Abra to escape—

"I am a soldier. I do as I am ordered. I was ordered to escort you to the grove whenever you wished." With a rattle of armored platelets, he strode past her down the hill.

Abra trotted after him, then dodged back to pull Judith along with her. They passed down the road lined with campfires burnt to embers, and tents full of snoring men. At the stream Ox lifted the torch for Judith to help Abra across. His brows tightened again, but he trod on in silence. Near the tomb he halted, dipped his head briefly. "Lady." He paced away to begin his slow vigil.

Judith blushed. Did Ox think Holofernes had already taken her? Their guard would be only the first to see her as unclean, though she was stained not by the general's body, but with his blood.

As the torchlight crackled away, Abra took several swift, plunging strides uphill toward Bethulia. Judith caught and stopped her. "Wait. Let Ox make his turn downhill. There's less chance he'll see us go."

"But it's over! We're so close to the gate!" Abra shifted the basket in her arms.

Judith crossed to Manasseh's tomb and leaned against the stone. *Beloved, I am here.* She stayed with one cheek pressed to the cool rock until Abra nudged her. "Ox just went past. Now can we run? Please?"

"Now we can leave." She wove between the trees and out onto the track to the village. The way home.

Though they were walking, Abra panted. "I want to run."

"I do too." Leaves rattled in the breeze. Or did she hear the platelets of Ox's armor? Judith knew they needed to move with greater care, not less. She broke into a jog. When they reached the final turn below the village gate, she grabbed her friend by the arm. "Run!"

Pebbles spurted underfoot, but many seasons seemed to pass before she saw the low arch set in the wall, with a rim of light streaming around the edges of the gate. A grinding sound—the key in the lock—and then the barrier swung partway open with Dorcas's slender figure in the gap. "Mistress, I knew you would come back tonight. I told Ezra you said you'd be gone five days, and today's the fifth day—"

She and Abra fell through the opening together, like runners at the end of a race. Judith whirled to shut the barrier behind them.

Her friend slumped against the wall, breast heaving. "We—made it."

"We're home." Judith watched Dorcas turn the key and then hugged the girl tight. Dorcas's bones felt frail as a songbird's wing.

"Ezra," she had said. *Ezra, not "Master Ezra."* The scrap of thought tumbled inside Judith. She put it aside. There would be time to sort out her little maid's situation later. Later, if the Lord's plan succeeded.

"Thank you, sweet girl. Thank you for being here." For still being alive. "I always seem to be sending you away with a message! I hope this will be the last for a long time. Run straight to the magistrate and tell him we're here. Uzziah must meet me on my housetop before the sun rises."

The girl darted off, torch sputtering. Judith and Abra fumbled their way along the dark street to the courtyard, where Abra dropped the basket on the bench against one wall. "Terrible thing. I never want to touch it again."

"You never will, I swear it."

Abra kicked off her sandals, then knelt to remove Judith's. "I want to sing, to shout. To wake everyone, including them." She bared her teeth at the wall that now stood between them and the Assyrians.

"You've wakened me, right enough." Huldah's crutch tapped out of the unlit kitchen. "So, that silly chit did right to stay up all night. Welcome home, mistress. Abra."

"Old woman, wait until you hear what we did—"

"Whatever it is, you will speak to me with respect." Huldah reached for the basket. "The plates must need a good wash, and you must need breakfast . . ." She dropped the basket back on the bench and stared at her fingers.

Stickiness had leaked through rags and woven reeds alike. A

puddle of darkness stained the bench.

Abra pressed both hands to her mouth while Huldah poked the rags aside to study the basket's contents. "It seems there has been a death." Her face creased in a fierce smile. "Well done, mis—Well done, Judith."

Staring down at the head, a ragged, gory line along the base of its throat, Judith heard the cracked old voice from far off in the distance. With a choked sound, she wheeled and fled crookedly across the courtyard and down the passage to her room. There she fought free of her fine garments. Jewelry pinged into corners as she tore it off. Naked, Judith curled up on the floor. She felt sticky all over, as if Holofernes's blood coated her inside and out.

Cool fingertips touched her shoulder. Judith shrieked.

"It's only me." Gently, Abra sponged off Judith's hands, then dipped another cloth into a fresh bowl of water before she washed Judith's face. At last Abra stooped and held out the sackcloth robe of Judith's widowhood.

She hugged the familiar garment, every thread of the scratchy fabric a blessing against her skin. "Thank you." Shakily she dressed herself, and then knelt up to clutch her friend's shoulders.

"You are a servant no longer. Stay in my household if that's what you desire, but any home you want is yours. Whenever you wish, where ever you wish it. Here in Bethulia, on a farm, even in Jerusalem."

Abra gaped at her. "It's too much—I never dreamed—"

"Nothing is too much." Judith kissed her friend's rounded cheek. "Because only you will ever know how it was. Only you can understand."

"Yes." Then Abra shook her head. "What would I do in Jerusalem? My friends are here. You are here. I want a house in Bethulia, on the same street as yours." She held Judith close. "Because only you know how it was," she whispered. "Only you will ever understand."

They hugged each other, laughing. Crying. At last Judith stood and helped Abra to her feet as well. "Go and rest, we'll talk more about this later."

She returned to the main courtyard, picked up the basket without hesitation, and climbed to the roof to wait for Uzziah and Achior.

Chapter Forty-five

SHE FOUND ACHIOR, EYES LIKE PALE FIRE, already waiting at the center of the roof. "Judith! You're safe?"

"Blessings and praise to the One! You are home." Uzziah stepped out of her tent, his garments limp and filthy. "Did you do it? Did you make a truce with the Assyrians?"

Judith staggered back from him. "Truce?"

"I believe Judith took more direct action, my friend." Achior touched the edge of the bloodstained basket with one fingertip. "Didn't you?"

She kept still a moment, looking at him across the basket and its burden. Then Judith tilted the basket. Rags flopped out, and the head of Holofernes bumped onto the bricks and came to rest at Uzziah's feet.

The magistrate stumbled backward. He dropped onto one of the low seats left from their meeting a few days before. "How did you—Who—" He stared at Judith like he had never seen her before. "Who is—who was—that?"

"Holofernes." Achior knelt close to the fallen head, fingertips extended, then drew his hand away without touching it. He rocked onto his heels to study Judith an instant, then stalked over to her black tent and jerked loose one of the support poles. The pole arced down like a spear in his skilled hands as he impaled the head on one end. He offered it to her with a bow.

"Show the Assyrians what you have done."

Shaking, Judith braced the pole against the wall so Holofernes's dead eyes glared down the hill toward his encampment. Exactly the way she had seen him in her last vision, on this rooftop the evening before she left Bethulia.

Uzziah's breath rattled like wind in barley. "What now?"

"We wait for dawn." Achior took a place close to the parapet and crouched down. "For light, so the Assyrians can see their general is dead. Killed by a woman on this, one of the luckiest days in their calendar."

Judith knelt beside him. Uzziah started to squat beside her, then shifted to be on Achior's other side. Neither man spoke, neither looked at her directly, but Judith caught the magistrate glancing at her, and then away.

I have seen death as a widow. Many women did. But she had also seen death from the hilt end of a sword. She had killed a man, and no matter how evil the man, Judith doubted men would look on her with lust again. She coughed. "Where are the elders?"

Achior answered her. "Chabris remained with his wife Shoshana, who is very weak." He shook his head. "And Joakim is with his wife as well, though for a happier reason. The girl is with child."

Judith smiled and shut her eyes. "I know." Then she leaned sideways until she could see the magistrate's face. "How is your mother, Uzziah?" Her voice sounded too loud in the dawn hush. "How is Naomi?"

"She longs to see you." Uzziah peered at her around Achior's shoulders, then away again when she nodded.

"This afternoon I will come visit her." And Shoshana, too—

Judith heard sounds down the hill, sounds that seemed both near and far in the gray light. Sounds familiar to her after days in the military camp. The grind of a hoof on hard ground, the chime of a bit. Chariot wheels clattered nearer, along with the salty tang of equine sweat and the stink of wet leather. A chill ripped through her. "They're coming."

A line of Assyrian chariots galloped, bounced and jolted over the crest of the hill to her right. A moment later a second line surged into sight on the left.

Both angled toward Bethulia's gate like the edges of a spearhead. The drivers shouted, bent low over their horses' flowing tails. The archers, braced and swaying behind each charioteer, stood with arrows already notched and ready.

Buzzing hisses slashed the air. An arrow struck the edge of the wall and a spray of chipped brick stung Judith's cheek. She cried out, one hand pressed against her cut face, as more arrows peppered the roof.

"Stay down." Achior pushed her lower against the wall.

Judith flattened herself closer to the cool bricks. Could the soldiers see Holofernes's head above the gate? Would any of them even notice it? Achior's long body tightened beside her, and she wondered if he thought the same thing. Another rush of arrows pelted down close behind them.

How did soldiers bear this mess of noise, battle after battle?

"Keep in line, men. I said keep in line!" A familiar voice shouted above the din.

Achior lifted onto one knee, then grunted and bent low again. "Sendal is leading the first wave, or trying." He grinned. "The charioteers can't form a solid attack because of the steepness of the slope." He nudged Uzziah's shoulder. "Your people planned and built this village wisely."

"Thank you." The magistrate dipped his narrow head.

Achior bobbed up for a second look. "The Assyrian chariots always clear the way for the archers on foot. The archers clear the way for the soldiers with ladders." He laughed. "So far, your hillside is breaking the rhythm of their attack."

Judith had to see for herself. She popped up on one knee, like Achior had done, just in time to see Sendal and another mounted commander gallop past. Achior's replacement held his sword high, heels drumming his mount's ribs. "Come on, men—"

Many of the chariots had peeled off to return to camp. A lone, deserted vehicle tilted at the brink of the hill directly above the spring, one wheel snagged on an acacia sapling, the other wheel snapped off altogether.

Up the wide path from the spring marched a block of Assyrian soldiers. As Judith started to duck, one of the men in front dropped his spear. "Look, above the gate," a soldier yelled. "Is that—it's the head of Holofernes!"

"Impossible. Our commander told me Holofernes gave the order to attack."

"I would recognize the general anywhere," came the voice of the first soldier. "That's Holofernes. Holofernes is dead!"

When Achior lifted his head to peer over the edge of the wall again, Judith joined him. Soldiers continued to march up the hill, then spread across the place of judgment just outside Bethulia's gates. But they no longer advanced in orderly ranks. Gathered in uneasy clusters, their shouts and cross-questions grew louder and more jumbled.

"Who killed him?"

"How did he die?"

Judith sweated all over. The outcry seemed far worse than the arrows. She had avoided the flying weapons by staying close to the wall. If she stood now, if she moved and even one of the men saw her, surely the Assyrians would storm the village and tear her to pieces.

Gradually the tumult swelled into a single cry from a thousand throats. It echoed off the walls and out toward the encampment. "Holofernes is dead!"

And then Achior leapt to his feet and pulled her up beside him. "Yes, your general is dead! The Bethulian woman killed him, she and her god."

Hundreds, thousands of soldiers gazed up at her. She must say something, do something, but Judith's tongue stuck to her teeth. She clasped the tent pole in both hands without looking at it, and held the grisly prize high. Blessed Lord, the pole was sticky.

"I am Achior of the Ammonites, and I warned Holofernes this would happen if your people attacked this place. Their god guided a woman to your general. That god helped her kill him." Achior took a half step back and left her at the edge of the parapet.

More and more soldiers spilled across the place of judgment, spreading along the hilltop to stare up at her and what she held.

Judith's lips shook, but she stood tall. *Blessed Lord, guide my words.* "I walked through your camp every day, and you saw nothing but a female body, soft. Easily used." She tilted the tent pole so the head drooped toward the men. One or two of the closest soldiers edged away. "Perhaps you see more truly now."

Spears and bows and short swords thudded to the ground. Soldier after soldier turned and forced a way downhill, against the wave of men still marching toward the village. Sendal appeared to be shouting orders, but Judith could no longer hear him above the buzz in her head, as if her mind was full of flying arrows.

The Assyrians were retreating. Everything her Lord had shown her had come true. *But I didn't die. I am impure, polluted forever, but I did not die—*

"You there! Halt! Come back. Come back, men, or I'll—I'll turn you over to the tartans!"

Not a single soldier obeyed the screamed command. Scarlet-faced, Sendal booted Desert after the retreating men. The stallion balked, and when the Ammonite whipped him, the stallion lashed out, heels high. Sendal sprawled on the horse's neck for a single rough stride, then crashed to the ground, half-hidden by the dust of the departing army. Desert charged into the trees.

Achior was on his feet. "Go, Desert! Gallop, my brave one. I will come for you soon, I swear it!"

"They're leaving?" Uzziah knelt up to gaze at the place of judgment.

"They're leaving." Judith clasped her gummy fist to her breast. And she had lived to see it, to know herself and her people free. *I come from a long line of warriors like David.* "Blessed art thou, oh Lord. Thank you." *Thank you!*

"They're leaving!" The magistrate whirled in a wild circle. "Praise our Lord, and Judith his handmaiden."

"No." She dropped the tent pole, and swallowed against sickness when the head bounced once and came unstuck from the end. "Give thanks to our Lord alone."

Achior stepped between Judith and her victim's head, and closed his hand on her sackcloth-covered shoulder. "I understand what Uzziah means. You are the one who did as your god asked."

For a moment Judith felt his warmth through the scratchy fabric. Then Uzziah gently moved between them and kissed her forehead. "Bless you, Judith. Ezra and I will bring my mother to see you soon, but now our people must witness this great victory!" He strode away. Despite his grubby robe, Judith glimpsed a hint of his former assurance.

In the encampment, armored figures swirled and tangled briefly, but more and more of them sped away, across the plain toward the mountain pass. Naked or skimpily clad slaves trailed cautiously after the soldiers. Perhaps Bagoas was among them.

As the noise of the retreat receded, different sounds began inside Bethulia. Laughter. Shouts of joy. Music. Achior perched on the wall, one leg bent up in front of him, and tapped his fingertips in time with a nearby sistrum. "You will always be known as the Defender of Bethulia."

"I hope not." Judith glanced at Holofernes's head, then gestured at her plain robes. "This is who I am."

"Widow of Manasseh?"

"Always." And yet she knew she had become more. When? Last night, when Abra tucked Holofernes's sword in her hand? Or on the afternoon of her first vision, when the sword of light cut through the air above Manasseh's tomb? Both, perhaps. And everything in between.

"You are Judith. Wife of Manasseh, Defender of Bethulia." Achior's healed mouth moved in its familiar, painful smile.

"I am Judith." She bowed to him. "Achior's friend." Judith. Perhaps not defiled forever. Touched, but not stained by the blood of the sacrifice she had made. Perhaps the Lord would send her a sign. She would never be able to ask Sirach. "I am still your friend?"

"Always." He stood and bowed to her in return. "Now, if you do not mind, I have a horse to catch, if I have to walk halfway to Babylon to do it."

"Not that far, I hope."

"But first—" Achior retrieved the general's head and tucked it inside the basket, wrapped in rags once more. "I will dispose of this."

"Thank you, Achior. Thank you." Judith bowed to him and watched him go, then frowned at her sticky fingers. She stood to peer down into the courtyard, to see if any water remained for the ritual washing of hands. As always after contact with death.

Tonight, she and Abra would collect as much water as they wanted from the spring. They would each take a bath! And then—

Tonight I will sleep in the bed my husband and I made. In the home they had both made safe.

Acknowledgements

THANKS TO THE KENTUCKY FOUNDATION for Women, Patricia West, the Uffizi Gallery of Florence, Italy, and Louise Hawes. The Kentucky Foundation for Women granted funds for much needed research for *Judith*, plus two weeks at Hopscotch House for work on the prequel. Patricia West provided funding as well as bi-weekly doses of friendship and writerly support. Thanks to the Uffizi Gallery and its staff for use of Artemisia Gentileschi's painting *Judith and Her Maidservant* for the cover of this book. And thanks to Louise Hawes for giving me the capacity to listen to my characters.

Thanks to Paschal Baute and his lovely wife for offering me a place to stay during research, thanks and blessings to Chana Cohn for help with the glossary—any mistakes are mine—and thanks to everyone who wrote a check or donated their time during my recovery from a 2012 stroke, especially Lori Taft Hurley and her husband John and daughter Marta, and JJ and Nancy Moïse Haws. I am grateful to Ellie Troutman and Melissa Swanner for caring for my horses through the first stage of my recovery. No one could have better friends or a sharper advocate.

Author's Note

WHEN I WAS A CHILD, I READ EVERYTHING that had writing on it that would keep still long enough for me to read. Cereal boxes, the encyclopedia, anything. Small wonder I was reading books beyond my reading level at school, sixth grade readers when I was in first grade. One rainy afternoon I discovered a book on the shelves my parents had built on either side of the fireplace. It was titled something like *Women of the Bible*, and it had my grandmother's childhood name on the flyleaf. I read it through.

I cannot imagine the book made appropriate reading for a young child, but I read about those biblical women. Ruth, Esther, and women not in the Bible, though I did not know it then. Judith, whose story did not make the cut into the Bible. She is in the *Apocrypha,* as I later learned, deemed too fictional a tale for the official text, and not quite historically accurate enough for the bishops who sat in judgment in the fourth century after the Common Era. I am sure the content of Judith's story had nothing to do with their decision.

But I didn't know any of that then, while I first read the book's summary of Judith's story or stared at the full color plate that accompanied it. I only knew I wanted to read more, wanted to know more about this heroine of her people. Unlike Ruth, who married her Boaz, I could not find Judith in the Bible my grandmother had given me.

Fast forward several decades. While I was at work on my Ph.D., I taught a class on everything cultural from Shakespeare to the present. I was forbidden to skip anything. Because I did not and do not personally know everything about architecture, art, drama, or literature from then until now, I brought in guest lecturers at appropriate times. When I didn't know someone personally, I visited the Humanities Resource Center and dug up a CD instead.

Which is how I encountered Sister Wendy Beckett's series on the great art of the centuries, where I met Artemisia Gentileschi's paintings of Judith. Which is how I got interested in her again.

This time I did what I had not known how to do as a nine-year-old child. I sought out and read the apocryphal *Book of Judith*. Imagine my surprise that Judith did not appear until the twentieth page of the thirty-page story. Shouldn't the character whose name appears in the title appear in paragraph one? Shouldn't the reader have access to her thoughts and feelings from the first page of the story? But no, in the *Apocrypha* we have nothing of Judith until she appears on the last day of the siege, two-thirds through the tale that bears her name. She remains a cipher. We know nothing about her except that she is a young, beautiful widow. A devout widow, at that.

In the first two-thirds of the *Book of Judith,* the reader learns more about the masculine side of the story than the feminine. We learn what the general is doing, how the magistrate is doing, plus how he feels about it. In a world where females exist only in their reaction to what the men are doing, the *Book of Judith* makes perfect sense. I thought Judith deserved her own story, where the character is more than a foil for the men. So I took the tools given to me by Louise Hawes and gave the full story back to Judith.

Speaking of history, no author could have a better publisher than Peggy Elam. Before *Judith* even had a contract, on the day she accepted the manuscript, Peggy suggested I find out if we could use Artemisia's painting that had so inspired me. After negotiations the museum in Florence came up trumps, and that is the partial image you see gracing the front cover.

I hope you enjoyed reading Judith's story as much as I did writing it.

LESLIE MOÏSE

About the Author

Leslie Moïse writes memoir, historical, and fairy tale inspired fiction, a logical progression since her Ph.D. included an emphasis on nineteenth century women's fairy tales. When not at work on her own writing, she loves to help others bring their stories to life. She lives in Kentucky above a forest near the Ohio River, with a whippet who thinks he's more intimidating than a Doberman.

Pearlsong Press published her memoir *Love is the Thread: A Knitting Friendship* in December 2011. In the spring of 2012, after she had completed a book tour for *Love is the Thread* and had signed with Pearlsong to publish *Judith*, she experienced a stroke. She is recovering and has returned to writing.

Praise for books by Leslie Moïse

"I was hooked...from the first page."
KNITTY.COM

"A gentle read."
GOODREADS.COM

"Dark as well as light threads and a substantial amount of the grit of everyday life."
LYNNE MURRAY
author of *The Falstaff Vampire Files*, *Bride of the Living Dead* & the Josephine Fuller mystery series

"*Love is the Thread* is beautifully written, chock full of wisdom and humor, and a nakedly honest and human memoir."
BARBARA BLOECHER
Shamanic Practitioner & Teacher

Also by Leslie Moïse

Sustained by the metaphor of knitting, *Love is the Thread* traces the way one friendship can change all our relationships. The memoir centers on two women, one snared in a lifelong struggle with bipolar disorder, the other reweaving her life after an abusive relationship. Spirituality, encounters with nature, and vacations on the Delaware shore form the threads of a friendship as varied and closely knit as the stitches in a handmade sweater. From the discovery of hidden colors in fresh snow to the satisfaction of teaching a young nephew to knit, *Love is the Thread* savors life's small glories, ultimate challenges, and all the moments of humor and tenderness in between.

Read an excerpt at
WWW.PEARLSONG.COM/LOVEISTHETHREAD.HTM

About Pearlsong Press

PEARLSONG PRESS IS AN INDEPENDENT publishing company dedicated to providing books and resources that entertain while expanding perspectives on the self and the world. The company was founded by Peggy Elam, Ph.D., a psychologist and journalist, in 2003.

We encourage you to enjoy other Pearlsong Press books, which you can purchase at www.pearlsong.com or your favorite bookstore. Keep up with us through our blog at www.pearlsongpress.com.

Fiction

Fatropolis—a paranormal adventure by Tracey L. Thompson
The Falstaff Vampire Files, Bride of the Living Dead, Larger Than Death,
Large Target, At Large & A Ton of Trouble—paranormal adventure,
romantic comedy & Josephine Fuller mysteries by Lynne Murray
The Season of Lost Children—a novel by Karen Blomain
Fallen Embers & Blowing Embers—Books 1 & 2 of The Embers Series,
paranormal romance by Lauri J Owen
The Fat Lady Sings—a young adult novel by Charlie Lovett
Syd Arthur—a novel by Ellen Frankel
Measure By Measure—a romantic romp with the fabulously fat
by Rebecca Fox & William Sherman
FatLand & FatLand: The Early Days—novels by Frannie Zellman
The Program—a suspense novel by Charlie Lovett
The Singing of Swans—a novel about the Divine Feminine
by Mary Saracino

Romance Novels & Short Stories Featuring Big Beautiful Heroines

by Pat Ballard, the Queen of Rubenesque Romances:
Dangerous Love | *The Best Man* | *Abigail's Revenge* | *Dangerous Curves*
Ahead: Short Stories | *Wanted: One Groom* | *Nobody's Perfect*
| *His Brother's Child* | *A Worthy Heir*